The
LIC... KASHMIR

Siddhartha Gigoo's books are *The Garden of Solitude, A Fistful of Earth and Other Stories* (longlisted for the Frank O'Connor International Short Story Award 2015), *A Long Dream of Home: The Persecution, Exodus and Exile of Kashmiri Pandits* (co-edited), *Once We Had Everything: Literature in Exile* (co-edited) and *Mehr: A Love Story*. In 2015, he won the Commonwealth Short Story Prize (Asia) for his short story, *The Umbrella Man*. His stories have been longlisted for Lorian Hemingway Short Story Prize, Royal Society of Literature's V.S. Pritchett Short Story Prize, and Seán O'Faoláin Short Story Prize.

Siddhartha's short films, *The Last Day* and *Goodbye, Mayfly*, have won several awards at international film festivals. His writings appear in various literary journals. He's also the co-founder of *Daalaan*, a Hindi literary magazine.

For more, visit siddharthagigoo.com.

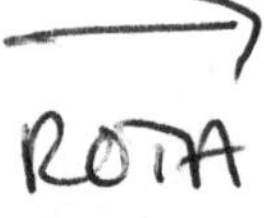

Also by the same author

The Garden of Solitude (2011)

A Fistful of Earth and Other Stories (2015)

Mehr: A Love Story (2018)

The LION OF KASHMIR

SIDDHARTHA GIGOO

RUPA

Published by
Rupa Publications India Pvt. Ltd 2020
7/16, Ansari Road, Daryaganj
New Delhi 110002

Sales Centres:
Allahabad Bengaluru Chennai
Hyderabad Jaipur Kathmandu
Kolkata Mumbai

ISBN: 978-93-5333-817-6

First impression 2020

10 9 8 7 6 5 4 3 2 1

Printed at Replika Press Pvt. Ltd, India.

Here we are always late by a certain interval of time of which we cannot define the length.

—BRUNO SCHULZ,
Sanatorium under the Sign of the Hourglass

Only two rivers flow here: Dead River and Red River.

—ARVIND GIGOO,
Gulliver in Kashmir

Contents

We have some more distance to cover. If we walk fast, we'll be there in no time. Do you see that embankment over there? We'll rest there for a while. Yes, that's where the fish are in abundance. And we'll take a boat ride too. The water in the lake isn't as cold as it seems; it is cold only on the surface. But down below, it is warm. The fish won't survive if the water is icy. And if you do exactly as I say, you'll learn how to swim like a fish. No one will ever tease you then. You trust me, don't you? I'm not fibbing, and I won't lie to you ever. I know you can do big things. I know how brave you are. Did you know I was about your age when I learnt swimming? I learnt swimming in a river, not in a lake. Dad taught me. It was difficult at first. I feared drowning. But I overcame the fear. Do you know how? Because dad was by my side! He never let me out of his sight even for a moment. When I got breathless in the water, he carried me in his arms and taught me how to breathe. Then, I started swimming on my own. Dad swam next to me. Every day we went swimming. Soon, I learnt how to dive off the bridge. People looked at me with awe and disbelief. They thought I was showing off. I wanted to do things that no one dared to. I dreamt of climbing the highest cliffs, walking on razor-sharp ridges, and summiting peaks where no birds lived.

You are my responsibility now. I will hold you tight in the water till you become fearless. We'll do this one step at a time. I'll hold you until you learn how to float. You'll then learn how to tame water. In no time you will be swimming like a champion. Until then, you should listen to everything I say. That is my only condition. Imagine swimming from this end of the lake to the other. You will be known as the youngest crosser of this magnificent lake. What I couldn't do at your age, you will. When we reach the other side, you will understand that everything that happened happened for a reason.

I know you never get tired. You're stronger than I am. Listen to me carefully now, pay attention. I have to attend to something urgent. I won't be long. I want you to wait for me here. Why don't you look at the fish till I return? Remember we are going to have an exciting day. It's your special day. We're going swimming finally. Once you get into the water, you won't want to come out. You won't be alone. Here, put on these headphones and listen to music. You can listen to anything that you wish to; your favourite tracks or any other songs you like. I will be back before the song ends.

I cross the road and the mist cuts me off. Zubair is out of sight. Then the mist disappears and Zubair is visible once again. He hasn't moved. He hasn't removed the headphones. I don't lose sight of him. I look at him and wait. I know he won't disobey me. My forefinger is curled around the trigger. I have everything figured out but somehow I can't get myself to do what I'm supposed to do. I've rehearsed this over and over again. It's been flawless every time. The desired result is just a shot away. A gentle push and Zubair will be in the water. He won't feel a thing.

If it doesn't happen here, then I must switch to Plan B. The railway track isn't far. The last train arrives in the evening. The job has to be done today. There won't be a tomorrow. It has got to be done today. Dad was right. I can't let Zubair go through an ordeal at someone else's hands. He must not come to any harm. He mustn't be left alone to…

Book I

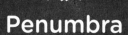

Penumbra

When we are away from home,
in new and strange places, we get to know ourselves better.

—Jokha Alharthi,
Celestial Bodies

Home Away from Home

1

I am on a flight that's about to land. A gorgeous countryside with lush green fields is in sight. Bountiful sunshine has carpeted the grasslands. Horses are grazing. Cows are asleep. Fields of hay run over the hills. What is this place? I have seen places like this only in the movies. I feel like I have been on board for hardly a second and the white outside has turned to green. How is it possible for winter to have turned to summer in no time at all? I rush to the toilet to pee. After I am done, I try to open the door to go back to my seat. The damn door doesn't open. It is stuck. It appears that someone has purposely bolted it from the outside to prevent my exit. I knock on the door. It makes no sound. The entire place is soundproof. I can't locate my spare trousers. People start getting off the plane, and I can't even remember why I was on it in the first place.

Your dreams can't compare with mine. If our dreams were to compete, I would win every time because my grandma was always the champ. I have inherited the dreams she didn't dream. She used to sit me down in the mornings and tell me about her dreams when dad hadn't shown up for days. That's how she kept me engrossed. I never believed in her dreams but now I do. Every dream she ever told me about is true. When she was dying, she told me about the funny dreams she had; chance encounters with animals and funny people like clowns of a circus. I knew they weren't true but I believed them. Even after her death, she didn't stop making unannounced appearances in my dreams. She is now making me dream her unfinished dreams.

Those who leave you or those you leave behind always return. In the end, the dog and the cat and the crows and the pigeons will return no matter how far you leave them and no matter how far you are. In the end, dad will come back. He will return and the dream will turn out to be a happy one.

Grandma used to say, 'If you rub a stone every day for seven years, it will come back to life.'

2

'This is the final boarding call for Zooni Aziz booked on flight AI 112 to New Delhi. Please board the aircraft immediately. The doors of the aircraft will close in exactly five minutes. I repeat. This is the final boarding call for Zooni Aziz. Please board the aircraft immediately. Thank you!'

I hear a whisper in my ear, 'Are you Zooni? The announcement is for you. You should hurry, else you will miss your flight...'

I gather myself and look around to make sense of my surroundings. A woman standing next to me is looking at me with mischief in her eyes. She seems to be either Japanese or Korean. Her features give her away. She is fair complexioned and shorter than I am. She sports a bobcut, and her hair is mostly black with an odd streak of brown. Her nose is flat. Her unusual features set her apart from the rest of the people in the lounge. A 4-wheeled trolley case is moving in circles around her. It's a nauseatingly slow rotation like that of a devotee going around a sanctum or a satellite orbiting a planet. In the woman's hand is a remote control. Her finger presses down firmly on a button. Somehow, she gives an impression of not being a stranger here. She seems unruffled at the comings and goings of people. Yet, unlike the others, she appears confused and clueless as to why she is at the boarding gate in the first place and what she must do. But then, the way she is looking at me, I get a sense that she is there for a reason. She seems to have come out of nowhere just to make me aware of something. No one else seems to be aware of her. She appears to be waiting for me to make a move. I can tell. She throws me a strange look which seems to say, 'You too?' It is some kind of a sign, like she is privy to everything that has happened in my life so far, and as if she has a clear sense of what I am thinking and going to do next. Maybe she knows what's going to happen. The expression on her face turns sly as she sees me regain a sense of purpose. 'You aren't going anywhere' is what her expression conveys.

My name is called out again. The airline attendant at the boarding gate looks at me, annoyed. Without saying a word, she points at the clock on the wall and gestures to indicate that the New Delhi-bound flight is about to take off with or without me and if I still choose to not come to my senses, I will be stranded here forever. That's all she does. She has no interest in what's happening around us. She's blind to the unfolding act. I'm just a vacant seat, 64-A.

I look at the clock on the wall. Someone is trapped in it. The person is trying to stop the big hand from moving. He's hanging off the edge of the big hand. He's about to fall. The big hand moves two-and-a-half places and then stops, unable to climb any further. The dial changes its appearance. The man falls and the hands of the clock start moving, slowly at first, and then at a terrifying pace until they can't be seen at all. The clock is about to explode and there's no sign of Time.

The woman with the flat nose knows she has my attention now. Success at last! But she's unfazed. We stare at each other without the slightest fear or embarrassment. I want to say goodbye and good luck to her before boarding the plane. Just as a courtesy! What if I strike up a conversation with her? Maybe she's in distress. Maybe she's waiting for someone. Maybe she's stranded. Maybe she has missed her flight. Maybe she has dropped the idea of boarding her flight and going away from here. Maybe she's just killing time and leering aimlessly at people like me to read minds for a lark. Maybe she's an aimless wanderer or a tourist or a vagabond. Maybe she's a contractor hired to do a job that she doesn't really want to do. Maybe she's a secret agent whose only job is to keep tabs on people in transit.

But then, what if I'm wrong and she's none of these. What if she turns out to be psychic? She might have been keeping me in her sight for as long as I have been here. Even when I fell asleep and dreamt a horrible dream in which I was plotting to get rid of Zubair by pushing him into a frozen lake on the pretext of teaching him how to swim. Maybe this flat-nosed woman is an interpreter of dreams. What if she has seen everything? What if she knows things I don't know yet?

She keeps staring at me as I walk away from her and board the plane. Her gaze follows me right inside the aisle of the plane. I can't stop thinking about the strange look on her face.

Why me? What have I done?

Has such a thing happened to you ever; at an airport or a train station? Just when you're about to leave, you chance upon a person—a fellow passenger or a stranger—who looks at you suspiciously, mystifyingly, as if she or he knows everything about you and the inner workings of your mind. What do you do at such times? Ignore the person thinking you might be reading too much into his or her expressions or stop to confront the person and try to find out the reason behind his or her fixation about you? Will you ever get to know the real reason?

The stalker's face seems familiar all of a sudden when I sit in the plane and look outside the window. In the sky, float small reflections of people familiar and unfamiliar. One such face is of a flat-nosed girl looking intently at me with a strange expression and a desire to make me remember her.

3

Unlike my classmates in the department, I hadn't gone home in the last two years. Everyone else had been home at least once or twice. And there are those who go home every four or five months. Sara and I have an apt name for them: Seasonal holidayers.

There are certain customs to be followed before one leaves for home. And I am leaving without notice. It's a strange departure. When Sara comes to know that I am gone, she'll panic and throw a fit. Who knows what she'll think about me. There will be consequences. She might not forgive me for not informing her. But explaining the situation to her would have been pointless. Sridhar is an exception, my feelings for him made me confide in him. That he is the only one who knows about my decision to drop everything—my research work, studies, friendships, and even him—on impulse and leave London, is a cause for concern.

He shouldn't have been my confidante. But the deed is done, and I have no one but myself to blame.

My decision to leave London and go back to Kashmir might seem impulsive and reckless to both Sara and Sridhar. But now that I have taken the decision to quit everything and go back, I realize I may have, over the past few months, taken many things about myself lightly. Sometimes you don't pay attention to yourself—your past, family, relationships, fears, complexes, abilities, likes and dislikes, ideals, principles and commitments.

Something has been looming in my mind for a long time now, and it concerns my father and my relationship with him. I assess the past two years of my life in London. Academically, there's been no problem. Everyone struggles in a new place. You dismiss the struggles as teething problems. So do I, sometimes. It is an endless marathon. There's no end to it although we are bound to forcefully conclude at some point in time. Hasty conclusions and early arrivals are scary. They make you lose confidence. You fumble and rise and fumble again. There are days you wallow in despair. There are days that bring comfort and show you hope. But hope is an illusion. And if you can't distinguish it from its real form, it makes you see things that do not exist. It assumes its real form in no time. And that is scary to deal with. You cling to things that you think will help you sail through turmoil and crisis. Then you lose your grip and fall. Friends come to your rescue. They help you battle your weaknesses and doubts. They offer words of wisdom, comfort and support. In doing so, their own weaknesses come to light and stand exposed, and you don't feel alone in the world and you don't suffer a nervous breakdown. Weakness sometimes becomes the source of strength. We are united in our weaknesses and fears. Weaknesses and fears bind us. I am no exception.

Well, maybe there are exceptions, such as Sridhar. He's bright and erudite and has a supreme ability to summon intellectual and critical faculties at will and in situations where we need them the most. Within him is a vast reserve of fertile ground that yields fabulous produce, day after day, month after month. The way he looks at the world and interprets it, sometimes precisely and sometimes imperfectly, is both intimidating and stunning.

When I first met him, I had no clue about his past academic record. But as I observed him inside as well as outside the seminar rooms of our university, I began seeing him differently. I began envying him. He has the makings of a great person. In some ways, he reminds me of my father. Strong-headed, mysterious, charismatic, influential, stubborn, puller of crowds…

On a personal front, I have done reasonably well so far, minus the ups and downs concerning my past associations and relationships. Some of them appear frivolous now in hindsight, as you would imagine. However, my relationship with Sridhar has blossomed. I wouldn't call it love though we have shared good and bad moments with each other. When we are together, life is beautiful and fulfilling despite our arguments over random matters. There are no worries. But then, night-time creeps in, when I look into the mirror or at the empty sky and come face-to-face with myself. Me versus me… the piercing gaze… the taunting voice… *What are you doing here? Is this what you should be doing? Will you ever be happy? What will you do if you fail? What sort of life are you leading? Are you on the right path? What if this is the wrong path? For how long will you depend on your father's money and fame? What if he's not around? What if something unforeseen happens? What will you do then?*

When I think of dad, there have been and still are only 'what ifs'. After all, he commands the Special Forces, an elite anti-terrorism unit of Jammu and Kashmir Armed Police, and Kashmir continues to be the most troubled place on earth. Kashmir has become a strange place. I feel attracted to it only when I see it in photographs. It seems unreal and hypnotic like a movie set or a fantasy. It entices with its false pretense. I am forced to call it home for several reasons, but is it really a home I wish to go back to? It is home because I was born and brought up there. It is home because dad and Zubair are still living there. It is home because of my dreams and memories of mom, grandma and grandpa. It is home because each one of us must have a place to call ours. It is home because that is where the seasonal holidayers go when there is nowhere else to go. It is home because everyone says so. It is home because, right now, I am headed there with a growing feeling that I might never return.

But the truth might be different than what I have believed so far. I don't feel like going there even though dad and Zubair still live there.

At this very moment, as I look back upon the times gone by and begin to assess my present situation, I must hold someone responsible for everything. Who could that person be? It's a terrible thing to pass on the blame to your father. I'm not going to do so. But I will let you judge for yourself. One of us has to be at fault, if not both. And you must get to the root of the cause.

Now that I am seated on a plane that's homebound, I am overcome with dark fears, fears that I have never experienced before.

Imagine your life's goal is to summit the highest mountain in the world. You prepare for it for years. Then one day, you set off for the foot of the mountain. It's a lonely and hazardous journey across forests, marshes, turbulent rivers, passes, glaciers and crevices. When you reach the foot of the mountain, you establish base camp, and for the first time, you get to set your eyes on the summit towering up to the sky. You realize how close you are to your goal. You say to yourself: 'It's achievable. It's possible. I will do it. Nothing can stop me now. Nothing will come between the summit and me.' At the foot of the mountain, you slowly begin your climb and then you climb back down after reaching the halfway mark. Along the way, you encounter dangerous crevices and you scale them using skill and perseverance. You set up camps where you will rest. These camps are for safety. They are the insurance should the unforeseen happen.

You keep going further up and then down again and, in doing so, you adapt to the extreme conditions otherwise you die. You become familiar with everything, not just with the unknown terrain—the mountain—but with yourself too. You leave your fears behind. You overcome the greatest obstacle—the fear of failure. Then, on the day that you finally reach the summit, you throw caution to the winds and risk your life to set foot on and touch the pinnacle where no soul has ever been. This is where madness takes over. And you're there at the summit. You are up there, alone, with no one to acknowledge your feat or to validate your claim. You leave no proof of your deed. But the trouble begins at the very top. When you're up there at the very top, you realize you can go no farther. It is all over. The only way forward is backwards. The only way for you to go is back down to where you began in the first place. No more heights to conquer. The mountain appears to tumble and spin on its peak. It is at this very moment that reality strikes you, harshly. Everything that you have done is of no use. You feel incapacitated. Is this the trickery of the mountains or of the demons residing on their summits? You are rendered bereft of any capabilities. You realize you can't do a thing hereafter. You even become incapable of investigating into the treachery of your own act.

Right now, as I wander aimlessly atop a lonely summit, I am going through the same treachery knowing very well that what ultimately kills you is not the ascent but the descent.

4

Through dark-rimmed glasses, Sridhar is looking into my eyes as if I am about to leave him forever. The night spreads forth its wings but its reins are with Sridhar. The hands of the clock are at his command. Such is his power. But he conceals the power as though he is waiting for the right moment to conjure it up and gift it to me one last time before I leave. He knows I am not going to stay. The quiver in my eyes gives me away. He places the tip of his forefinger on the mole on my face. When he lifts his finger, the mole is gone as if it never existed. How does he know my secret desires? That I am better off without the mole and that the mole was a curse!

What have you done, Sridhar?

'You want it back?' he lisps. He already knows the answer. He knows I will never say yes. But I don't want him to know that I am lying and that what he has done is sinister.

'If you want it back, tell me,' he says, seeing the fear and ecstasy in my eyes.

But how will you make it reappear now that it's gone?

'Do you really want to know?'

I run my fingers over my face. The skin isn't mine. The mole is gone. I grasp Sridhar's hand and run my fingers over his palm thinking that the mole has stuck to his hand and that it will come off. But nothing of that sort happens. I am scared. I want him to tell me to go away.

The mole was a birthmark, and he rid me of it. When I was in my mother's womb, an eclipse took place. Mom had been debarred from going out of the house that day. 'Don't go out during the eclipse' had been the diktat. But true to her nature, she did just the opposite. Defying everyone, including her husband, she stepped out exactly at the time when the moon turned black. Dad wasn't home. When mom was outside, looking at the black moon, she had a fall. When she returned, she realized that something was wrong. But it was too late to do anything or to rectify the mistake. The deed had been done. A tiny mole appeared on my mother's face that very instant. When I was born, everyone saw the big mole on my face and panicked. They thought it would bring me bad luck.

'Nothing is my doing,' Sridhar declares.

Soft light falls across his face and mine.

Could this be the dawn? This is your doing. You had promised you wouldn't hurry.

'I am not the one going away,' he says, sarcastically.

I had hoped he would make me stay. He had cast a spell over me. But I had made up my mind. Nothing in the world would make me stay. My bags were packed and I had no choice but to go.

You know that only you can prevent me from going but you won't. It was a mean thing to say, but I was merely testing him. I didn't want to take the blame. He was beyond blame. But one of us had to bear the burden of guilt should we never get to meet again or should the unthinkable happen. Regret is the worst thing to happen to any person.

Sridhar has his reasons to be happy, confident, content and unperturbed in all situations. Pinning my hopes on him would have been the biggest blunder. He is from a village you have to look up on the map of India, a tiny dot in South India. He was born in a farm on the outskirts of Tiruvannamalai in Tamil Nadu. His schooling took place in a missionary-run institution there. His parents are farm dwellers. He is the first of his clan to have earned a scholarship. He is also the first of his clan to have set foot in a foreign country to study and earn a living. He supports himself by taking up jobs such as giving tuitions to the children of underprivileged refugees and asylum dwellers. Yet, invariably, he ends up waiving off the fee. His explanation: 'There are times when you don't accept money.' But he possesses something that none of us possess.

5

At dawn, Sridhar comes to my room. 'I've to show you something. Come with me right away…'

I am in no mood to go anywhere. There is little time left for anything. I'm getting ready to leave but I don't know what all I have to do before I leave. Things are scattered all around me. I have lost interest in everything—what I should do and what I shouldn't do. Things lying in front of me and around me seem useless. I must simply take my bag and run away from here. I don't need anything.

I must reach the airport on time. You can never predict last-minute hurdles.

‘I will wait,’ Sridhar says, with a patient look on his face.

When I come out of the shower, I see an unbelievable sight. My shoes have been polished. Even those I am not taking along—three pairs of sandals and three pairs of shoes. My clothes have been ironed. Even those stacked in the cupboard.

‘It’s going to rain,’ he says.

I sling my bag over my shoulder and rush out with my hands over my head. He stands there and watches me go. Then in an instant, as if by magic, I stop, stand still for a moment, and turn around to face him. I feel something I have never before felt in my life. A mysterious force! It isn’t letting me go. It’s trying to hold me back. It isn’t Sridhar’s doing though. He is merely looking at me and waving a reluctant goodbye. He isn’t trying to hold me against my wishes. He isn’t even trying to shield me from uncertainty. I stand there, gazing at him bemusedly with a sting in my heart, trying hard to not abandon my goal. The summit is far and there will be pitfalls—some of which I have perceived during the last few days. I pull myself together. There is no deception in Sridhar’s heart and I am blaming him for my own weakness.

I am about to leave his world and enter another. In the sky is the remnant of a cinder. Until last night it was a burnished moon. I walk towards the bus stop. The longest walk ever. Church bells start pealing. My steps are shaky. The bridge of departures is ahead. It is my favourite place on campus. I love it because Sridhar first discovered it for me. It has been my go-to place when no other place existed. We have been the lonely walkers when no one else was around.

The bus arrives on time. It is half-empty. I sit at the back of the bus and take a look at what all I am leaving behind. The road ahead lengthens. It seems to be spreading forth out of nowhere.

And then, a raindrop falls on the windowpane.

At the airport, something unexpected happens. The attendant at the check-in counter inspects my ticket and my ID as if something is amiss. He takes a long time to clear me for the flight. His expression, as he looks at me, seems to suggest that I am an imposter trying to fool him. He appears unsure. To make matters worse, he throws an unlikely question at me: 'Is this you?'

What kind of a question is this?

'The ID says you have a large mole on your face. It's there in your photo. But I don't see the mole on your face.'

He denies me boarding. People start queuing up behind me. They become impatient, 'What's taking her so long?'

I'm not the cause of the delay. Stop blaming me.

I plead with the attendant to permit me to board the flight. He calls someone else to verify my identity, 'Is she the person she's claiming to be?'

I make several pleas in my defense, '*Listen, I am the daughter of a distinguished police officer in India. I have proof of that. Why won't you believe me?*'

'Listen, Miss,' he says, 'we need to follow a procedure for identification. Will you please step aside and let the next passenger be attended to?'

You're mistaken, Mister. You think I am causing the hold-up. Come to your senses and do your job properly.

'I am doing my job. Now step aside or else…'

Are you threatening me? How dare you? Who do you think you are, you pathetic….

'Security…' the man yells.

I'm not going to do what you say.

I am handcuffed and pinned to the ground as if I am a

criminal. I plead my case politely once again: *I am not what you think I am... I have my rights...* And then, losing my cool: *Bloody racists... morons... pathetic brats... do whatever you will but you will repent this act... I will make sure you pay for this...*

My phone is seized and my bag is confiscated. I find myself in a dingy room. Some sort of foul-smelling antechamber where the scum of society are made to blurt out unpleasant truths after being meted out remedial treatments. A fiendish-looking interrogator enters the room along with his sidekick. Such people are nameless and faceless. They don't smile, ever. They deal only with the worst kind—those who don't deserve to exist. They just stare at you. Their unblinking stares are meant to not only test your emotional threshold levels but also to end your tolerance to pain. It then becomes easy for them to extract anything from people no matter who they are and what powers they possess. At the slightest hint of pain, people will simply blurt out anything and confess to things they never did or can't even dream of doing. 'Out with the truth or else' is the warning given to me. The scariest question is asked of me: 'Who are you?'

How many times do I have to tell you? I'm a student at the University of London. Is this not enough proof of my identity? I'm also a human rights and an anti-racism activist. What the hell are you doing?

My pleas fall on deaf ears. All because of a damn mole! It is Sridhar's fault. He shouldn't have done this. Had I known this would happen I would not have allowed him to do this! How stupid of me to think that the mole was a curse. I am a damn fool. I run my fingers over my face. The mole is there. I beg them again: *Look, it's there. Let me go. I am not lying. Look at me. The mole is there...*

'Where? We don't see it,' growls the interrogator's assistant.

What is wrong with all of them? Why can't they see my mole? Is it some kind of an evil spell that only I can see it and no one else can?

'We need someone to identify you.'

Alright, his name is Sridhar and his number is...

'What about your father? You said he's a police officer in India?'

In Kashmir.

'You're from Kashmir?'

Check my passport. I have been living in London for the past two years. This is my home now.

'We are going to call your father...'

Don't call him, please. He doesn't know I am...

'We will give him a call.'

No, please, wait.

Taking a closer look at me, and seeing me shaking with fright, the interrogator does the unexpected. He grins and does an about-turn. My bag and phone are handed back to me.

A boy taps me on my shoulder and says, 'Ma'am, is this where you get off?' The bus has come to a stop outside the Departures terminal at Heathrow. Some people are getting off and others are getting in.

London, do not be horrible to me. I'm begging you. I must get back to Kashmir in time.

Sridhar's doing is not going to come in the way of my mission. It is not going to prevent me from doing what I have set out to do. It is not going to stop me or be an impediment in any way. I have spent many nervy days with a sense of foreboding that something terrible is about to happen.

At the airport, nothing untoward happens. The attendant at the airline check-in counter is courteous and kind. He even compliments me: 'Zooni! What a musical name? What does it mean?'

Moon, you stupid! You're supposed to know.

He wishes me a pleasant flight and asks me if I would be coming back to London soon. To avoid any unexpected hassles or embarrassment, I pull out a scarf and wrap it around my face so that I don't have to explain the absence of a mere mole.

'Happy journey to you, Ms Aziz,' says the attendant. I don't look back and rush over to get through Security. My only baggage—uncertainty, anxiety, worry! The security official asks me to remove my scarf. *Oh no! What if?* I have no choice but to comply. Sensing my hesitation, he says, 'Take it off for a moment; it is all right unless it is there for a religious purpose.' I take it off and touch my face exactly where the mole is supposed to be. No one seems to notice its absence. I shall search for it only when no one else is looking.

At the boarding gate, I hear frantic and repeated announcements bearing my name: 'This is the final boarding call for Zooni Aziz booked on flight AI 112 to New Delhi. Please board the aircraft immediately. The doors of the aircraft will close in exactly two minutes. I repeat. This is the final boarding call for Zooni Aziz. Please board the aircraft immediately.'

And then appears the flat-nosed Japanese woman standing aimlessly in the lounge with a perennially rotating and revolving trolley case. She stares incessantly at me as though I am the culprit of a grave immoral act. 'You, too?' her look conveys.

You can't scare me. Stop pretending to be someone you aren't and go and intimidate someone else.

6

Sridhar and I met for the first time at an anti-racism protest on campus. Our introductions had been brief, but the first sight of him hadn't left a favourable impression on me. He appeared unimpressive. Dark-rimmed spectacles, insipid attire, disheveled hair. Barring an odd sparkle in his eyes, there was nothing that made him stand out. Sara and I seldom paid attention to him. It was later when I learnt that he had secured a prestigious scholarship to pursue his master's degree in economics, that I started wondering about his past record. A fully funded scholarship is no mean feat in our university. I, for one, didn't have a scholarship. My dad paid for everything and deposited money in my bank account from time to time. There was no paucity of money or resources. Sridhar didn't give an impression of being extravagant. He needed little. He ate frugally. He didn't even own a proper wardrobe. He regarded many things with irreverence. He never borrowed money or books or anything else from the rest of us. Many people shared things to make the most of their resources. He didn't and yet, he was rarely in need of anything. His hostel room was sparse. He walked alone, ate alone, never formed a team during seminars, and yet managed to impress the faculty. But he looked at them with disdain. At least that was what Sara and I felt. Maybe we were mistaken or presumptuous, but he didn't give us a reason to think otherwise.

Then the situation on campus took a strange turn of events. Britain announced its intention to part ways with the European Union. Outsiders felt insecure. Some of us were ridiculed by you-know-who. Overnight, protests erupted on campus. Students went on rampage. It didn't take some of us more than a day to decide what to do and what not to do. We were up in arms against the decision. It was clear. We wondered what would unfold. Sara led the protests on campus. She steered the creation of placards and graffiti. She was the feisty rebel amongst us. Everybody lost interest in studies and class work. After all, it was a matter of principle and conviction, and a make-or-break deal for the immigrants.

The protests became fierier as days went by. Students and faculty made speeches in the university parks and cafes. 'The city must burn until order and people's votes are restored,' Sara went on to say. The slogans reverberated: 'Save our future… We belong… Down with racism… We all bleed the same colour… All lives matter…'

The campus scene was tense. Mobs were everywhere. Groups were continuously being formed. A divide among people came to the fore. Them versus us. Supporters versus the dissenters. Some of us were singled out and mocked at.

During one such protest, Sridhar stood in a corner, all by himself, and watched us raise our hands and chant slogans. I didn't like the look of detachment and disdain on his face. He seemed unperturbed. It looked as though he was taunting us. 'How smug he looks!' Sara quipped. Maybe Sridhar believed that he was above all such politics. The very politics that sought to impact our lives, define the rules of our existence, set absurd and preposterous parameters based on nationality, race, and identity rather than merit.

'Why aren't you protesting?' Sara asked Sridhar. She couldn't stand his uncaring attitude. She went on a tirade: 'What good is your education if you are not standing up for those who can't stand up for themselves? You are neither an outsider nor a mute spectator to what's unfolding here.' The poor fellow listened quietly without saying a word. Then, upon repeated snide remarks by Sara, he broke his silence, 'Your friend doesn't know which side of the divide she's on.'

'Who are you talking about?' said Sara to him in an admonishing tone. 'Do you even know her? Think before you talk...'

Clearly, he was talking about me, mistaking my passivity for ignorance and indecisiveness. His eyes were fixed on me and no one else, as though he was trying to test me and question my intentions and belief. Sara was our leader. I marched alongside her. She led from the front because it impacted her the most. She was passionate, impulsive and emotional about everything, especially about her position and status in the country. Her rebellious streak was not just for the heck of it. It had a clear and distinct purpose. It was founded on the question of her existence. Her ideological conviction was the strongest amongst us all. It was non-negotiable. Her arguments were lucid and convincing. We immigrants gathered around her when she rose to speak and address us. Although as Asians, we were in the minority, we were too strong a force to be ignored. Drums and tabors made an appearance. We wore black scarves. We held one another's hands and sang in unison. Everyone's solidarity mattered. Sara brought us together.

'You know who I am talking about,' said Sridhar, not taking his eyes off of me. It was a piercing gaze. Sara pulled me by the arm, and said, 'Do you even know him? Who does he think he is? He is, at best, a spoiled brat, a snob. He seems to have had a smooth ride so far in his life, doesn't seem to have been with people at all.'

Sridhar's remark filled me with disgust. It was mean and made to make me feel unsure about myself. He continued looking at me, inscrutably, almost as if he wished me to confront him and get into an argument with him. I took the bait. I couldn't resist it any longer. I agreed with Sara. He shouldn't take us for granted. I decided to take him on: *You are supposed to be on our side.*

It didn't take him even a fraction of a second to retort. It was almost as if he already had a ready reply. He was prepped for the situation, and it occurred to me that he had done his homework well. 'What do you know about protests, injustice, deprivation?' he jeered.

You are talking as if you have seen everything in life. If we don't protest, what will become of us when we are targeted? We will be sent home. I don't want to go back home. I want to be here.

'It will never happen. We will have to go back eventually. You will also go back. You don't belong here and never will. You don't want to be answerable to others here. Moreover, all this will benefit you. You don't get the picture at all, do you?'

Then why are you here in the first place? Why not go back?

'What makes you think I won't?'

But what if we are humiliated? What will you do? Sit and watch quietly like you're sitting and watching right now.

I wanted to tell him what it felt like to live in a place where you don't know if you will survive the next moment. The meaning of real fear! Where daily life is rife with uncertainty and deceptions. Where to live is to die.

For all your erudition and scholarship, you should already be aware of it. Or are you one of those who brushes everything under the carpet? Are you someone who turns away from the ugliness of life and looks the other way when helpless people turn to you for support?

You have blinkers on, like so many others.

We argued for days. Neither of us budged. Ironically, we weren't supposed to fight each other. We were supposed to fight those who wanted to oust us from here. The next morning, he joined a protest march. 'I came for you' is what he seemed to convey with a slight wave of his hand and a glint in his eyes. Of course, he didn't express it in those exact words. But the haughtiness that had adorned his look earlier hadn't gone away. I acknowledged his presence. *Good for you! You are forgiven.*

But then, something unexpected happened. He grabbed my hand when he saw a mob storming at us. I freed my hand instantly and raged towards the mob. He ran alongside, conveying: 'Hey, don't worry, I am here, I will protect you should anything bad happen.'

As if I cared.

'You are a Kashmiri. Did you ever protest in Kashmir?' he asked me later, as we sat in the park.

His question was unwarranted. I wanted to slap him. I ignored the question. It was a trap. His intent was to not only distract me from my immediate pursuit but also to corner me so that I would appear defenseless and have no solid justification of my existence and the way of life at the university. But I gave him an answer anyway.

Who are you to question me? What do you know about me?

Days later, as the protests ebbed and normalcy returned to the campus, Sridhar and I started hanging out. I realized that our encounter with each other during the protests hadn't been, in fact, a matter of chance. He had followed me. He knew about me. He had dug up every bit of information about me. Facts, perceptions, opinions, rumours, trivia, everything! It was the easiest thing to do. The extent to which people can go to find out details about other people baffles me.

Sridhar knew of my Kashmiri roots right from the very beginning. Like many others, he, too, followed news about Kashmir for the wrong reasons. I was not the problem. It was my father and the nature of his job, his position and his authority. He is no ordinary person in Kashmir. He's been in the news for various reasons. All you need to do is to look him up on the Internet. There are snippets about his extraordinary accomplishments and feats everywhere. If you don't trust me, then here's what you should do. Google 'Commandant Abdul Aziz, Special Forces, Kashmir' and the results will stun you. You will know what a legend the man is. If you're too lazy to type so many keywords, you can simply try 'Commandant Aziz, Kashmir'. Just the name is enough. He's feared and feted at the same time. You will come across my name too. And that's not because I am his daughter but because of my association with the Human Rights Watch forum here in the UK. Some of my research work has been noticed. I am not boasting. It's the truth.

My purpose was, to put to rest, Sridhar's well-meaning doubts about my ideology and to expose his connivance in that 'fortuitous encounter' on the day the 'parting of ways' was announced.

Nowadays, one is perceived through a faulty prism. A Kashmiri girl with a seemingly elitist mindset... studying law in London... part-time human rights activist... fervent campaigner for the rights and aspirations of Palestinians and Catalans, but not for her own people who are fighting a lonely battle to reclaim their right to live peacefully and freely...

Now here's the catch: Daughter of a high-ranking Special

Forces cop, who's in charge of counter-insurgency operations in Kashmir and who's an agent of the state and who's perceived as a Kashmiri against Kashmiris... someone who's a witness to the daily brutalities of his own force against his own people there... a Statist in a place where the State is perceived as an oppressive, unsympathetic and occupying force working against its own people... Where does his daughter stand on the question of Kashmir and the goings-on there? Is she with the Kashmiris who are against the security forces or with the forces that are often accused of stifling and putting an end to people's voices? Those UK-bred Kashmiris who are vocal in their support to the secessionists shape people's perceptions.

How is Sridhar ever going to reconcile to my seemingly ambivalent position on Kashmir? These are the question marks that have punctuated our relationship during debates and discussions on campus. It's convenient to arrive at quick conclusions. Therein lies the conflict in people's minds. How is it possible that a Kashmiri Muslim girl is comfortably living with the fact that her father is a pro-state cop?

Yet, I forgave Sridhar. Don't ask me why. I wish I knew. It just happened. I didn't even tell Sara. I never gave it much of a serious thought in the beginning, though it bothered me when Sridhar wasn't around. He wasn't drawn to my charms in any way. He was a loner but he didn't mind my company.

It was an incident that occurred during a seminar on human rights at our university which brought our feud out into the open. My father had been in news. He had been awarded another medal for his feats. People exchanged their personal perspectives. There were haters, and there were admirers. Some pretended while others couldn't fake it. We were having a fierce argument, when in front of everyone Sridhar asked me a question he shouldn't have. The question prompted other speakers to hurl some more unwarranted questions at me. 'You are usually at the forefront of human rights protests in town, Ms Aziz,' they said mockingly, 'but do you ever consider the terrible situation with regard to the human rights of your own people in your own home state?' I got their drift instantly. I knew what they were trying to do. They thought they could corner me with their insinuation. They would then say things like what a sham she is behind my back. They would mock me in private and applaud me in public. But it was not them that I was concerned about. It was Sridhar, whose carefully planted and mischievous question had triggered an unpleasant situation. I said what I had to say and left in disgust. Why give a damn about them! They are mere armchair activists with little understanding of what goes on in homes in Kashmir. Their arguments were dodgy and inconsequential.

The next day, Sridhar apologized to me. He said that he was only trying to prove some other point by considering an ideologically dichotomous perspective, and unintentionally, the spotlight had drifted towards my dad and me. I forgave him yet again. He said he hadn't meant to insult me in front of the others.

What insult? It was a bad joke. Do you even realize at what cost you wanted to prove a point? I reiterated for the last time. *Do not mess with me. Do not try to analyse an unanalysable human situation. For that you will need to be in my shoes. It's not a contradiction or a paradox. It will never be for either my dad or me. I can explain it, but I won't. Even if people think I am conflicted, so be it. I don't give a damn.*

It was then that I decided to make my position clear. I joined a massive protest. I made a speech in which I spoke about my father and his duty and love towards his people in a place where common people live in constant fear of being killed. I bemoaned the loss of innocent lives in Kashmir. I held up a placard, not to prove a point but because I had done so, many times; just not outside in the streets and in full public display to garner attention, rather in solitude. Certain grievances and qualms must remain a private matter, not to be shared with anyone, not even with friends.

The deed was done and I geared up for the consequences.

'If Kashmir becomes free sometime in the future, your dad will become the top cop of independent Kashmir,' joked Sara. 'Or maybe he will have retired by then and both of you will settle down here in London.'

The very same evening, attention-grabbing headlines and posts flashed across news sites and social media platforms:

> Daughter of a Top Commandant of Kashmir's Special Forces—an infamous Police unit accused of frequent human rights violations in Kashmir—leads a protest in London

> London-based Kashmiri law student distances herself from her police officer father's misdeeds in Kashmir

> Kashmiri student-activist upholds human rights—Doesn't spare her father, a top cop in Kashmir accused of corruption and fake encounters

Accompanying the headlines were distasteful images: a policeman trampling a small boy holding a rosebud in his hand, a weeping girl silhouetted against coils of concertina wire, a woman beating her chest with her son's body in her lap, a map of Kashmir torn to shreds under the boots of a cop, blood dripping on tulips, red snow. All of this was the conspiratorial handiwork of the usual suspects! When you get a photo wrong, you get everything wrong. I received phone calls from some beat reporters and social media news junkies, hungry for stories that show even the slightest potential to create sensation. Calls and messages asking me nauseating questions and seeking clarification and further details about what I had said at the protest march. 'Is it true that your father is accused of dozens of false encounters in Kashmir and that he's enjoying complete impunity? Does he confide in you? Do you agree with his actions? Why have you now distanced yourself from him and his actions? Do you intend to speak more on this subject in future? Are you going to take your activism to Kashmir?'

Sara stood by me. 'You realize I don't have a cause. I am neither here nor there. I belong nowhere. But you must do what is right…' she said. She was furious too. She was enraged at what people were saying about me. She took them on.

'She's the brightest and the most principled of us all,' she said to the others about me. 'She won't spare even her father in matters of truth and justice.' Sara's intention was right. She wanted to shut people's mouths. 'These people are stupid,' she said about those trying to malign me and typecast me to suit their vested interests. 'Don't talk to them anymore and don't let their stupidity bother you.'

Thereafter, I decided to keep mum about my father, although certain truths can't be kept private and will always be presented as doctored and twisted versions in the public domain, courtesy of those obsessed with the developments in Kashmir. Especially those who want to constantly stoke the fire, create rifts and partitions within the society, and tear our relationships apart. Dad had warned me against such people. Then there are those fund-seeking conference-hoppers, who choose to keep tabs on my dad and create an outrage over almost everything good or bad concerning him and his men. This is the reason I find myself regretting having talked about my father with anyone on campus or outside. Even with Sara, although she shared everything with me. We had a no-secrets code between us. It's an important code between two close friends. 'There should be no secrets between us,' she would say.

But now there are and I can't disclose them to her or to anyone else.

Sara has been there for me, both in times of crisis and joy. She's the only one who can read my mind and interpret my silences. She feels the same way about me. Maybe she's mistaken. Maybe both of us are mistaken. We often have heart-to-hearts, but I always dread bringing up the topic of my dad and his work in Kashmir.

Sara's parents aren't British by birth. She is. Her mother is Portuguese and her father, who's originally from Lahore, is a British citizen now. Having migrated to the UK in the 80s, he is now a successful real estate agent in London. He has had his share of struggles and misfortunes though. But then, as they say, 'fortune favours the brave'; he found his calling in real estate and did exceedingly well. Well-to-do and well-respected by those who know him, he continues to inspire Sara with his austere way of life. It is very evident in their relationship. She idolizes him. His office is a huge space, in the very heart of London and he has some very prominent Londoners and immigrants amongst his clientele. His business punch line—Creating Homes For You—is apt and reassuring. Sara knows what she's going to do once she's done with her PhD. She plans to expand her father's business and establish a law firm, especially for the immigrants living in the UK. She's on course to realize her dreams. 'Good things will happen, god willing,' she prays. Nothing gives me more happiness than seeing the glimmer of hope in her eyes whenever she talks about her father and his struggle to make London their home. Purely out of filial affection, she would imitate his funny accent: 'Everything is for Sara, my only child.'

Now the worst is happening. I am leaving without informing her. I haven't even left a note. Will she see this as a betrayal? I don't want her to forgive me. But the opposite will happen. She will forgive me. It's not in her nature to forgive so easily but she loves me.

Now that there's no time, I feel a strong urge to confide in Sridhar and tell him things I haven't told him earlier. The flight is about to take off. I want to hear his voice. I am not sure if he wants to hear mine.

An unlikely conversation is already taking place in my mind.

7

The memory of a similar day of parting comes alive.

Dad has come to see me off at the Srinagar airport. I am to board a flight to Delhi and then fly to London from there. Dad doesn't make use of his privilege and power to accompany me to the boarding gate. There isn't an entourage with him. He has strictly instructed his staff and security detail to stay away that morning. They know the consequences of not following his orders. In the past they have tasted repercussions. They are in a fix. How should they not do what they are supposed to do? They don't want to disobey their commanding officer. But they still have an important job to do. After all, it is a matter of the security; the top cop's daughter mustn't be left alone at any time, not even when she's inside an airport. Dad whispers these parting words to me, 'We shall meet sometime next spring. Zubair and I will come over to see you. You know how impossible it is for me to leave everything and go anywhere. I will have to obtain a No Objection Certificate from the government to leave the country. You know what all it takes. Duty takes precedence over everything...'

Hasn't it always?

'I am going to give it my best shot' is what Dad wants to say but doesn't.

At the airport, officials greet me. They escort me right up to the plane. To them, I am a very important person, a dignitary of sorts. They accompany me to the plane, and they wait next to me until the announcement about departure is made.

Dad's 'next spring' never came.

I'm about to take off. What if I don't return? Will you... ?

My question remains unanswered. 'You should have told Sara,' Sridhar says, emphatically. 'What will she think? She'll ask me. What am I supposed to say?'

You know what to say.

'Stop talking to me and tell her now. It's important.'

It is too late. There is no time.

'There is time.'

Will you make it stop?

'Sara will think, she told Sridhar, and not me?'

What a terrible thought! That I might never get to see Sara again is making me think things over again. I must stop thinking this way or I will never be able to face her again. I am just beginning to understand the true nature of my relationship with her. In this battle between reason and emotion, reason must win.

Sara's name flashes on my phone. I am seated inside the plane. We are now taxiing on the runway, seconds until take off. I realize what a blunder Sridhar has committed by telling Sara about my sudden and unannounced departure. I didn't want to break her heart and disappoint her. But someday if I do meet her again, I shall plead guilty and not justify my betrayal. I shall beg for forgiveness.

If the day has begun in such a way, how will it end?

The plane takes off and the phone screen goes blank.

Quit or Die

1

The trouble really began in spring when I decided to take Sara to Kashmir. Why did I even think of it? It was my idea, and Sara was thrilled about it. Sara's dad would often share his memories of Mirpur. His mother's family came from there. Somehow, the topic of life in Mirpur always came up whenever I visited Sara's house in London. 'We are Kashmiris too,' Sara's dad would say. There were times I wanted to explain the difference between *his* Kashmir and *my* Kashmir, but out of respect I kept quiet. And, by Kashmir, I didn't mean the geographical landmass; I meant people and their way of life, the culture, the attributes and the peculiarities. Sara, on the other hand, was well-versed in such matters. She saw her dream—of travelling to Kashmir with me—on the verge of coming true.

We started thinking enthusiastically about the trip and what all could be done to make it happen. Sara's elation knew no bounds—for the first time I saw her child-like excitement at the very thought of being able to set foot in *my* Kashmir. The prospect of going to Kashmir with me, and spending an entire month there gave her food for thought; the rebel-activist in her never slept. She had a knack for spotting opportunities. She was picturing our trip in her mind already, 'Imagine what all we can do... We shall explore the hinterland.... We will get a first-hand view into things… You will take me to places where you spent your childhood and wonder years… Your dad can show us places that we otherwise wouldn't be allowed to see…' She went on and on visualizing us having the trip of our lifetimes, a trip to remember.

The first hurdle was informing dad and getting him to say yes. Not just a maybe yes, but an emphatic yes!

We started drawing up a list of places to go to. Some of them were in far-flung areas that even I had not been to. Uri, Neelam, Gurez, Lolab and Bangus were on the list. Places I had seen only in photographs. You take one look at the photographs of these places and the heaven-on-earth epithet stands justified.

But the thought of persuading dad was a cause for concern for me. What if he acted pricey or simply brushed the idea aside or dismissed it for some reason or the other? Sara believed my dad would help us and arrange everything if I argued the case well. 'We will constantly have people at our beck and call,' she said, excitedly. 'He will make sure we achieve everything on our to-do list. After all, he rules the roost there.'

Well, I thought, this wasn't just wishful thinking; it was very much possible and doable!

When I first tossed the idea to dad, casually, he didn't say anything, except that I should think things over carefully before bringing Sara to Kashmir. His exact words—let's give it a careful thought—seemed positive though. Caution is always his first reaction, I thought. Nothing wrong with being cautious!

From my perspective, the first conversation on this topic was just to test the waters and to see how dad would react and respond. It wasn't a complete disaster thankfully. I couldn't imagine dad doing the same, as in gauge my reaction to his mannerly and well-intentioned request for some additional deliberation on the matter. At least, he hadn't dismissed the idea. His considerate reaction bowled me over. That's normal, nothing wrong with it, I thought. *We must and we will, for sure, think carefully.* But we had already thought carefully, very carefully. All he meant was if we had indeed given everything a good thought, then we could go ahead with the plan. At least, that was what I inferred from his 'let's give it a careful thought.'

I realized my fears were unfounded: *I needn't be so paranoid. Dad would never say no to me. How stupid of me to think otherwise.*

Then, in the next conversation on this very topic, dad left me with more things to reflect upon. 'Think about it carefully and rationally.' The word 'rationally' being the only addition to his sentence! It took me some time to comprehend that his tone sounded warning-like, hinting at a possibility that we were rushing into things and weren't taking enough time to mull over the idea properly. The tendency to read too much into words…

The third conversation began with the same request but ended with a different proposition: 'There are other better places in the world to go to.'

'What better place than Kashmir?' said Sara when I told her what dad had said.

We had already made up our minds; therefore, there was no point in mulling over the plan or coming up with alternative plans. Kashmir was the only plan. But so far, no luck with dad! However, I did get a feeling that our plan was not something he had written off completely.

Thereafter, in all subsequent chats with dad, he kept repeating the same thing, but added a few enticements to lead us on to a different track: 'Think about it. Go to places you haven't seen.

Both of you! Explore new habitats. See new people. Discover new cultures. Create new memories. How about South America? Don't worry about money and expenses. Everything will be taken care of...'

My 'but dad' pleas kept falling on deaf ears.

I didn't want to impose dad's contrarian and unjustified proposition on Sara, lest she felt unwelcome. What would she think of him? I wondered. That he's heartless and that she would be a liability in Kashmir! Also, the thought 'what would she think of me?' tore me apart.

Then, in the next conversation, citing security-related reasons, dad said spring wasn't a good time for the trip. I saw a ray of hope and took a chance. I proposed summer. A few days later when I brought up the topic again, he said summer wasn't a good time either. I didn't give up: *How about autumn? Nothing happens in autumn. People prepare for winter and life comes to a halt there.* He said he would think and let me know. Autumn was still a good six months away. And six months was a long time.

Dad stuck to his excuses: 'You don't want to ruin your vacation especially when you're bringing Sara along.'

I stuck to mine: *Why won't you make things happen for us? Just this one time! Am I asking too much? It's important because I have promised Sara. It was my idea in the first place. What will she think if I tell her now that we should drop the idea? If it were her dad, he would certainly help us out.*

It was a nasty thing to say, but it just came out at the spur of the moment. I didn't mean to draw comparisons between the attitudes of two fathers towards their daughters' wishes, but justifying dad's refusal to Sara was a disconcerting thought.

'You have got to explain things to her...' dad kept on saying.

'And more importantly, to yourself… What's wrong with you…?'

I didn't want to dampen Sara's spirits and become the cause of her disappointment. I knew what she would say in case I told her dad's consistent and unwavering stand on our plan: 'What's the big deal? We can go ourselves. Let's not be a bother to your dad. He has far more important things to do and we shouldn't burden him. It's just a trip. We can figure things out ourselves. Book tickets, take a flight, and land up there. Haven't we made many such trips here in the UK? You're such a worrywart. Leave it to me. You just relax. We will not tell anyone about this. Nobody will come to know. And tell your dad we will take care of ourselves and won't do anything that will cause him worry…'

'What's the big deal?' was her mantra in such matters.

It was summer, time for Sara to apply for her visa. She got all her paperwork done and we geared up for Plan B just in case Plan A should not materialize. If not autumn, then winter; if not winter, then the next spring. We were adamant on going to Kashmir come what may. But dad was still suggesting we go to some other place. I didn't yield. I remembered what dad had once said to me, 'You know there are no such things as desires and wishes. You either do it and make it happen or you don't.'

Therefore, I persisted: *How about we come home first to Srinagar, stay there for a few days, assess the situation, and then decide where to go and if at all to go? We won't do anything against your wishes. It's a promise.*

'What places do you have in mind?'

How about Gurez Valley? It's far from civilization and very safe. Nobody will come to know…

'Gurez?'

Why not? You once talked about it, remember?

‘I never talked about it. You must have dreamt it.’

So what? Can’t we…

‘Foreigners aren’t allowed there, Zooni. Your friend will need a permit to go there…’

What good are you, dad, if you won’t make it happen for us? Even if you think it is risky, you know ways to protect us. You safeguard everyone else but what about your own daughter and her best friend? Dad, are you listening? Please…

His terrifying silence meant only one thing.

Dad’s rebuke—‘You and I should speak in one voice when it comes to matters like this’—led me to think: What should be done now? How should I handle the situation? I couldn’t come up with any more excuses. I didn’t want to. Sara would say the same thing: ‘let’s go, you and I; nothing will happen.’

It doesn’t work that way in Kashmir, was what I decided to tell Sara. Daughter of a top cop roaming with a friend attracts undue attention.

But come to think of it, dad only had to agree to instruct his staff and everything else would fall into place. That’s how it works for many others who are in power. His colleagues would do anything for their children.

The voices in my head drove me insane, ‘Maybe you should stick to usual things and join the seasonal holidayers. If that doesn’t work, then how about a solo trip to Cornwall? Rent a bike and ride along the coast. Go to a club and drown your worries in you-know-what. Things will happen. Or better still, forget everything and stay put. No, don’t give up so easily, stay focused, try harder…’

Then, one last desperate attempt at eliciting a considerate response from dad: *I have no one to curse but myself. How I wish the idea had never occurred to me. I will lose face in front of Sara. Because of you, dad, your daughter's dignity is at stake.*

'You're behaving very immaturely, Zooni. And you very well know it.'

Now who's behaving immaturely?

'Ok, here's the deal. How about Iran? Grandpa always wanted you to go there. It was his dying wish. Don't you remember? It's still on your bucket list, right? I think it's a fabulous idea. As far as Kashmir is concerned, let's keep it for next summer. I promise.'

Iran? Isn't it unsafe there as well? But if you don't want us to come, then I will end it right now. No point in keeping on about it.

Dad looked upon our Kashmir plan as a predicament. And he wanted to solve the problem his way. His solution—drop Kashmir, go to Iran instead—was clever because to end the stalemate and still be seen as the guardian of his only daughter's dignity, he had to invoke grandpa and his dying wish. I almost fell for the emotional blackmail.

But now that dad had involved grandpa, then what ought to be taken into account is what grandpa would have said and how he would have dealt with the case. How would he dole out justice? What would his verdict be in this battle of ideas between his prosecutor son and defence counsel granddaughter?

My case was watertight. In the court of law, I would have argued: 'Kashmir first, and then Iran, because grandpa would also have wanted that, and there's enough evidence of it...'

'Never give in' was what my dad had taught me. I would have dropped the idea if Sara hadn't been the prospective fellow traveller. But then the question of my doing this all by myself would never exist. The whole purpose was to go to Kashmir with Sara so that she could do and see all that she wanted to. I agree some of the things on her to-do list appeared reckless but that was the bloody point. To do what we had thought of doing. All I expected from dad was to relent and play an important role in defending our trip and making it happen for Sara and me. It was a mere trifling. I wasn't asking for the moon.

It was a matter of prestige. Resting the case was not even a remote possibility.

Time started slipping by. June made way for July and July for September. Autumn was just a month away. The time to go was in November. Winter was going to be impossible. The roads to those beautiful valleys are closed during winters. No one can go there, but nothing was impossible for dad. Day after day, he refused to surrender to his daughter's wishes.

There was nothing I could do. Nothing that could change his mind!

Dad, it's been two years, don't you want me to come home and see you?

Dad's silence concealed his answer. I was not to bring the topic up anymore. Thereafter, he stopped answering my calls and messages until the only sound I heard over the phone was a beep-beep-beep.

It was time to tell Sara the unpleasant decision. But I feared what she would say in such a situation: 'If not *your dad's* Kashmir, how about *my dad's* Kashmir? You know what I mean. My dad has connections and he knows how to pull strings. We land in Lahore and take a SUV to Mirpur. Bangus and Lolab are not that far from there. We can sneak in if you're up for an adventure. A win-win, don't you agree? It will be a secret mission. Are you game?'

Imagine dad's face at the very thought of it! He might well shoot me in the head even if it were a joke.

What a pity! It's almost laughable. Sara's dad creates a distinction between two Kashmirs and we begin evaluating possibilities. We were torn between an uncertain binary of *her* K and *my* K. It was almost like a serious joke.

Sara was beyond persuading. She had made up her mind. I was in a quandary, but I didn't want to play spoilsport. Dad may be right. I evaluated possibilities—worst-case scenarios and next best options. I readied a justification for Sara just in case. I prepared arguments and counter-arguments: *What if dad is right?* Yet, I saw hope in dad's silence even when there was none. He hadn't ruled out the possibility of making it happen for us next summer. Iran wasn't a bad idea. We should give it a serious thought.

But the K plan was on and it was still Plan A. We kept it on the front burner. As dad would say, 'Never quit. Cowards quit. The brave get what they seek at any cost and in any situation, no matter if they live or die.' I would never disregard his teachings even at the cost of not listening to him on this particular occasion. Both of us were right in our own ways and neither of us was ready to relinquish our position.

The last recourse was to leave everything to the stars.

2

In December, just a day before Sara and I were to depart London for Tehran with a stopover at Istanbul, I got a message from Uncle Dar, dad's second-in-command and his most trusted deputy: 'Come home immediately. Do not tell anyone there anything, and even here after you land. Pretend everything is okay and wait for me at your house. I will come for you. You won't be able to reach your dad or me. But we are together.'

Little had I thought that Uncle Dar's message would become the cause of my last-minute betrayal of Sara. Who would have thought that the grand plan—doing big and small things, things we had never done before, and compensate for the lost dream—would crumble to bits? But it happened and, in a twinkling, I took a call. There was no vacillating between let's-wait and nothing-bad-will-happen. There were no maybes and ifs and buts. I booked myself on the first available flight to Srinagar via New Delhi and readied to leave without informing Sara. Sridhar came to know. Well, I had to tell him. To be honest, I told him for reasons I am still unable to explain to myself. It just came out of me. It shouldn't have, at any cost. I couldn't keep it to myself. I should have. Weakness is the most terrible of things. So is love—stupidest of emotions.

I read Uncle Dar's message again and again. What was he trying to say and what is he concealing, I wondered. I imagined dad and him camping quietly in a remote place, readying a surprise for me. But this wasn't a prank. They were no longer reachable on the phone. My messages to dad went unanswered; my calls were met with a beep. Uncle Dar had said that there was no point in even trying.

I would be able to find out everything only after I reached home.

Uncle Dar's cryptic message ended abruptly. At first, I thought there was more to come. But I was wrong. Dad would never think of dictating such a message meant for me to anyone. Not even to Uncle Dar. He's not a person who hides behind the nuances of language. He gives orders himself. I had seen enough evidence of that lately. But then the abruptness of the message made me jittery. Was it on purpose? I had no clue. Dad would never let his guard down with anyone, let alone his own daughter. Was I reading more than needed into this? Or was this message a means to dissuade Sara and me from landing up unannounced? If so, it was the worst ploy. Dad would never employ such wily means.

It was going to be a long night before I could reach him and find out these answers. Home was far away and time was slipping through my fingers.

It was at that moment I tuned in to the news from Kashmir. The skirmishes between the Special Forces and militants and their supporters were almost a daily affair. But because these things happened routinely, they didn't even make the headline. However, on that particular day something stirred in me. It was the first time I felt this way.

I read a headline:

> Militants kidnap 3 Special Police Officers in North Kashmir

Then I read another and another and another:

> Two Special Police Officers resign after the abduction and killing of their commandant in Kashmir
>
> Six more officers of Kashmir's elite Special Forces quit after receiving warning letters from militants
>
> Four more kin of Special Forces Officers abducted by militants in South Kashmir
>
> Abduction and killing of Special Police Officers in Kashmir casts a shadow on the future of security in the valley
>
> Kashmiri cops targeted again—Militants abduct and kill two Special Forces cops and post a video online

> Militant-turned-cop killed on his first day of duty

> Militant avenges the death of his slain kin. Kidnaps and kills the kin of Special Forces Officer

Then a shocking headline:

> Valley-based militant groups give final ultimatum to Special Forces Officers: 'Quit or Die'

3

I glance upon the map on the screen in front of me. The plane—a blinking dot on the screen—is hovering over Central Asia. This is the closest I will ever get to Iran. My grandpa's dying wish won't go unfulfilled now. Part of Sara's and my grand plan has come true. Ahead lies the Hindu Kush range, and in another four hours the plane will enter Indian airspace.

I surf the channels on the in-flight entertainment system. I choose Film. I make a random selection and press the button. A movie starts playing on the miniature screen in front of me. I put on the headphones. Moments after the opening credits, a scene catches my attention.

A uniformed man with his hands tied behind his back and mouth taped has been pinned to the ground by two masked boys with guns in their hands. The place—a wooden shed with a thatched roof—is deep inside a thicket and surrounded by verdant paddy fields. It is summertime, and there are streams nearby, shimmering with water from the mountain springs.

A young boy points the muzzle of a gun at the captured man's temple. The boy is taller than his partner who's holding a piece of paper in front of the captured man. Pointing his pistol at the message written on the paper, he screams into the man's face: 'Didn't you heed the warning? Read what it says. Doesn't it say you must quit and repent or face dire consequences? What part of it didn't you understand?'

Two other boys are silently filming the entire scene using their mobile phones. Their hands are steady. One of them steps forward and rips the captured man's shirt. He tears the rank insignia—three five-pointed stars—stitched on the shoulder loops of the hostage's shirt. Then he stamps on it with his muddied boots and signals to the short boy for further instructions.

'Read,' the short boy yells at the detainee. 'We are warriors of this holy land, you traitor. We are the guardians of our faith and land and you're siding with the usurpers…'

'He's not a traitor,' cries an old man sitting nearby. 'Spare him. I'm begging you…'

'Quiet,' admonishes the tall boy, signalling at the old man to stop intervening. 'We know what we're doing.'

'You're too young to understand. You're like my children. The man is one of us. What sin has he committed?' asks the old man with an empathetic look in his eyes.

'You should know what he's done,' the short boy growls, giving the old man a fearsome look.

'He's just doing a job. It's his duty to protect us and this beautiful land of ours. He's helpless before his children. He's doing this for them. Think of them. What will they do? They will die. They will curse us…'

'He's the curse,' shouts the tall boy, turning his fierce gaze back at the handcuffed captive.

'Someday this man will save you. He will save us all from

ruin. He's innocent. In god's name, let him go. Set him free…'

The tall boy squeezes the trigger of his gun and fires in the air.

'God is with us,' the boys roar in unison.

'Stop! Don't do it,' the old man implores. 'He's a poor soul. Think of his mother and father and children. What will they do? Where will they go? What will they eat? What will they wear? Who will look after them if he dies…'

'Looks like you also haven't read the letter,' says the gun-wielding short boy. 'Everything has been explained to him and others like him. How many times does the obvious have to be explained to our own people who are hell-bent on betraying us?' He starts circling the hostage in an intimidating manner. The prisoner is motionless. His head is bowed, and he seems to have resigned to his fate partly out of helplessness and partly out of a sense of revulsion at how the situation has turned out.

'But his old father and mother…his small children…?' stammers the old man in a desperate attempt to seek the hostage's release on grounds of mercy. Little does he realize that he has run out of excuses and that merely citing the man's family won't melt the hearts of the resolute boys, who are determined to carry out the sentence no matter what.

Raising his hand at the old man, as if he's about to breach the line, the short boy screams, 'You are worried about his father and mother and children and the fathers and mothers and children of others like him? What about our fathers who sacrificed their lives? They laid down their lives so that we would someday take up their noble cause and purify this land so that our children can breathe freedom.'

The tall boy jumps in: 'This holy land is smeared with the blood of our fathers. Don't you remember their supreme sacrifices? Do you think we will let their martyrdom go in vain?'

'But children are children,' says the old man. 'They must not be made to pay for the deeds of their fathers...'

'You talk of this traitor's children?' howls the short boy. 'Don't you know the facts? His children are well settled in foreign shores. They will never return to their homeland. They don't even think of this country as their homeland. They don't like it here. They think this place is no good. They don't see the blood of our fathers in the soil. They visit their own homeland as tourists. Horrendous tramplers of our ancestral blood! That's what they have become...'

The old man tilts his head sideways indicating that he's paying attention to every word thrown at him. He moistens his lips with the tip of his tongue and bends down submissively: 'What will his children do in case you...'

'Look at our children. Do you even bother about them? Do you care what will happen to them? They will be orphaned tomorrow. Who will take care of them then? Who will pay for their food and clothing? They will have nothing. This traitor might even hunt them if we let him go alive. But we know that they too will rise against the tyranny and oppression for they are not like this traitor's children. They have conscience and real education. Their education is in taking up our cause. You think this traitor's kith and kin will starve to death if he dies?'

'But what if...?'

'No more buts and ifs,' chides the gun-wielding tall boy, tightening the hold over his prisoner, and looking intently into the old man's eyes. 'You know how much he and his ilk are paid to kill us? You know how many of our brothers he has killed so far and how much money he has made? Look at the mansion he has built. Look at the fortune he has amassed. Whose blood do you think is in it? It's blood money his mansion and fortunes are built on. This traitor has traded his faith and morality for money and fame. If he wishes, he will trade this holy land and all its inhabitants for more money. Such is his greed. And it is people like you who make him think he's some kind of a legend. He will pay for his unholy acts now...'

'No, no, he's not a traitor,' persists the old man. 'He's the son of our soil. Give him another chance. One last chance...'

'Shut up, you fool!' fumes the tall boy furiously with a look that signals the end of the argument.

'We gave him enough chances, didn't we?' interjects the short boy. 'We are not like him who ambushes his own people and shoots them in the back without a warning. Unlike him and his gang, we are humane, as god would expect of us. We warned him in advance. We waited for him to comply. We gave him enough time. And what does he do? He tears our letter in front of everybody. He makes a joke of us in front of the whole world. He ridicules the noble cause we are fighting for. Remember what he said, "I warn these wayward boys against lifting a finger against my men. None of my men will quit." He calls us terrorists. Who does he think he is? A saviour?'

'Forgive him then. It is god's wish to forgive people...'

'Read the letter again. He's a traitor and a blasphemer, and you're equally to blame,' the short boy says.

The old man sits motionless as he listens to the boys' arguments passively. He is unflustered as if he has nothing to lose. He goes on chanting, 'It is god's wish to forgive...god's wish to forgive...'

'You have no idea about god's wish,' refutes the short boy.

'Brother,' the tall boy interrupts, sensing that their whole plan is going awry. The expression on his face changes as he suddenly comprehends the old man's diversionary and devious tactics: to buy more time until either he or his partner are convinced of the immorality or the futility of what they are about to do; or until they fall out with each other and then one of them either gives up or ditches the other.

Dragging his partner closer, and in a final bid to keep him from engaging into any further argument with the old man, he whispers into his ear: 'This good-for-nothing senile man is the least of our worries. We will deal with him later. Let's not waste any more time in doing what we were supposed to have done hours earlier.'

'You're right, big brother, but I want to...'

Seeing a window of opportunity, the old man mumbles, 'God, grant these innocent boys wisdom to distinguish good from bad. Grant them knowledge and forbearance to bear the unbearable. And save this poor man's children from becoming orphans...' He goes on and on, persistently.

'It's pointless, brother,' the tall boy mutters again into his partner's ear while allowing the old man to babble on about children, mercy, compassion, conscience, good, bad, forbearance and god. 'He is a foolish old man, past his prime. He sounds like a broken record. He will go on repeating the same stupid excuse endlessly...'

'But shouldn't we...? We must not let him...' The short boy doesn't seem to be convinced. He wants to give it one more shot. He doesn't want any loose ends.

Running out of patience, and yet not losing his composure, the tall boy murmurs: 'No, brother, no, don't get carried away by the deceptions of ignorant and uneducated fools like him and others. They have been made to believe in lies and fabrications. They have no morals. They can't even think straight. They have lost the ability to tell a lie from truth, good from evil, just from unjust. They have neither reason nor foresight and judgement. It's because of people like them that we have been subjugated this long. That's why we have not seen victory so far. They, too, are an obstacle to our war against oppression and corruption. But we won't let people like him come in the way of our worthy cause and deter us from taking the right decision. We will kill each one of the traitors until this land becomes pure again. We will purify it with or without anyone's help. The old man has done his job by bringing this traitor to us. But right now, it's up to us to finish him off on time and without any glitches.'

He gears up for the inevitable by clenching his left fist, expecting his partner to follow suit.

The old man's prattle is unending. 'Spare him! God! Please save him! What if he was your father? What would you do then?' He is relentless and hopeful that his ploy—to trigger a discord between the two boys—will work if he doesn't give up. His voice gains confidence, 'Spare him! Please save him...he's innocent... you know he's innocent...you don't want to do this...'

'Go back to your farm, old man, or else watch us do our job,' warns the tall boy. He signals his partner to stay mum.

'O kind fathers and mothers,' the old man goes on tirelessly, feeling more and more invested in the dispute, 'where is the compassion you claim to have instilled in your children?'

'If it comes to choosing between our father and the cause of this land, you know what we will choose. We will kill our own mothers and fathers if it comes to that...' lectures the tall boy convincingly and in a manner as though he's addressing a large gathering. He turns his gaze back at his partner and then at the other boys filming the proceedings. A discreet yet cautious signal is exchanged.

Facing the old man, the boys begin to chant, 'Someday you will realize the cost of your happiness and freedom. You will repent that day. You will beg for forgiveness but we won't be around. You won't even find our bodies. We won't even have graves. But, at least, this land will be pure once again.'

'Someday you will repent…' says the old man to the boys as he begins to cover his eyes with his hands.

The gun-toting short boy walks up to a beehive in the shed and lifts the lid. The chanting continues. A swarm of bees is unleashed upon the captured man.

The scene changes. A figure silhouetted against the dying sun is running towards the captured man in the shed. It's a girl with golden hair. No one can tell if she's happy or sad. She reaches the shed and throws her arms around the captured man. Behind them is a burning beehive and the bodies of the boys. The old man is dead from a blow to his head.

Marvelling at the golden sky, the girl whispers into her father's ear, 'Look dad, sunset.'

Holding the hand of his little girl, the man walks up to a stream nearby, fetches water and pours some of it into the dead man's mouth.

Soft music plays and the scene fades out.

The music is interrupted by an announcement: 'Ladies and gentlemen, this is your captain speaking from the flight deck. We're cruising at an altitude of 31,000 feet. The air can't be clearer than it is right now. If you're occupying window seats, do take a look outside. It's a magnificent view down below. You will see a river meandering through dunes of sand. We're flying over Iran and the river is Karun. We also have a special message for Ms Zooni Aziz who's flying with us today. Ms Aziz, a very happy birthday to you! This is going to the longest birthday of your life as we traverse long time zones. Sit back, relax and enjoy the flight. We wish you happy times ahead.'

4

Dad and I are camping in the woods. He returns in the dead of the night. It is snowing outside. Dogs are barking. Dad enters the cabin dressed as a snowman. He holds a dead game bird in his hands with its head chopped off. Blood is dripping off the bird's long, slender neck. Its claws are still trembling. I have never seen a bird like that. I'm scared to ask dad what it is. It's a horrifying sight. Dad places the bird on the floor and lights a fire. Unable to bear the sight of what he's doing, I look away. After some time, Dad serves both of us. He puts a handful of meat into his mouth. I look at him sheepishly. I inspect his hands carefully. The look in his eyes and the movement of his jaws do not betray either guilt or remorse. He looks at me and asks me to taste the meat. I am terrified. He licks his fingers, moves his hand to the plate in front of me, mixes some meat with rice, kneads a morsel, picks it up in his fingers and moves it towards my mouth. I open my mouth and... I lick his fingers. The next morning, the sky clears up. Dad readies for another hunt.

Days later, I realize it was not my dad's first kill. He's an ace hunter. He takes me hunting the following year. For the first time in my life, I see birds in the sky and atop trees waiting to be brought down. Birds with long necks, wide feathery wings and large beaks are all over the place. It's the largest ever gathering of birds from unseen lands. At first, I practise using a slingshot that dad has made for me. But dad soon teaches me how to use a bow and arrows. There are plenty of missed targets and wasted arrows, especially when the targets are high in the sky or hidden in the trees. The real fun starts when I lay my hands on an air rifle. Dad doesn't say no to me. I become indiscriminate. Then, once when I am about to bring down a majestic bird sitting atop the highest branch of a tree, dad stops me. 'Not that one,' he says. 'She always sits that high to keep vigil. If you observe her long enough, you will get to know a secret.' I ask dad what the bird's secret is, but he smiles and says, 'You shall have to spare her, give her a chance, and a day will come when you will either discover the secret yourself or the bird will reveal it to you. But you shall have to wait till that day and keep your eyes and ears open when no one else is looking.'

Then comes the day when I go hunting alone. I collect trophies, and I don't know what to do with them until dad says we could give them away to neighbours. They don't believe him when he tells them whose doing it is. That very moment, I want to show them how I do things. I want to give them instant proof by aiming at something high up and bringing it down with just a single shot. But I remember dad's words, 'Don't be impatient when people don't believe you, a day will come they will see you in action and be stunned at what you are capable of.' So I remain calm and revel in people's disbelief at my claims. From that day onwards, hunting becomes a 'thing'. Everyone looks at me oddly, as if what I'm doing isn't the normal thing to do. They believe a girl my age isn't supposed to do such things. I don't pay attention to these people. Dad is always on my side. And it is my job to do things that nobody else can. Nothing else matters!

5

The truth is that I didn't quite know that my father was a police officer until I was about eight or ten. I hadn't seen him in uniform until then. By the time he returned home from work, I was asleep, and by the time I woke up, he was gone. Then one day, I dreamt of him and in my dream he was dressed as a police officer. The next day, I told my classmates that my father was a police officer. At the time I didn't know I was merely borrowing an image from a dream. Once when dad came to visit me in school, I hid under a table because he wasn't in uniform and I thought everyone would get to know what a liar I was and then I would stand exposed before everyone. In the evening, I confessed to dad that I had lied about him. 'That I am a police officer,' he said, laughing. 'But I *am* a police officer.'

The next day, he showed up wearing a uniform with stars and medallions all over it. He seemed unreal. A sudden realization that dad must have rented the uniform just to please me and make me happy dawned on me. Forest Lane was full of such shops where you could rent fancy clothes and uniforms worn by people like policemen, fire brigade officers, construction workers, mountaineers, and adventurers. Fancy dress partygoers often went there to pick outlandish gear and fashion wear.

One summer's day, dad said he would take me to his office. We got ready and left. It was a bright Sunday afternoon, and I got to sit next to him in his jeep. A shiny medal adorned the pocket flap of his jacket. But he didn't take me to the police station as he had promised. We drove to the meadows in Pahalgam where we had picnicked many times. A large crowd greeted us, and we drove through the crowd as though we were the chief guests in a grand celebration. Dad didn't tell me anything about what was going on but I guessed that preparations were under way for a large carnival. There were cameras and lighting equipment all around. Big buses decorated for the occasion were parked along the road leading up to the meadow. People wore colourful clothes. Had I known that we were going to a film shoot, I would have told my friends about it; or at least I would have told them that I was going to see film stars. Dad was in charge of everything. He was greeted with salutes. So was I. Everything unfolded perfectly that day. Nothing went wrong. There was order even though the crowd was impatient to mingle with the hero and the heroine. Children wearing colourful dresses flocked the place. And then loud music started playing. A song to which the hero and the heroine started dancing echoed off the face of a mountain. And then came the moment of disbelief when dad introduced me to the hero and the heroine. He told them I was his daughter and I shyly hid behind him, not knowing what to say or do. The hero and the heroine shook my hand and then told dad how grateful they were to him for making the security arrangements. Dad said he was simply carrying out his duty and it was his job to make sure everything fell in place for the cast and crew. 'Come to Bombay and meet us,' said the hero. The day ended on a happy note and, the next day, I told my friends that I had been to an actual film shoot and to my shock, nobody except Nusrat believed me. Everybody else thought I was fibbing. I had no proof to furnish in support of my claims of having met the hero and heroine. Dad was the only proof and he wouldn't talk about it.

A year later, when another film crew came over to shoot for

a film in the same meadow, the situation was no different than it had been in the previous year except that it was the chilliest winter in years and there was abundant snow everywhere. Dad and an entire contingent of policemen had to jostle with people to keep them out of the way, though the entire meadow had been cordoned off for days so that nothing untoward happened during the filming. The whole place was under dad's command. Nobody was allowed to come or go freely. The liberty the onlookers and residents of the meadow had enjoyed during the previous shoot didn't exist. The trouble started when, not very far away from the meadow, dad performed a daring act by jumping into the icy waters of the river nearby to save a boy from drowning. But something else happened at the same time as the boy's accidental fall into the river. A short distance away, a girl had fallen into the river, too. She struggled to save herself from being dragged under the turbulent current.

Seeing dad jump into the water and swim towards the drowning village boy, the crowds of people started praying for a miracle. When dad was in the water, he saw not one but two kids. That girl was me. Dad had to make a choice between the two—the village boy and his own daughter. Seeing dad swimming towards the village boy, one of dad's daring officers jumped into the river to pull me out of it. The entire village witnessed the act. There was disbelief in people's eyes. Later, many things were said about dad. That he risked the life of his own child to save the poor boy. Others said that he couldn't differentiate between the two children who had fallen into the water and that he had had no idea that one of the children was his own daughter. Nobody knew the truth. The village people carried dad and his officer on their shoulders. Women hugged them and children saluted them. For saving the village boy, dad was given the title 'Lion of Pahalgam.' When the news about the incident spread across the whole of Kashmir, dad came to be known as the Lion of Kashmir. Tales of his valour were splashed all across the newspapers and narrated in homes and schools. A news report carrying photos of dad and his junior officer read: 'Police Officer Abdul Aziz prevents a catastrophe, saves a boy from drowning in the Lidder.'

The officer who had plunged into the turbulent river and saved me from drowning was none other than Salim Dar.

The Arrival

1

The plane begins its descent into the valley. I look out of the window and see nothing but a pristine whiteness that seems to have swallowed up everything—trees, houses, distant mountains, even the sky. It is a misty morning.

Outside the airport, a gigantic snow globe hangs precariously in the sky. A crack in the grey sky through which some light is escaping starts to close. At a distance, the lofty summits of a mountain range are sitting atop a black cloud. This is the same place where two years ago dad had seen me off and left me with a parting promise: 'Next Spring.'

A half-torn poster of 'Lion of the Desert' is pasted on a wall. If any outsider were to look at it they might think it is still 1985. There's a reason why no one has ripped the poster off the wall. It shows a messiah-like figure ready to be hanged.

At the taxi-booking booth, I ask for a taxi to take me home. I give the booth operator the address. To my dismay, things start falling apart. The booth operator says that no taxi is willing go to the city because the city is under curfew due to the ongoing violence.

What has happened?

'There is bloodbath in the city,' says the operator with an expression of anger and sorrow on his face. 'They torched the shrine at Khankah,' he adds. Other drivers gather around me to join the conversation.

Who is they? Who torched the shrine?

'The agents of the state, who else...they burnt it and are now blaming the liberators to give them a bad name.'

Is the news confirmed?

'News? How will you even get news? The government cuts off the Internet whenever we need it the most. They don't even want us to stay in touch with one another. They don't want you or anyone else to know what's going on here and what's happening to us. They want to send us back to the dark ages. They want us to perish along with our families...'

What are the Police doing?

'The bloody police know everything and are complicit. The whole thing is their doing. They are the real culprits.'

Are you sure it's the Police's doing?

'Everybody knows,' whispers a bystander, dejectedly. 'It is to give us all a bad name and to defame our legitimate struggle. It is the state's doing in connivance with the police agents...'

I plead with other taxi drivers loitering nearby: *Will someone please give me a ride?*

Nobody even looks at me. My pleas fall on deaf ears. I continue begging: *I'm not a tourist. I am a Kashmiri. All I want is to reach home.*

'It's too dangerous to go there,' they say. All of them refuse. 'Wait until the curfew is relaxed,' says somebody with a hint of assurance and hope.

But what if the curfew is not lifted? Where will I go?

At a distance, a bunch of foreign tourists get into a taxi and drive away.

How come you're taking the tourists but not me?

'It is because nobody else is going to the city. These tourists are going to Pahalgam.'

Pahalgam? I almost blurt out the truth about myself. But after hearing what the man had said about the burning of the shrine and whoever was responsible for the burning, I stay mum.

I make frantic inquiries and plead with the rest of the taxi drivers to consider my desperate request: *Is there no one?* Seeing me at my wits' end and in despair, an elderly man walks up to me with compassion and pity in his eyes. He has been standing nearby quietly listening to everything, until now.

'I'll take you, come with me,' he says, approaching me with steady steps. A child-like confidence in his gait and gestures sets him apart from the rest. 'Come on, let's go,' he says, rolling up the sleeve of his tunic and extending his welcoming hand towards me. The other taxi drivers begin to surround him threateningly as if he has committed a big blunder by agreeing to drive me to the city.

'Are you mad, Ali?' they warn him. 'You can't do this. The union's decision in inviolable. There will be consequences.' His expression changes from compassion to disdain. He grins at his fellow taxi drivers.

'She's like my daughter,' he says, without even looking at them.

Sensing resistance by the union people, he urges me to hurry towards the parking lot. Just then a tall man with a thick beard comes out of the booth and blocks our way to the parking lot where all the taxis are parked. He is evidently their union leader.

'Ali, you can't do this repeatedly,' says the union leader authoritatively. 'You know what is at stake. After all, it's everyone's life that's at stake not just yours. You don't have kids, but we do. Enough warnings have been given to us. Moreover, the holy shrine of Khankah is still burning. The entire area has been cordoned off. Not a soul is going to get through. You will be shot on sight and so will this innocent girl. I know you don't care about yourself but you are going to put her life in danger if you take her there…'

'Yes, yes, I know how to handle it, don't instruct me…'

Thank you! I express my gratitude to everyone for their concern but the kind-hearted taxi driver interrupts me: 'You don't speak to them and there's no need to thank anyone except god. I will make sure you reach home safe, come what may. Hurry up now…'

With a wave of his hand, he gestures to the taxi drivers and the union leader that he's neither inclined nor obligated to obey any rules and that he's going to do what he feels is right. He looks towards the sky as if someone up there is looking back at him and conveying some sort of an approval for the daring and risky mission he is about to undertake.

'Let him go,' says one taxi driver to the others, stubbing out his half-smoked cigarette and stomping it under the heels of his boots. 'He's incorrigible but lucky. Nothing will happen to him. He always escapes, and it is people like us who land up in trouble.' He then looks at me, and says, 'Go my dear, god be with you!'

The roads wear a deserted look. Fortunately, the policemen keeping vigil in the armoured vehicles parked on the roads don't stop us. The taxi driver talks to me and sensing my anguish, tries to comfort me. 'God will be kind to us,' he says with a look of compassion in his grey eyes. 'Humans are powerless, but we must be fearless in times like these.'

I look at my cell phone to check if there're any messages.

There's no signal. I turn the phone off and on several times to try my luck with the network. It is as good as dead, just like the city. Through the rearview mirror, the taxi driver notices my desperate attempts to revive the signal. 'No point trying,' he sighs. 'All phone lines are down. There's no cell network anywhere in town. The government has cut it off.'

For how long?

'No one knows.'

I try and make a random call in a hopeless bid to awaken the dead phone. Hopefully, it will work. An automated message greets me: 'Your call cannot be completed at this time. Please try again later…' The message keeps repeating. I keep at it. I don't want to give up; therefore, I keep trying. But, no luck. Maybe since we are driving through a bad network area, there's no signal. After all, we're still on the outskirts. Maybe I will get a signal once we are out of this wilderness. Every time I dial a number, a different message plays: 'All phone lines are down… All lines in this route are busy, please try again later...'

Sick of listening to the automated messages, I hang up. Seeing me give up hope, the driver casts another pitiful look at me.

Doesn't anybody know what's going on? Is it because the shrine is burning?

'It isn't just the shrine,' says the taxi driver with a sense of foreboding. 'This is just a precursor to a larger calamity. Doom is yet to come. God save us!'

What do you mean?

'It looks like the government is going to strip Kashmir off of its special status. We will be finished. It will be the end of us. More shrines will burn. Everything will burn and no one will come forward to douse the fires. Those who try to resist will be rounded up and thrown into trenches. We will be cut off from the outside world. Nobody will be allowed in or out.'

How can that be?

He pauses for a moment, takes a deep breath and exhales, and then casts a furtive glance at me through the rearview mirror.

'Yours was the last flight to land. The highway and the airport will be closed from tomorrow onwards. We will never know what is going on. Nor will anyone come to know about us. Whether we live or die. This wasn't supposed to happen… But you don't worry. I shall make sure you reach home safe…'

Thank you for…

'You should know everything—the truth,' he interjects. 'After all, you are expected to plead our case when you go back to London and America. Who else do we bank on?'

He falls silent.

I am home after two years. Dad is unreachable. I'm alone in a taxi and being driven into a city under strict curfew. It's the most unusual thing to happen to me in my entire life. The daughter of the head of Special Forces in Kashmir having to beg taxi operators to take her home and having to travel alone in a taxi with little assurance of a safe arrival! I don't even know the way home because dad has moved again. He keeps changing houses for various reasons. The place I am going to is his seventh residence. This house is in a colony on the outskirts of the old city.

Whatever is happening in the city right now, dad is in charge. And his only daughter is alone in a taxi and might possibly become the target of one of his own policemen who will suspect her to be in violation of the curfew. Now I know the meaning of shutdown and having nowhere to go.

Should I have told dad that I am coming home? But how? He was right. This place is not what Sara and I had imagined it to be.

As we enter the city that's under dad's command, ravages of destruction start showing up along the roads. Not a soul is to be seen. There's not a bird in the sky or on treetops. Even the strays are absent.

2

I am sitting next to dad in his car. It's snowing outside. We are going to the hospital where mom is admitted. We reach the hospital and it's heavily fortified. Guards are keeping vigil. Dad is greeted with salutes. We enter the hospital and the guards shut the gates. The hospital appears vacant. No one except us is allowed inside. Hospitals aren't this quiet and empty. They are noisy places teeming with patients and doctors.

On the windowsill is a pigeon's nest. Nestled against its mother's warm belly is a newborn chick gasping for air. Its mother is pecking at the chick's left wing to remove the ticks. She strokes the feathers of the chick with her beak. She's doing everything to save the chick. She doesn't give up either hope or will. She goes on and on relentlessly. The chick makes an incredible effort to ape its mother and to impress her with a daring act.

We walk along a long, narrow corridor. At last, we stop in front of a room. It's the only lit room in the darkened corridor. I hear sounds. Dad holds my hand and takes me into the room. Mom is alone inside. In her lap is an infant with blue eyes. Mom hands him over to my dad. Dad lifts the boy in his arms, gives him a kiss and places him on my lap.

'He's your little brother,' whispers dad. Mom utters a name.

'Zubair,' she says, looking at the little one on my lap. For the first time, she looks at me as if I have brought her joy and hope. As if I am the sole reason for her existence. As if she's alive only because of me. I hold the little one on my lap for a moment and then hand him back to dad. He has the kindest look in his eyes. So has mom. She closes her eyes and goes off to sleep as if she hasn't slept in ages.

On our way back, I stop by the windowsill to inspect the chick hoping that its mother's efforts have borne fruit. She has done the unimaginable in my absence. The chick is immobile, its deformed head and featherless wings bear puncture marks, and it has been thrown out of the nest. The mother is now tending to her other two chicks. Sensing my presence, she gives me a threatening look, spreads her wings over the two chicks and stiffens her body like an eagle. It's too late to do anything now. The chick will die any moment, and the crows will come and take it away. I should have stayed.

At home, I ask dad why the hospital was empty. He looks at me and brushes the question aside. When he senses my sadness, he takes me to his room and comforts me. He talks about mom and Zubair and says we should prepare to welcome them home.

'He's your little brother, and you shall have to play the big sister's part now,' he says. 'You shall have to take on big responsibilities.'

Such as?

'Such as keeping a watch over him, protecting him, and making sure he's okay. Will you do that for him and mom?'

But that should be mom's responsibility. Won't she do that?

'She may not be able to take care of him all the time.'

But why is that? What's going to happen to her?

'She will need time to recover.'

Why was the hospital empty, dad?

Dad's explanations fall flat.

3

After mom's death, the burden of responsibility shifted to dad. It became evident when he couldn't conceal his worry. He was never at ease at home and whenever he was away on duty, he would send an officer to check on us. His name was Inspector Dar. I called him Inspector Uncle or Uncle Dar. He would come on his bike, bearing gifts of all kinds. He showed me a photo of his daughter and said that he would bring her to visit us someday.

'She is a little younger than you and very shy,' he said. Inspector Uncle sported a fearsome moustache, which I didn't like. Dad would sometimes ask him to pick me up at school and bring me home. On those days, dad would send his jeep, and Inspector Uncle would ferry me around. He would take me to the shops in the market and ask me to choose anything I liked. He never paid for the things he bought for me. The shopkeepers pampered me and wanted to shower me with gifts. Inspector Uncle would take the things the shopkeepers gave willingly and out of respect. I believed he took them for his daughter. I believed that everything came for free because of Inspector Uncle's moustache. The only thing I wanted to lay my hands on was the black coloured pistol in a shiny leather case attached to Inspector Uncle's belt.

I wanted to meet his daughter.

'When she's older, I will get her here,' he would say.

Why can't I come over to your house so that I can meet her?

He made a promise: 'I will ask your dad and then take you home, or I can bring her along one day when you are picnicking with your dad.'

❧

One day, dad took me aside and asked me if I had noticed anything peculiar about Zubair. *What do you mean?* I asked him, unable to relate to the question. Physically, Zubair was fine, and I hadn't noticed anything odd in him other than his sharp reflexes, mood swings and reticence. But as days went by, dad remarked that Zubair shouldn't go to school for some days, and I suspected something was wrong. He said Zubair didn't have friends there, and he didn't like to be around anyone.

But dad, that is no reason to skip school. I hadn't been given the same privilege so I didn't accept dad's assessment. Sensing my curiosity, he dismissed the matter hurriedly: 'It's nothing, let's forget it.' But his eyes gave him away.

I kept asking dad what the matter was. I thought he was being overprotective about Zubair. *You worry too much unnecessarily. He's just fine. You should stop worrying. I will keep a watch over him. You mustn't make him miss school.*

I noticed a change in dad's behaviour towards me too. Something was bothering him. Was it Zubair or I? Or was it his work? Was he worried that something bad was going to happen to us? That we would be kidnapped? What if someone did and demanded a ransom? This was the only possibility that occurred to me at the time.

I decided to do something I would never do under any circumstances. I sneaked into dad's room when he was away. Hoping to discover some clues, I rummaged through his things in the drawers and the cupboard. Stashed in a drawer was a doctor's prescription for Zubair. It said: PTSD. The four letters aroused my curiosity.

The very next day, dad came to know of my trespass. But for some reason he refrained from asking me about it. Though it was a serious matter, he didn't think bringing it up would be an easy affair. I had readied an explanation just in case he brought up the topic. Later, when I brought up the topic of the prescription, he dismissed it by saying that doctors wrote such prescriptions for almost everyone who visited them. 'They will write one for me too if I were to tell them about all that goes on in my head and all the crazy things I do sometimes,' he said. But he knew I wasn't a fool to buy such a flimsy excuse.

After some days, dad explained to me that I would have to be very vigilant around Zubair, and in case I noticed anything odd, I was to bring it to dad's notice. He said he would take us on a holiday and it might benefit all of us. There were some dos and don'ts to follow though. Dad's words were reassuring. He didn't give an impression that anything bad was going to happen to Zubair. I just had to follow his advice. I started observing Zubair closely. I kept a watch on his behaviour, whether he ate well and whether he spoke politely without creating a scene or throwing a fit. I was looking for signs of abnormality because the doubt had been planted in my mind.

I became worried at not being able to spot any oddity in Zubair and his behaviour. He did nothing out of the ordinary. Maybe his sickness was unlike any other I had seen or known or heard about. The only thing he was scared of was water. He never learnt to swim despite all efforts to teach him. He sleepwalked at times. I saw him talking to himself when no one was around. But so did I at times. I think we all do, especially if we are confined in our homes with nothing much else to do. There were times when I didn't know what to do and how to deal with him because he seemed absolutely fine. However, I did start spending more time with him.

One day, while exploring his room, I discovered a secret hideout full of empty matchboxes. I was led to it by the strange sounds emanating from there. I had been hearing the sounds from time to time. Upon further scrutiny, I found that the source of the sounds was the stacks of matchboxes. There was a whole cupboard full of them. Sounds came out of each one of them. When I opened one matchbox after another, I was shocked. The matchboxes were teeming with insects, some alive, some dead, and some battling for their lives because they had been tied to pebbles or small nuts and bolts that you sometimes find abandoned on roadsides. I saw insects I hadn't ever seen. It could be that I had never seen them at close quarters. Some were from our backyard. They lived under the soil in the garden, in crevices in trees and anthills and mounds. They were now suffocating in matchboxes. There were beetles, locusts, caterpillars, earthworms, silverfish, centipedes, sandflies, crickets, stoneflies and moths.

What on earth is Zubair up to, I wondered. There was no way to find out unless I caught him in the act. I couldn't understand how he went about doing such gross things to these insects and why he did such things in the first place. In some matchboxes were tiny strange-looking insects that resembled plastic toys. They seemed to have metamorphosed into neither-dead-nor-alive creatures. Their bodies had undergone some form of alteration. A strange state of being!

The next day onwards, I began spying on Zubair. I saw him

go out into the garden with a bag full of empty matchboxes. I observed him from a hidden spot, not wanting to be discovered. His secret must remain a secret if I am to find out more, I thought.

There was no way Zubair could have done all this all himself. I wondered if his weird obsession—capturing insects and then keeping them in captivity in dingy and stuffy matchboxes—had something to do with the sickness he had been diagnosed with. *Is this what PTSD does to you?* What worried me more was that dad didn't know anything about it. What if he came to know? But then again, what if all this wasn't a secret? It wasn't possible that dad knew nothing about it. Nothing escapes his watchful glare.

I couldn't simply ignore Zubair's doings. Instead of informing dad, I did just the opposite in order to get to the very cause. I knew the places we could go to in search of insects to add to the collection. The fact that Zubair hadn't told me about any of this was worrisome. I deserved to know. When I next went for a walk with him, I purposely went off course and kicked up stones with my shoes just to see if we'd chance upon an insect or two. And when an insect did pop up, I stopped to have a closer look at it just to notice Zubair's reaction. He didn't react initially, but as days went by, he noticed my interest in insects too. Maybe he thought it was a coincidence. Then quite unexpectedly, he disapprovingly dragged me away from the insects, as if he didn't trust me. But I didn't give up. I wanted him to know I was on his side. In doing so, I wanted him to be on my side and to reciprocate and acknowledge my act. It turned into a long game with no end in sight until one day he saw me rescue a tiny insect from certain death when a bigger insect was trying to make a meal of it while it was still alive. Half of the insect's body was inside the mouth of this monster insect and the other half was struggling to get free. Zubair performed a daring rescue mission and we brought both insects home and kept them in two separate matchboxes. Unfortunately, the small insect lost its life. I told Zubair that he had done an act of kindness by trying to save the insect though I knew the act wasn't as kind as I made it sound. But I didn't know what else to do. The mystery deepened. What I didn't know was whether Zubair was trying to save the insects or destroy them. But it gave him a strange sense of satisfaction. On the other hand, he was still giving dad a hard time by making him wonder and worry about his mental state. Dad's worry was justified. He felt saddled with all the additional work and concerns that came up owing to the situation at home. There was his own work and duty and then there was the uncertainty around Zubair. He was torn between the two—commitment towards his work and responsibility towards his children.

There were days when Zubair threw a tantrum just to annoy us so that we would leave him alone. It was never easy to get him to calm down whenever he did such things. Dad never lost his cool though. I wanted to ease his burden. I wanted to take over charge of Zubair. I grew protective. But I began to worry as well. What would happen to him if he was not allowed to do the things he liked? What would happen to him if his obsession came to an end or was made to stop? Zubair's insects were his life. He caught them and put them into tiny matchboxes, imagining that he was saving them when actually he was causing them pain. He arranged them in a manner that didn't seem random and without reason. I didn't intervene, afraid that my intervention might bring about some undesirable change in his attitude towards dad and me. I played along and tried to win him over. And he didn't seem to mind my tagging along, although I didn't know if he wanted me to. All I wanted was to gain his trust. I felt responsible for his well-being. Not just because dad had told me so and had given me the charge but because I had no other choice.

There was another reason. I didn't want the cicadas in the matchboxes to stop singing. They sang most beautifully when they were dying. Zubair may not have had a reason for doing what he did. Or maybe he had and only he knew. He knew how to silence his captives when the singing grew louder. And his ways were gruesome and ingenious.

The day I saw some boys in our neighbourhood teasing Zubair and calling him names, I lost it. Don't ask me what I did. I taught them a lesson they would never forget for the rest of their lives. A few precise kicks aimed at where it hurt the most drove the point home once and for all. I let Zubair watch me that day. I wanted him to learn how to fight and defend himself. He screamed at me that day. He even tried to stop me from bashing up one of the boys. He dragged me away forcefully, and I wasn't happy about it. Despite his attempts to stop me, I did what I wanted to do. I acted on impulse. But seeing Zubair cry made me sad. I realized that sadness was a pointless and terrible thing. The next day, when the errant boys saw me, they ran away and hid in the barns of their houses. I looked at them warningly so that they would never have the guts to crawl out of their holes and mess with Zubair. I didn't care about the consequences.

Then came the summer of misfortune. And to this day I blame it on the errant boys though everyone else thought otherwise. The thrashing I gave them had ignited revenge in their deranged minds. But I don't regret it except that Zubair's menagerie was destroyed. Our house caught fire and everything was gone and burnt to cinders. I am certain that it was no accident and that our house was intentionally set on fire. I suspected it was the handiwork of the boys in connivance with some miscreants. These children had earlier been blamed for wanton acts of arson. The real culprits were never caught. When the fire was raging, Zubair tried to drag me towards the burning house. This really alarmed dad as it appeared that he was trying to get rid of me. But no one understood the real reason behind Zubair's act. I wasn't scared. Dad caught hold of him and carried him away as he shrieked and threw a fit. Zubair yelled and called out my name over and over. That was the first time ever that he looked at me with such sadness, expecting me to help him and come to his rescue. I saw fear and desperation in his eyes. He didn't give up until dad forced a sedative down his throat. He didn't even give up in sleep. He moaned and groaned.

The fire destroyed everything. After some days, I went to inspect the debris, hoping to chance upon any remnants and salvage things that might have escaped the fire. I found nothing. Everything was gone, burnt to ashes.

Zubair didn't recover from the shock. I secretly wanted to help him re-build his menagerie in our new house. The cicadas stopped singing and nights were not the same anymore. To look into Zubair's eyes meant inviting trouble. He looked at me, as if I were the cause of his loss and as if I were to blame for everything; like I did nothing to stop the fire or to save his treasure. I felt helpless. In a wakeful stupor, he rummaged frantically, digging into the soil to find something underneath it. His nails turned black. When I touched him, his skin was ice cold. His eyes turned red. I gave him a sedative so that he could sleep peacefully. But he remained awake. When, after many days, he finally fell asleep, the look on his face made dad shut the door of the room and go away.

It was as if Zubair had been forcefully put to sleep, against his wishes. When he awoke, he wasn't himself. He was transformed into something else. Like an insect, he crawled. He crawled into a box and didn't come out. He groaned and made strange sounds. He called himself by some other name. When I asked him what it meant, he showed me by curling his body in an awkward fashion. His insects had taken over his mind but he didn't fear them. He suffered, imagining them suffering. What he loved during the day, he feared at night. Those *things* had done strange things to him.

Some days before I was to leave for London, Zubair was put in the care of a caretaker. Dad was allotted a new house. He had to be away from home a lot because of his duty. In the attic of the new house were pigeons. The caretaker reared them. Some pigeons were of a rare breed. Dad thought the company of pigeons might be good for Zubair. And it would do all of us good. The caretaker believed pigeons brought good tidings.

One day, a blind mystic visited us because the caretaker was one of his ardent followers. I had heard incredible stories about this mystic. People thought he possessed healing powers. He was a venerated person in the entire neighbourhood. He was believed to have healed many children with strange illnesses. Everyone spoke highly of him. 'He is our saviour and the saviour of our city,' said people. He was believed to have saved the city from a disastrous flood that had wreaked havoc for days. People had gone to him for help. They had begged him to use his powers to placate the river. The river's rage had been boundless. Until then it had been a placid river. No one had thought it would swell and pose such a threat. The mystic had walked out of his house, stood on a bridge and uttered some words addressing the river. His followers claimed to have seen cranes with long necks fly from a distant mountain and land in the city. 'The cranes then gulped down the floodwaters,' people said, enacting the scene. Others said giant fish and birds came to rescue them. Maybe these were hallucinations or mere visions caused by the sudden change in the river's course and the temperament of its waters. Or perhaps the mystic's spiritual powers had done the trick.

The caretaker made the necessary arrangements for the days when the mystic's followers visited him in his house. They came for revelry, food, music and blessings. The mystic's utterances were not easy to understand. People interpreted them in different ways. The mystic had a certain power over people. Such was his aura. That day when he came over, he placed his hand on Zubair's head and mumbled some words. Maybe it was a prayer. 'He sees things that none of us see,' said the mystic about Zubair.

But Zubair remained the same. I thought back to the day I had seen him nursing the healthy insects and ignoring the ones that needed nursing. He looked happy that day. Happiness of a kind that no medicine can give! It didn't come to him magically. He had worked for it and earned it. Such was his devotion and love for the insects. It got me thinking. I needed him more than he needed me. He placed his bets on the good things he chanced upon; things that showed hope and promise. He never connived such things. Such things just happened to him. But why, I wondered. Maybe he would teach me someday.

Dad started to convene his meetings at home. The meetings would go on and on for hours. Dad didn't mind Zubair's presence in the room. Everybody liked him. He would be hugged and given all sorts of presents. During one such meeting, I saw things going awry. Dad raised his voice several times. I heard voices of others. Then more voices came out of the room: 'This isn't a good idea, Sir…it will be disastrous…if you have made the decision, we will stand by it…but this could get us killed…we mustn't do this… Sir, you're placing your trust in the least trustworthy person, knowing that he would betray you and us all…'

4

Reaching anywhere has never before felt like such an ordeal. I feel as if I have been in this taxi for years now. The house I am headed towards is nowhere in sight. Time seems to have slowed its pace. Grandma was right. 'In Kashmir,' she had said, 'Time strays off course in winters and you have got to be mindful of its trickery and help the person next to you stay awake and alive.' Right now, I am witnessing the wickedness of Time, and its sorcery. The gentle taxi driver seems to know the reason for he's not in the least concerned about reaching the destination. It shouldn't be taking us this long. After all, it's a small city. Going from one end of the city to another in a taxi and that too on empty roads, shouldn't take more than half hour. The taxi is crawling forward. You can almost outrun it if you run alongside.

Can we speed up?

My plea remains unheeded. The taxi driver is unable to hear me. He seems to have forgotten about me. That he is to take me home isn't on his mind. Such a thing happens in dreams when one has no control over anything. In dreams, time passes in the strangest of ways. You feel that you are going somewhere yet you never reach anywhere, and then you realize that you never set off in the first place. There's a wall between the taxi driver and me. We are two separate entities without a common purpose. My purpose is to reach home and his purpose is to keep delaying the arrival. He's complicit in whatever is happening right now. I look outside the window.

Somewhere at a distance are hordes of people. They are running towards a gigantic snow sculpture of a man who looks familiar. He has a moustache and a beard made of charcoal. The people throw snowballs at the sculpture. I wonder why they are doing so. Why do they want to bring it down? It is a magnificent sculpture of a leader-like figure. A stately beard, a high-rising forehead, an elegant moustache and broad shoulders! He's perfectly chiseled, like a hunter. Snowball after snowball is aimed at the bust to bring it down. At last, the people taste victory. The sculpture collapses to the ground.

It is an unfamiliar world. And then, the gates of the city are seen one more time. This is happening again and again. It's a vicious cycle. How many times will we keep entering and re-entering the city and not reach anywhere? We're going around in circles.

As we enter the city, a mob is marching towards a police station with firepots in their hands. The look on the faces of these people scares me. What are they up to? Their faces are not visible. But this seems to be the unfolding of a terrible act.

Don't do it. Please don't do this. Go away. Go back to your homes.

My pleas fall on deaf ears, as if I don't even exist. The people march on. They are screaming. The past has returned with a vengeance as if it has one last trick up its sleeve.

People are marching towards the police station with the firm intention to storm it. They seem to be coming out of nowhere and growing in number. A man throws a ball of fire into the premises. In a matter of minutes, there are flames everywhere.

‘Quit or face the consequences,’ the voices blare.

My worst fears… Some people start dragging the injured out of the station, putting them on stretchers and carrying them away. Dad comes out of the police station. He starts tending to the injured. There’s a sound and dad falls to the ground. I run towards him. He’s bleeding. His men carry him towards a vehicle. They drive off. I run after the vehicle and reach the hospital. Dad is inside the emergency ward. It’s a gruesome scene. The injured are scattered all over. They are unattended and left to fend for themselves. People are scrambling for help. At the ward, a doctor refuses to look at dad. Dad’s men scream at him. The doctor looks away.

‘Look at these people, they need help too,’ the doctor says, pointing at dozens of injured people in the ward.

‘You must treat him or else I will kill you with my bare hands,’ says a policeman. There’s fear in his voice. The doctor turns around. The expression on his face changes from remorse to fear.

‘I’m sorry,’ he mumbles, trembling with fear. ‘I don’t know what’s happening to me.’ He draws the curtain and starts examining dad. His expression changes again. He turns towards me and gives me a kind look. Dad acts as if nothing has happened at all. Then he notices me hiding behind the curtain and looking at him helplessly. He turns his gaze away and then he turns it back to me as though he isn’t sure whether I am a dream or reality. His expression gives him away. Fear turns to anger and then back to fear. He narrows his eyes and gives me an angry look. I hear his unspoken admonition: ‘Why are you here? I told you not to come. What is wrong with you? You disobeyed me. What am I going to do now? Leave everything and protect you? You will get us into trouble…’

Moments pass in trepidation and disbelief. 'There's nothing to worry,' the doctor whispers into my ear, seeing me cry. 'Your dad is going to be okay.' He moves away, handing over the care of my dad to a young nurse who has the most compassionate hands. She attends to dad as if he is her father. Her hands are steady as if she has been doing this all her life. She's not afraid. She nurses the wound with softness and care. At a distance, the doctor's eyes are moist with regret while he examines the other patients in the ward. A stranger walks up to the doctor, and says, 'you saved yourself from ruin.'

Dad looks at me and gives me a triumphant smile, as though he's just performed an impossible feat. He knows I won't disappoint him in reciprocating the gesture. I hold his hand in mine. It's a code between us. His anger and fear are gone. He's himself once again.

'I'm waiting for the day when you become a doctor and I will be placed in your care,' he whispers.

But what if I don't become a doctor? What if your prediction doesn't come true?

'You will still not let anything happen to me...'

Dad could have been anything—a teacher, a doctor, a businessman or a scholar like my grandfather who was a tutor of Persian and whose dying wish was to go to Iran where he believed his ancestors were buried. Dad had studied history and was supposed to follow in his father's footsteps but he chose the police service. He gave up his real passion for this job. He never told me his actual reason for his decision to join the forces. I always wanted to know, and I hoped he would share the secret with me someday. Who knows what compulsions he might have had at the time?

He wanted me to study medicine, but I was more interested in law. He never said no to me and made sure that I didn't have anything to complain about. He was very happy the day he sent me off to London. He thought I would change my mind but I didn't. Seeing me off at the airport, he had said, 'you are right; there can't be any life if there's no law. Someday, we will take the flight together...'

5

It is the winter solstice. The sun won't make an appearance. The sky is grey, the air is frosty, and inside my heart lies a deep desire to see dad and Zubair. It's a day of absent shadows. The day will be short, and the night long.

Back at the University, everyone must be celebrating in different ways. There will be parties in the hostel rooms. Everyone will be getting drunk and dancing. Sara and I had grand plans. But none of them were to come to fruition. Plan C had been to go to Cornwall and spend the holidays there by the sea. We were going to rent two scooters and explore the villages along the cliffs. Plan D had been Iran. Plan E, *that* Kashmir. Plan F, *this* Kashmir.

Smoke-filled roads greet us as we enter the city for the tenth time. Police pickets are lined up on both sides of the road as we make our way through toxic fumes coming out of busted teargas canisters lying on the road. Suddenly, I hear a siren. I turn to look out through the rear window. A squad vehicle is on our tail. The siren is for us to know that we are to stop immediately or else brace for consequences. The driver looks at me and shakes his head, as if he's gone through this ordeal several times and knows what's to come. With the shake of his head, he signals to me that he has no choice but to comply with the warning. Without panicking, he pulls over immediately. His lack of panic is partly reassuring and partly worrying.

'Don't worry. Stay calm. I will handle the situation,' he mumbles.

In an instant, four masked troopers wearing camouflage combat fatigues get out of the siren-screaming vehicle, force open the doors of our taxi and instruct us to get out. They don't say a word. Their gestures say everything. Their faces aren't visible; except for the hideous blackness they are wrapped in and the muzzles of their slick assault rifles, nothing else is seen. The insignias attached to the pocket flaps of their jackets read: 'Commandant—SPECIAL FORCES'.

One of them grabs hold of my arm and starts demanding answers to his questions: 'Where are you going? Don't you know this area is under curfew? Do you have permission to be here?'

Folding his hands, the taxi driver starts his defense sheepishly: 'This is an emergency, Sir. This girl's father is in a critical condition in the hospital and we have no time. She wants to see him. She's come from Delhi and we're already late. I volunteered to take her to the hospital. After all, hers is a humanitarian case. She doesn't have a curfew pass. Her father might not survive. I beg you to let us go. I will drop her at the hospital and go home. I have no intention to break the law...'

'Is that right?' asks the masked trooper.

Desperately struggling to conceal my fear, I nod.

'What is your father's name and which hospital is he in? We will take you there.'

My heart skips a beat. *I'm doomed.*

I begin to explain: *My father's name is Aziz and he's in the city hospital. If you wish, you can drop me at the gate of the hospital. I will be eternally indebted to you for this favour.'*

'Which hospital? Does it have a name?'

I blurt out the only name I remember: *Lalla Memorial Hospital.*

'Really? That hospital closed down two years ago. Moreover, this road doesn't lead to any hospital. This leads to the Police Colony. This is a restricted area. You need to have permission to be here,' he says.

Staring suspiciously at me and examining me closely, the other trooper demands my ID.

It's over, I think. I will be taken into custody and this poor driver will be… I shouldn't have lied but I can't even say the truth. They must have gathered something is not right. Who would dare risk their lives in such a situation?

I live in London. I'm a student there. Inspecting my ID, the trooper says something even more troubling: 'We will take you to your father but since you have no curfew pass, you need to come with us first.'

Go with you? But why? He has just explained that we have no time. I am racing against time. My father is…

'No, you have to come with us.'

Where?

'If you don't comply, we will have to use force.'

Listen, please. Let me go this time. I promise never to come out again in the curfew. I would never have committed this mistake had my father not been in the hospital. Please understand. My father is battling for his life. Do I have to produce permission to even see him in his dying moments?

The two troopers don't let go of my hand and begin to forcibly drag me toward their vehicle. At this point, I lose it completely and start screaming: *Please don't do this to me. Save me. Someone help me. Where is your senior officer? I want to talk to your officer. I don't want to talk to you. Let me go. You can't drag me like this. Do you know it's a crime to treat a woman like this? You can't do this to me… Help… Someone help me…*

'You must know when to open your mouth,' screams the trooper, dragging me towards the vehicle. The taxi driver starts pleading: 'Let her go, please. She's innocent. I will take her to the hospital and you can take me instead. Let her go…'

Don't touch me. Let me go. You have no idea who you are messing with…

Fearing that I will be forcibly taken somewhere from where there will be no coming back, I almost blurt out the truth. This could be the end. There's only one way out of this mess.

In a flash, another vehicle comes to a stop next to us. Two more masked troopers climb out of the vehicle. The four troopers of the first batch change their attitude, stand to attention, and salute the new arrivals making it apparent that they are senior officers. But one of them still has a firm grasp on my arm. One trooper steps aside and begins to explain the situation to the two officers. My heart starts sinking at the presence of two more troopers who seem to wield more authority and power than their juniors. One of them steps closer to me. Unlike the others, his eyes aren't behind dark shades. A black cloth covers his face. He's tall and well built. I steal a look at his outfit to ascertain his rank. His badge reads: CC—SPECIAL FORCES. Attached to the shoulder flaps of his jacket are his rank emblems—three five-pointed stars and the head of a lion. Our eyes meet and the two of us exchange a strange, frightening look. There's something about his eyes. Fear grips me. I start trembling. I struggle to conceal my fear. I keep observing him and the movement of his hands and eyes until I can no longer look him in the eye. There are no words. Sensing that I might faint out of fear, he turns away from me instantly. With a slight wave of his hand, he signals to his juniors, and then he boards his vehicle and drives off. The trooper lets go of my hand and the four of them step away. At this point, it becomes clear to me that the officer's gesture was an order that I wasn't to be touched and that I was to be freed immediately.

'You may go,' says the trooper. 'It is your lucky day.' The four begin their walk back to their vehicle. The look on the taxi driver's face betrays disbelief and relief. 'Thank you for letting us off... thank you for showing mercy,' he says to the troopers. 'Let's go,' he gestures to me, and we board the taxi once again.

We are back on the road. 'You should cover your head with a scarf,' says the driver pensively. 'It is for your own good.'

I wonder how much more distance we have to cover to reach the house. 'We're about to reach,' says the driver.

I can't take my mind off the tall officer's eyes. Is it possible that I am mistaken? Am I imagining things once again?

I ask the driver about the burning of the shrine. I want to know what he thinks. The truth! He would know it.

'You know,' he says, 'they are made to do such deeds like setting a shrine or a house on fire. But someone else does it and blames it on them so that we hate them more and their killing is justified. Their lies are our truth, my child. You will not understand such things yet. But, someday you will...'

A lone cyclist appears at a distance. He's cycling agitatedly towards us as if in panic. The taxi driver takes his foot off the accelerator and the taxi slows down.

I lower the window of the taxi. A strange occurrence outside makes me shiver. Dragonflies are dancing a ritualistic dance around the moon, as if they are going to swallow it up any moment. The moon swells until it can swell no more. It is at its largest indicating that the end is near. More and more dragonflies are flying towards it, narrowing the distance between them and the object of their desire. It is a race to the end, until the night and the moon cease to be. Nothing will remain, not even a faint trace. The moon puts up a brave fight. It doesn't give up. It sails quietly and invites the invaders into its luminous sphere. The tide turns in its favour. The dragonflies begin to perish one after another.

The cyclist gets off the bicycle and parks it by the roadside next to a lamppost with no light. Looking at the approaching taxi, he puts the bicycle up on its stand but keeps pedalling so that the dynamo keeps rotating and the bicycle light stays on. The taxi stops a few metres from where the bicycle is parked. I get out of the taxi and open my wallet to pay the driver.

The driver looks at me, lowers his eyes and then shakes his head. 'I can't,' he says, refusing to accept the money.

But you did me the greatest favour by bringing me here when no one was even willing to look at me…

'I didn't do you any favour, my child,' he whispers softly. 'You did me a favour by making me stay strong and fearless. Anything could have happened today. The police could have… It's over now. You saved us…' An enigmatic smile flashes across his wrinkled face.

But you must take some money at least. I want to tell him to accept some money for the sake of his kids, but I remember what his fellow taxi driver had told the others at the airport: 'He has no kids and that's why he's taking the risk of going to the city when no soul should go there.'

'What will I do with the money? What will it fetch me? I have got my dues today,' the driver explains.

You have been lucky for me. I don't know how I should thank you.

'No, you have been lucky for me,' he says. 'But if you insist on showing your gratitude to an old man, allow me to ask you a question.'

You can ask me anything.

'What brings you here?'

I shouldn't have said yes to his request. How do I answer the question truthfully? I can't lie to him after all that he's done for me.

Why are you asking me this?

'The response to my question can't be another question, my child,' he says. 'I won't insist, and if you don't wish to answer, it's fine. It's none of my business, but may I tell you something? Whatever has made you come here, do not commit the mistake of going into that colony over there... Even birds do not fly there,' he says, pressing down on the accelerator and driving off into the thick mist.

Into the Night

Ismail, the caretaker, receives me by the roadside as if he has been expecting me.

How did you come to know? I haven't told anyone.

'The area ahead has been cordoned off, no one is allowed here,' he says, ignoring my question and taking his bicycle off its stand. 'I came to pick you up and take you home.'

You knew it was me in the taxi?

He nods and we start walking. Casting a sorrowful glance towards the smoky sky, he says, 'Look at what they have done to the shrine… It is gone… Everything has been reduced to embers… A curse will be unleashed upon us now… May god shower his kindness…'

What an unfortunate mishap!

'It's not an accident.'

Who's responsible then?

'You know who… They have brought ruin upon this place. They will rot in hell…'

I remember the words of the taxi drivers at the airport: 'The culprits are the agents of the state. The Police are to blame for they are complicit in this sacrilegious act.'

We walk past newly built and under-construction houses. 'Some of them were being constructed when you were here,' explains Ismail. 'But look at them now. They are mansions. Would you have imagined? Your house is still unfinished owing to several reasons. You dad wanted to complete the renovation before winter was upon us but it couldn't happen. Winter arrived early this year. Now the contractors are refusing to work, as if the cold is going to kill them. It is tough to build a house in this place. The labourers throw insane tantrums. They have become greedy. Their antics know no bounds. They don't even work properly. One's got to supervise them all the time otherwise nothing ever gets completed. Contractors are the worst of the lot. You should hear their demands. They behave as if they are kings and everyone else is at their mercy. You can't even argue with them. It's pointless. Their fathers would be ashamed of them. But who cares? Nobody gives a damn these days. The old values are dead. Now everything is about money...'

You know what the taxi driver said to me about this colony?

'I know what he might have said. He's not the only one who believes that this land is...well, all I know is that a major land dispute is going on here and people are superstitious about coming to this colony...'

You mean they are building houses on land that isn't theirs. Is that what it is?

'It is nothing to lose sleep over,' Ismail says, interrupting me. 'These are routine things... As long as your dad is around, nothing will happen.'

Where is he?

'Haven't you told him that you are coming?'

You know what he would have said had I told him. He forbade me from coming here...

At last, we arrive at the house. It is a fortress. The wooden nameplate bears no name. The iron grills of the gate rise tall. The house is flanked on all sides by four cemented walls with loops of barbed wire coiled around the top plates. It is bigger than the house we occupied before my departure for London. This is the seventh house I have seen. Every two or three years, dad changes houses.

Whitey comes out of nowhere and barges in through the gate. I hold out my hand to her. She wags her tail and licks my hand, as if I am the one who raised her. She has grown.

'She's been expecting you. How do you think I got to know of your coming?' says Ismail placing his hand on my shoulder. 'You should see her throw herself all over Zubair. She is very possessive about him. She protects him like a mother and will do anything to keep him from harm's way. Neither your dad nor I can come between her and Zubair.'

Where are her pups?

'The first litter didn't survive. There is one from the second litter, and the little fellow keeps showing up once in a while.'

I can't take my eyes off Whitey. She doesn't take hers off of mine. She seems to be conveying something to me. This has happened to me many times. Every time I have looked into her eyes, she has tried to warn me about something. On one occasion, when she was little, she saved me from a bunch of mad dogs prowling in the street. Having her around is comforting.

Our old car is parked in the driveway. The windows are frosted. Two more vehicles—a jeep and a SUV—are parked in succession. They are black in colour. Sand, stones, bricks, tiles, marble, logs of wood and iron rods are scattered all over the courtyard and buried under a thin layer of snow.

In the dimly lit corridor, I get a closer look at Ismail. His right eye looks damaged as if a sharp object, like a knife, has pierced it. He has lost his looks but he doesn't do a thing to conceal the deformity.

'It's not as bad as it appears,' he says.

Why don't you get it fixed?

'What is the point?' he says. 'It is going to keep happening.'

He talks about the battle between the crows and his pigeons. 'The crows,' he says, 'are hell-bent on gouging my eyes out so that they get to take a pigeon or two from the loft. But I won't let them. The war will never end as long as I am alive. I am worried for the pigeons. What will happen to them if I am not around? Who will look after them?'

Ismail's pigeons are his life. They are of a special breed. He believes that his pigeons are the messengers of god and that they will someday bring good luck and will keep the evil forces at bay.

But there is another reason for Ismail's obsession with his pigeons. And that is their supreme ability to resist and counter disease. They never fall sick. It is because of a genetic condition. The pigeons are immune to viruses that most birds aren't. They are supreme fighters and no disease can harm them. They are known for their longevity. These pigeons also possess a strange trait. They side with the strongest of humans. The weak stand no chance. They leave you the moment they detect weakness in you. They have a knack for sensing weakness. But if they sense strength, they will never desert you. They will give up their life for you. It's a bond for life.

Rani is astonishingly gorgeous. A long glittery neck with a tapestry of colours, a majestic crest, a broad crown, a spotted beak, and red claws set her apart from the rest of the pigeons and from all other birds I have ever seen in my life. Two years ago, when she was just a squab, a crow had attacked her. But her mother—an ace fighter—had put up a brave fight. The battle had lasted an entire night and Ismail had been forced to intervene.

Crows had surrounded him and he had thought the end of Rani was inevitable. Rani's mother had been severely injured in the battle. Her wings had gotten damaged. The very wings that had shielded Rani from the crooked beaks of the crows had grown weak in the days to come. But she never abandoned the will to fight. She had battled a dozen crows to save Rani. Rani owed her life to Ismail. But the battle was far from over. Rani and Ismail versus the bloodthirsty crows...

Ismail speaks about his foes: 'They remain undeterred. They will return, and maybe meet the same fate. They have tasted failure so many times yet they will continue having a shot at us until they succeed. They have no ambition left but to take revenge. The sole purpose of their existence is to take one pigeon from this house. But as long as I am here, their hunger will remain unsatiated. Rani might not be able to kill them, but she will not give them a chance to win either. The crows now want to come for her young ones as they came for her when she was a squab herself. They have unfinished business in this house.'

What kind of a life will Rani and her chicks have here? The crows will keep coming for her and them. The chicks will always be at risk. They should just die in their eggs. How long will Rani fight the crows? Someday she will lose and the crows will win. This is not the place for her to be. She doesn't belong here. This is a place of defeat. The crows are invincible. Nothing can destroy them. But they don't want to get rid of Rani straight away. They keep her waiting. They grant Rani a reprieve because it keeps hope alive. They want to stay in the game. It's the only game they have. To terrorize the meek, because the meek think they will get to live for one more day.

Ismail thinks otherwise: 'Someday Rani will surprise us all.'

Zubair hasn't grown. He's still the boy he was when I last saw him. He tiptoes into the kitchen, grabs hold of whatever he can find, places them on a plate and brings them to me as though I were a guest. Then he crawls into a corner and sits, quietly conveying with a look that I must eat.

'This is how he serves guests when they come,' says Ismail.

Zubair brings me magazines from dad's bookshelf. Then he invites me to his room. It's full of paintings, sketches and photographs. Photographs of dad and all of us adorn the walls and the shelves. There are photographs from my first year of college in Srinagar before dad sent me to London to study. It pained him to watch me going to college in Srinagar so he spent a fortune to send me off to London.

In one of the photographs, I am standing next to Nusrat and her brother. She is married now and has a two-year-old son. Nusrat loved the city but she wanted to go away from here. 'Anywhere but here,' she used to say. But she wasn't able to leave for reasons unknown to me. When I was leaving, she was both happy and sad to see me go. She wrote to me every day for a month and a half. 'I'm in a cage,' she would say repeatedly. 'There's no escape and I have to learn to live with it.' Then, when her son was born last year, she gave up all hope of going away from here and focussed her energies on her son's care. 'What I couldn't do, he should,' she wrote. Then all of a sudden she stopped writing to me. I never heard from her again. I had so much to tell her. We had parted on a sombre note: 'We will meet again…'

I know she must still be in the city but meeting her or informing her of my arrival isn't the most important thing on my mind. It is pointless.

The first year of college wasn't fun because most of the time there were no classes. Dad wouldn't allow me to go out alone. And he didn't even trust his own security detail. There were days he would accompany me to college and when my classes got over I would find him waiting at the college gates. When he was away on duty, I was under strict instructions to remain indoors and look after Zubair. I obeyed him. I had no choice but to follow his instructions. I didn't want to betray his trust in me. I was sworn to the code. He kept tabs on us and enquired every now and then about us.

Zubair shows me more photographs. In one photo, dad is receiving a medal at a function. Several medals and rewards and citations adorn the room. There's a photo of dad and Inspector Uncle. Dad is carrying me on his shoulders. Inspector Uncle is carrying another little girl on his shoulders. Both of them are youthful and handsome. They aren't in their uniforms. We're in a large meadow. The mountains have snow on them.

In dad's room is grandfather's old bookshelf. There are books on politics, religion and history. In the cupboard many sets of uniforms are kept neatly. It is at that moment I hear a familiar voice: 'I have come for the alms.' A cloaked figure is all that is visible to me. The person repeats his entreaty. He is the same beggar who has been coming to every house that we have ever lived in. It is a moonless hour of the night. Ismail goes to the gate with a bowl full of leftovers. The beggar accepts the food, retraces his steps and vanishes after taking a turn at the end of the street.

'Something is amiss,' Ismail says, looking intently at me. 'What have you done to your face? You don't look like your mother anymore.'

It is the mole he is curious about. Ismail has figured it out.

I come across an old photo of grandma. Dad, mom and I

are by her side. She looks youthful and radiant. She's holding my hand firmly in her grasp to prevent me from slipping away. Our bags are packed. We seem to be ready to leave for somewhere. I faintly remember the day this picture was taken. What must have happened that day, and later in grandma's life when I wasn't around? I want to know everything about her. Who she was? What she did? How she lived? How she died? The mysterious look in her eyes makes me curious about her.

Dad is asking grandma to hurry. He's mum about where he's taking her and doesn't tell her anything. But why is he being so secretive? I begin to wonder—are we going to that place in the mountains where there are waterfalls, a lake, and the shrine grandma always wanted to visit? Year after year, dad had promised to take her on an outing. His words—we deserve an outing; it will do us good—had been most reassuring and comforting.

There's just one problem. Dad is taking grandma against her wishes. She's too old and weak to resist and she can't comprehend what's happening and why she's being taken along. Her legs have no strength but she plods on despite the pain in her limbs. Dad walks ahead and keeps looking back as if this is his only chance to take grandma on this trip. He's scared for her. He knows she might collapse but he's adamant. Grandma follows him like a child without knowing where she's going and what will happen to her if she continues to be dragged along in this manner, against her wishes. She has had enough but she willingly submits to her son's authority. She suspects it is a stratagem but she doesn't say anything that will annoy dad. She doesn't want to prove him wrong. She loves him. She's more worried for him than herself.

The road ahead is endless. Dad carries the bags. Grandma clings to her purse—her only possession. Dad is forcing grandma to move at a brisk pace like him. She's left with no choice but to match his pace so that he remains in sight. At times, dad doesn't even wait for her. When he realizes she's far behind him and unable to keep up, he stops and waves frantically at her indicating that she must rush or else be ready to be left behind forever. Suddenly, grandma is bestowed with some kind of mysterious power. A kind of strange strength is leased to her and she starts walking faster. 'Faster, faster,' dad urges her, almost as if they are being chased by some hoodlums.

Dad, don't be so cruel. Grandma is not a horse like you. Take pity on her. Look how hard she's trying to obey you. She will die if you harp on making her run. What's the hurry? Why the rush?

'Look,' blurts out dad. 'We are not alone. Everybody is leaving. She must hurry or else…'

She's exhausted. She can barely stand on her legs. Where are we going? Are we going to return soon…?

'Nobody knows when they will return or if at all they will return.'

What are you talking about, dad?

Dad points to an old man who's standing by the gates of the city and begging everyone not to leave: 'Wait, this too shall pass, don't leave.'

'There's going to be mayhem,' argues dad.

'Don't believe in the rumours. Nothing that hasn't happened before will happen. We must hold on to one another and save one another. If you save one person, you will be saved too…'

'But our children… They are scared…'

'They aren't scared. You are. Go back to your home. Do not leave.'

'But you were the one who foretold the arrival of dark days. If we stay, we will perish. It's better to leave and save our children. If we survive today, our children will return tomorrow.'

'Don't go. Nothing bad will happen…'

'You are saying so because you have nothing left of your own.'

The old man doesn't give up. He continues waving his arms to stop people from leaving. But nobody listens. Dad thinks the man has lost his senses.

But dad, there's no one…

'I've lived here my whole life,' murmurs grandma, 'but I will do as my son wishes.' She musters all her strength and starts running. Soon, she overtakes dad.

'Slow down,' dad says to her. She doesn't pay attention to what he's saying.

'It is the wrong way,' he screams. 'We have to go to the right.'

Grandma thinks she has no other choice but to keep running. She doesn't want to disobey dad and see him lose his patience once again. Dad follows her. Then, all of a sudden, grandma stops and collapses. Dad rushes towards her and helps her up. She's trembling.

'I can't walk anymore,' she mumbles to herself and cries, but doesn't give up, as if she has been promised a reward at the end of the race if they arrive at their destination.

Dad throws an enticement: 'Zooni will be there. She is waiting for you.'

But I am here, dad.

Grandma gathers herself and then mustering up strength and the last of her reserves, she takes off again. 'Zooni, my Zooni,' she cries, 'I'm coming my child…' That's all she says. Her eyes light up, and she runs like a person whose last and final wish is about to come true. A boon is granted to her. But the boon isn't her union with me. It is strength. Strength she doesn't have. She had sacrificed her happiness and health for my happiness. Yet she never gave up. I was her life. I am still her life, her only hope. But I am not elsewhere. I am with her, holding her hand, but she can't even see me.

Dad yells again: 'Let's go. Let's rush. Let's not keep Zooni waiting.' Never before have I seen grandma so excited at the prospect of seeing me. Such is her love for me. She's also blinded with her love for dad. She's doing everything to please her only son. She's risking her life for him and me. She doesn't question dad and his intentions. He might be wrong. He might be on the wrong path. His paranoia might be irrational. He might have lost his mind. He might have become selfish. But he should not go through this torment. Grandma endures the agony because all she wants is me.

She stops and lowers her head partly in obeisance and partly out of fatigue. She raises her eyes skywards and breaks down again as if something bad is going to happen at this very place. She drags herself along laboriously.

This could kill her, dad. She won't survive the ordeal. Please stop. Let's not go any further with this.

Dad doesn't realize that grandma is ready to do anything for him. Even if it means she has to… Let me not say it. Dad should know that grandma has no wishes of her own and that her only wish is to see her son happy. Grandma points her finger towards the sky. Thousands of dandelions are falling from the sky. I see faces of people I have never seen before. Am I supposed to see these things? They don't seem to be meant for me. I become worried. Is this a sign, a foreboding that something isn't right? *Do you also see that?* To even ask you seems insane. How am I to describe those things?

Anything can happen. There is no one around. What if something happens to grandma? Who will help us?

One moment dad is with us. The next moment, he's making a speech somewhere because I can hear his voice loud and clear. He seems to have forgotten about us. I leave grandma there and run after him. He leaves us behind and boards the bus that all of us were supposed to board. I wait for another bus. There's none in sight. Dad has gone far ahead. He seems to be running away from us deliberately. The bus recedes into a distance. I beg someone at the bus-stop to give me a ride. I empty my pockets. I give him everything I have. He lends me his ticket and asks me to get on the bus. I hop on but the bus doesn't move. I look for the driver and the conductor. They are nowhere. I look at the ticket and realize my folly. It is a fake ticket. I have been duped. I get off the bus and inspect its condition. The bus doesn't have wheels. Half of it is burnt; the other half is in complete shambles. I can't even complain. There's no one around to listen to my woes.

Someone, please help me. A cyclist stops to inquire what I am doing in the middle of the road and why I am running around like a mad person. Without answering his questions, I ask him to give me a ride. He seems to be a kind soul. He creates room for me and asks me to sit on the carrier rack of his bicycle. I sit behind him and hold on to the seat post. He begins to pedal. I beg him to speed up. He picks up speed but something is not right. The bus carrying dad is going in the opposite direction.

It's the wrong way. We need to follow the bus. Turn around. That way. Go back. I beg the bicycle man to stop. He doesn't listen and goes on pedalling as if I don't exist. I jump off the speeding bicycle. Time is slipping from my hands. This isn't the road the cyclist had taken. The bus has gone out of sight. I run through a road full of slush and mud and dung only to reach a dead end. A lone auto driver is sitting in his auto rickshaw. He seems to be waiting for a passenger. I ask him if he can give me a ride in his rickshaw and chase the bus. I give him my word that I will pay him after I find my father. I have nothing left except a noble intention to repay the kindness and return the favour. The auto driver looks at me, gives my request a thought, and shakes his head. I beg him to say yes.

'Which bus,' he asks, looking in the direction where my finger is pointing. 'There's no bus.'

Look at me, Sir. Don't say no to me. This is my only chance of finding my father. The man shakes his head again, partly out of annoyance and partly out of disgust, and then takes his stony gaze off of me. I shout at him: *Look at me. I am a police officer's daughter. You can't do this to me. You must help me. I am not lying...* The man's expression doesn't change as if I don't matter to him at all. He thinks I am either boasting or telling a lie. He looks at me pityingly, thinking that I have gone mad. Then he says the most shocking thing: 'Listen, my dear, yesterday when you came here, you said the same thing—that you are the daughter of the so-and-so top shot who rules this city. Why do you keep losing your dad every day? You keep coming and going and nothing happens. Go away and your dad will come back to you.' I look at him with tears in my eyes. He's unmoved at my plight and unapologetic for his response, as if I am the one who is to blame for my father's willful desertion of his family. There's nothing I can do to make him believe.

It is the end of kindness and mercy. I resume my chase. My feet are sore. My clothes are grimy. The bus passes by me once again. It is going around in circles and doesn't stop. Once more, it passes by me. I look inside the bus. It is empty. My chase has been futile. Dad is nowhere in sight. The bus picks up speed and goes out of sight once again.

'You won't ever find your dad,' a bystander remarks, looking at me. I don't cry because I know I will find him. Dad isn't in the bus because he is far away, waiting for me. But I can't stop the bad thoughts from ruining my hope. What if he isn't waiting for me? What if he has left me behind on purpose? He has taken Zubair also with him. Maybe he thinks he's better off with him than with me. I will be doomed to chase them forever. They are nowhere. I can't locate grandma. I have left her far behind. It's my fault. What must she be going through? What must she be thinking; that all of us left her behind to die? I am losing time. But soon I will run out of time and I won't even die. Because it's the end of humanity and I will be condemned to run after dad through roads full of slush, grime and mud.

The light that is shining is just an illusion. The day is black and endless. I resume running. I say to myself: *Hold on to this moment and to yourself, for if you don't, everything will vanish forever. Don't give in to deceit. Let go of everything. You won't be on the losing end for long. When the spell ends, dad and Zubair will come back, and grandma will still be in her house.*

In my dreams, I am the weakest of all.

Then all of a sudden, I hear a faint whisper: 'This isn't your dream. This is my dream, you stupid girl. You are dreaming my dream. You weren't even supposed to dream it. It isn't in your share. But now everything will be okay.'

Will you always keep going away like this? Does it not bother you to see me suffer and pine for you eternally?

'I will always keep coming back to you.'

Will we still be happy?

'We will still be happy despite the comings and goings.'

Dad is still talking to me. But I can't see him. He says I'm in his sight.

❦

A black cloud opens its mouth to swallow the white moon. A man barges in through the gates of the house and Whitey wags her tail—a sign that the stranger's scent is familiar. Ismail opens the door to let the man in.

'Zooni,' the visitor says, looking intently at me as if he has known me for years, 'your father has sent me. You must come with me.'

The man looks familiar. And suddenly an old recollection of a camping trip comes alive.

Is that you Uncle Dar?

He is surprised at my delayed recognition of him. He has grown old but his moustache is as fearsome as it was when I first saw him. His hair is white and he isn't in uniform.

How did you know I have reached?

He looks at me with an expressionless face, but I notice how hard he's trying to conceal his emotion. He doesn't answer any of my questions. *How have you been and how's your daughter? She must be…*

'We must hurry, Zooni,' he instructs authoritatively, interrupting me and putting an end to my excitement.

Is something wrong, uncle?

A look of assurance flickers across his face and he shakes his head: 'Everything is fine, but we need to go from here. There's little time.'

And what about Ismail?

'Don't worry! He won't go anywhere. He has his pigeons to look after.'

I look at Ismail and he gives me his old reassuring look conveying that I should go with Uncle Dar and do as he says. He has kept a bag full of necessities ready. In the bag is a change of clothes for Zubair. Nothing else. He has already gotten Zubair ready as if we are to go on a picnic.

I don't want to go anywhere. But I am left with no choice. There must be a reason why Uncle Dar is here. He's the only one I trust. I don't want to know what is going on outside. In the dead of night, Zubair and I set off with Uncle Dar in a vehicle. We drive along the long winding boulevard circling a lake. When we reach the very end of it, we make a turn and then it's difficult to tell where the road ends and where we are headed.

The moon sails alongside us. Like a sentry, she's keeping an eye on everything that's going on down below.

Book II

Umbra

...time was not passing...it was turning in a circle...

—Gabriel García Márquez,
One Hundred Years of Solitude

The Safe House

1

'This is a safe house,' says Uncle Dar, parking his vehicle by the gates of a house that resembles a mansion. The trees are still and moonlight appears to be stuck to their branches. There is not even a faint rustle of leaves. Not even the sound of crickets or any other insects of the night.

At a distance, towards the far end of the avenue, are two guards standing to attention and keeping vigil. Their frozen salutes are reassuring. They don't even turn their heads towards us.

'This is where both of you shall spend the night,' Uncle Dar instructs. 'You will have enough room here. There's a dining hall where you both shall eat. You're not to indulge in any sort of adventure. You won't be here for long.'

But what if...

'There are no ifs and buts, Zooni. You know the drill, don't you?'

How long will we be here?

'Just tonight!'

And what about dad? You'd said you would...

Pointing toward the entrance, Uncle Dar asks us to get off the vehicle and go inside. 'Don't worry,' he says, giving me a look of regret, reminiscent of an unfulfilled promise. 'You will be okay. The house is guarded as you probably noticed. Go inside and take some rest.'

As we step inside, we find ourselves in a circular lobby with a domed ceiling. A bowl of apples is placed on a table in the centre of the hall. A frosted circular window frames a garden dotted with poplars. A zigzag pavement made of red tiles leads to the backyard. Another window frames a hill.

'There's someone else here,' Zubair lisps, narrowing his eyes and inspecting the vicinity. He seems to have a keener sense of the surroundings. So far he's behaved as if nothing abnormal has happened. As if he's used to all that's happening. He steps towards the bowl of apples, picks one and tosses it up to catch it.

Don't eat it. Put it back.

Disregarding my order, he rushes to the window and wipes the frost off its pane to have a clearer view of the backyard.

What's going on over there, Zubair? What are you looking at?

He signals me to come near him. We peep outside through the frosted windowpane. There is a shed in the backyard. In the shed is a cow. She's mooing softly. A girl rushes down the stairs. Her hair is short and her nose is pierced. She's wearing green boots. She seems my age and as tall as me. Her features are striking.

'Come and help me,' she utters, looking at me as if she's been expecting me. 'Come on, will you? What are you waiting for? We're already late...'

A deep-throated moo is heard.

'Why're you so still? Hurry up,' commands the girl again.

What exactly do you want me to do?

'I will tell you what to do.'

She leads the way and drags me along through a backdoor. I signal Zubair to tag along and stay in sight. He obeys diligently. A pungent smell wafts around. It's the smell of dung and ammonia.

'Look, amniotic fluid...' says the girl, pointing her finger at the cow. 'She's calving finally.'

Shouldn't we leave her alone?

'No, no, we've got to be by her side when the calf comes out.'

The cow moos again. Clearly, she is annoyed and our presence is accentuating her discomfort. The look in her eyes is terrifying. Maybe she thinks we are a threat to her or that we are trying to intrude into her space. Her tongue snakes out. She lies down and licks off the fluid oozing out of her dilated birth canal. The girl sits next to her and begins to caress her hind legs. And then it begins to happen. The head and legs of a calf make an appearance but...

Zubair's gaze is elsewhere. It is fixated on a window as if someone else is peeking at him from there.

'Someone is watching us,' he whispers into my ear. The cow moos again, drawing my attention to it. A tiny calf wrapped in placenta plops out of her birth canal. The cow chews off the umbilical cord and begins to eat the placenta. She licks the fluid off her newborn. But the calf isn't moving.

I look at the girl. Something is wrong. She too senses that something is not right with the calf. The calf doesn't seem to be breathing. My heart starts pounding. This is not a good sight. *What if?*

'C'mon! Help me. We've got to help her,' says the girl, readying herself for action.

What should I do?

'Are you saying you don't know how to revive a calf? What will you do in life? How will you...?'

Listen, I'm not a...

Zubair doesn't take his gaze off the window. I notice something strange. Framed by the window is a shadowy figure.

It seems to be making weird hand signs that look like instructions.

The girl takes over. She tries several tricks to revive the calf. The cow acts in tandem. The girl inspects the calf's mouth and inserts her fingers into it. Some fluid comes out of it. She continues doing so until there's no more fluid in the calf's mouth. She does it with the confidence of an expert. Then she rubs the neck of the calf right where the windpipe is. She doesn't stop and keeps at it. Moment after moment passes in trepidation. Nothing happens. The calf remains still. The girl waits for a response. I don't want to be here. I feel like going back inside. The very sight of the stillborn calf is unnerving. Its mother continues licking the fluid off its face and mouth.

Some more nervy moments go by. Just when the calf's revival seems impossible and I am about to give up all hope, something miraculous takes place. A stroke of luck and the calf begins to display its first signs of life—breathing and movement, though very feeble at this stage. The memory of a similar moment—Zubair's miraculous revival shortly after his birth—comes alive.

Strange-looking birds gather and sit on the fence of the shed. The chirping begins. It is unusual for birds to chirp at such an unearthly hour. They are cheering the birth of the calf.

The shadowy figure by the window is silhouetted against a pale light. 'What are you looking at?' the girl asks, looking at the window.

There's someone at the window.

'You see it too?'

Who's that?

The figure climbs on to the windowsill. It looks like a girl. Her face is veiled in the darkness. Down below her, the surface is icy. If she jumps off the window, she will break her skull and crush her bones.

'Don't pay attention to anything,' the girl says, dismissively.

But she's about to jump off the windowsill...

'Oh! Nothing will happen, not yet at least,' she says with a sneer on her face.

What about the calf? Will she survive?

'The calf will live. My job is done. We must celebrate. Are you in for a celebration?'

Where did you learn all this?

'All what?'

You know what.

'I know what you're thinking. You think I'm from some village up north where all I do is be around cows and help them give birth...'

I didn't meant that... I mean you don't look like a...

'Rustic girl?'

She looks like a rustic girl, but she's full of sarcasm. She seems so full of herself. I look again towards the window. The shadowy figure is gone. The window is shut and there is no light in the room as if no one has been there in ages.

I want to find a room for Zubair and myself to sleep in. It's been a long day, full of twists and turns and I don't want the night to be endless or to bring me more upheavals. I drag Zubair back into the lobby. The floor is smudged with foot impressions. The dining hall is empty. There's no sign of any food except the unripe apples in the bowl. They look silvery. I inspect them. I pick two and hand one to Zubair. He rubs his fingers on it and places it back in the bowl. As I take a bite, the girl screams, 'don't eat them. They are not ready yet. Spit it out or else...' She snatches the apple out of my hand. Then she forces me on to the floor and puts her fingers into my mouth to empty it as if I have consumed a forbidden fruit. I don't feel a thing. The light begins to fade and everything becomes hazy. I hear footsteps.

❦

A storm is raging outside. A man barges into the house and shakes the snow off his coat. He's alone. He looks rugged and weary. He's wearing the same coat I had given dad before leaving for London. He unwraps the muffler from his face.

'Happy birthday, Zooni!'

Dad?

I touch the cuff of his coat. It's the same one I had bought for him. He shakes his head and smiles. 'It is your grandfather's coat. You gave it to him and I took it after he attained jannat. Do you remember?'

But he died before I was born.

'No, no, sweetheart, he didn't die before you were born.'

What's going on, dad?

'Listen Zooni, I want to show you something,' he says, pulling me by my hand and taking me to the window. Pointing toward the foothills of a distant mountain engulfed in a haze, he explains: 'Look over there. That's where I am right now. You mustn't worry. I know you are brave. You mustn't give up on me. I will come for you, and we will go home. Until then, you must look after Zubair. He has no one but you...'

But dad...

The next moment, I open my eyes and dad is gone.

'Good to see you are not dead,' the girl says, washing her hands in a basin.

Was that you? Were you talking to me in the voice of a man? I know it was you. How can you be so cruel?

'Do you get panic attacks?'

You think I was having a panic attack?

'Then what was that? I saved you. You were going to die. You weren't even breathing. The least you can do is thank me. Now, don't do or eat anything without asking me. The apple you bit into was not meant to be eaten. Not yet at least. Look how grimy you are…' Her hands are still smeared with mucus from the cow's birth canal and she's struggling to wipe them clean. She sniffs at them to ensure the smell is gone. She grabs my hand and takes me outside once again. The calf is suckling blissfully.

I can't bear the smell. Is there a room I can get for my brother and myself?

'The entire house is yours; you want me to give you a tour?' the girl says, grabbing my hand and pulling me closer to her. 'And don't worry about your brother. He's eating happily. I gave him an apple, a ripe one. The poor boy was starving.'

She takes me to the attic of the house. In the corridor, I hear hushed voices. Looks like some other people are hiding here. Seeing me tag along willingly, the girl becomes ecstatic. She opens a door and we are in an alcove bedecked with flowers. It resembles a miniature garden. She opens another secret door and in front of us is a field. Without letting go of my hand, she takes me further ahead. We're in the middle of a field. The sun is burning bright. It is springtime and almond buds are tossing their heads. The girl lies down on the grassy soil strewn with leaves and petals. She makes me lie down next to her and starts caressing me slowly. Running her fingers over my palm, she slowly makes a reach for my face. She places her forefinger on my lips indicating that I shouldn't talk or resist. Seeing me lie still, she grins. Then as she begins to do the inconceivable, I scream: *Stop! Stop! What are you doing? Take me to my room.*

Grabbing hold of me, she bursts into a fit of laughter. 'Is that what you think? That this is some grand resort and I am its caretaker… And that I am here to serve you?'

I struggle to free myself from her tight grip. At last, I force myself out of her firm grasp, and stand.

If you aren't the caretaker, then who are you and what are you doing here?

'Suppose I told you a secret… Would you believe me?'

Only if you tell the truth…

'I came here to die. But now, after seeing you, I'm tempted to change my mind…'

Oh no! Not only is the girl mad, but she's suicidal too. She wants to die and she wants me to play along. And now, suddenly, she is thinking of abandoning her plan. She barely knows me, yet she's already acting as though we are going to change each other's destinies. I can't fathom who she is and what she's going to do, but here in this creepy place and at this unearthly hour, she can do anything to get me into trouble.

Die as in take your own life? Why would you want to do that?

'Don't be so suspicious,' she whispers softly, giving me a sympathetic look. 'You may be thinking that I am mad. I am not. Seriously! I'm in control of everything—my senses and my life. You have seen the evidence, haven't you? You mustn't think otherwise. The moment I saw you, I knew I could count on you. All I want is a favour. Will you…?'

But didn't you just say you are thinking of dropping the idea?

'Only if you agree to… Will you?'

Oh please!

'Then my plan is on. Will you help? It's not a big favour to ask…'

Suppose I do help you, what do I get in exchange?

'A favour for a favour.'

2

I should not have left my house. Now I am stuck with this mad girl. She seems to be in some kind of trouble. But if I leave her alone now, she might do something crazy. I can't let anything happen to her on my watch. If I abandon her and something happens to her, I might get into worse trouble.

It's a very harrowing situation to be in. Trying to flee from someone—a girl like me or like any other—who is about to die and who's looking at you and pointing a finger at you, daring you to leave her alone. She doesn't say anything, yet she's not expressionless and silent. The mysterious look in her eyes conveys you should do something. You know what it is. It is the power that a dying person transfers to you in their final moments. It's a power of a kind that you have not known before. You are bestowed upon with that power and you can instantly feel its immense weight and limitless capability. It's that power which puts you on a pedestal. But instead of accepting it, you run away because you can't stand the sight of the dying person and because you find that you are imagining yourself in her place. Then all of a sudden, you feel utterly powerless. You hear voices. The voices don't stop. You don't want to hear the voices but you can do nothing to stop them. The dying person hands you something you can't hold on to. Something you can neither keep nor discard. She hands it to you and leaves you alone. And you turn it into something else. It's a reason to forget and to live.

In this terrifying moment, I see dad. I see what he sees. I feel what he feels. I hear what he hears. I'm hiding fearfully behind him while he is teaching me how to be fearless and protect my little brother from people with blackened faces. He slips his service revolver into my hand, raises it towards his chin, inserts the muzzle into his mouth, places his fingers over mine, and begins to squeeze the trigger.

It is me, dad. It is me you are about to shoot.

'Tell me when you wake up,' he whispers into my ear.

Will you still be around when the dream ends, dad?

'Tell me when you stop dreaming.'

Don't do it, please... I beg you... You are going to get us both killed...

❦

'You are wrong. Tonight will be our night. We will do what no girls have done before. We will rejoice. We will experience freedom and life...'

Was that you again speaking in the voice of a man?

'What makes you think I can speak like a man? Don't you know my name?'

You haven't told me anything about yourself yet, not even your name.

'Call me Muknas.'

What sort of a name is that? Why would your dad and mom name you Muknas?

'Haven't you heard the legend of Muknas?'

What legend?

'She belonged to the bloodline of a great warrior tribe.

Singlehandedly, she took on an army of invaders—those who were hell-bent on seeing her tribe perish. While the war was raging on, her mother and father came back to life to fight everyone who threatened their only progeny. For days, the girl's mother and father fought against an army of thousands. Together, they defeated the enemy. When the battle ended, the mother went up to the little girl and laughed at her funny-looking nose. But she didn't reveal that she was related to her by blood. She named her Muknas—the flat-nosed one.'

No such legend exists... Tell me your real name...

'I have only one name and it is Muknas. It is the name my mother gave me and I like it. You had better get used to it.'

But your nose isn't flat. Its tip is pointed toward your feet.

'It is because the girl's mother set it right. It was her wish.'

You give me no reason to believe you. Prove it.

'You will have proof tomorrow. Be patient.'

What's going to happen tomorrow?

'As if you don't know! I will be gone tomorrow. What are you going to do then?'

What do you have in mind?

'To do what no girls have done before... You won't regret it if you do as I say. Here, take my hand. All your wishes will come true. You won't see me tomorrow. I will have come and gone as if I never existed. Come and let me take you where no one has ever been. Look, the moon is shrinking once again. After all, she has taken after you.'

3

It is autumn. Dad, Zubair and I are walking along the railway track strewn with withered, rust-coloured leaves. Our shadows stretch out long behind us. There is no sight of the train. Dad keeps turning around. He points toward the distant bend where the train is expected to make an appearance—engine first and then the coaches. It's meant to be a sign but I can't understand its meaning. Dad is timing our pace. We are walking as if there's no turning back. Dad looks toward the sky. An eagle with a large fish in its talons is soaring above us. A sign that I am not dreaming! Dad seems to be running away from something, and he is taking us someplace far where no one will find us. As if someone is after us. He keeps a firm grip on my hand, as if I am going to break free and run away. The leaves crunch under our feet. I can't hear dad's voice. I am trying to read his lips. The whistle of a train is heard. But there is no train in sight. It doesn't show up even when the whistle grows louder. Dad doesn't leave the track. We go on walking and walking. This is a dangerous undertaking.

Dad, what are you doing? Look, the train is approaching. We should get off the tracks.

Dad is out of earshot. He can't hear me.

Are you testing me again, dad? I will not run away. Look at Zubair. Look how excited he is but he can't run fast like you.

We go along the same path endlessly. As I look back at the bend where the train is supposed to make an appearance, my fear transforms into courage. The more I feel afraid the more I want to go on. There are no people around but dad suspects otherwise. He doesn't even have anything to defend himself and us with.

Eventually, we turn up at a place that resembles a clinic.

People are waiting in hordes. They seem to have been waiting for days because some are lying on the floor and the faces of some appear sunken. They seem to be hiding their afflictions. Everyone is silent. Are they mad or sane? No one can tell. They glare at us and it is scary. The doctor arrives and doesn't know what to do and where to begin. Inspecting the faces of people, he tries to figure out the cause of their presence here and the nature of their afflictions. Everyone is unsure about what the doctor is about to do. The doctor seems unsure of his own abilities as well. He's unsure of the people he has kept waiting for so long. He doesn't know if they are waiting for him or someone else. He remembers nothing. He could be a patient himself. He can't even bear the sight of his patients. He wants to run away but the people form a wall around him. He is trapped. Every child here looks like Zubair. Dad can't tell the doctor from patients. He rushes to grab hold of the doctor. 'I am not the one,' the frightened man screams. 'What am I doing here? I am not supposed to be here. Let go of me.'

I see the rope to which I am attached. One end of it is coiled around my ankle. I wonder if it is long enough to let me go anywhere. I don't know where it will fall short. It is curtailing my freedom. I won't go any further unless I am able to see its other end.

If this is a test, then it is meant to make me fail. But it isn't a test I will always pass.

Zubair is behaving normally. But something is wrong with dad. He's looking around for someone but he doesn't know whom he's searching for and what he must do. He has mistaken an imposter for the doctor. Or maybe the doctor is pretending to be someone else to escape the wrath of the people. Suddenly everyone freezes. Except dad and us, no one is able to move. People seem to be tied to the floor. When I take a closer look at them, their true condition is revealed. They are cripples.

4

The voice of Flatnose echoes through the hallway: 'When the time comes, will you be with me?' She's singing and dancing like a girl possessed. It's a celebratory dance. I know how this is going to end. I know where this will lead. Tomorrow, she will go back to her house. I will go back to mine. She's just looking for paltry excuses. She won't do anything silly or even remotely dangerous. She might be looking for a reason to live but she gives me strange looks which suggest that it could be my turn next. I'm at my wits' end and running out of patience. I want to tell her what I really think about her. That she's such a put-on. That she must stop faking it and that her pretentious behaviour won't lead her anywhere.

She falls down in a fit of rage. Strange sounds like that of a cow about to give birth come out of her. She stretches out her legs and writhes in pain. She rips her clothes apart and takes them off. A strange fluid seeps out of the pores in her skin. She cries and moans: 'Help me. The baby is about to come. Don't leave me alone.'

There she goes again, I think. She falls silent and begins to breathe deeply. I hold her hand and begin to caress her legs the way she caressed the legs of the cow when she was about to give birth. She wants me to do this. My hands are covered in mucus. She gives out another cry, and then: 'I can't feel the pain yet… Is it out…? Head first, right? Do you see the head? No? Okay, let me push harder… Now? Do you see it now? Yes, yes, I see it… Don't touch it… Oh, a boy… Look, how adorable he is… More adorable than your brother… Don't take him away… Give him to me… He's mine… You will kill him…'

She goes on screaming and blabbering in turns. Her face turns red. She clenches her fist around my fingers. She bites her lip. Blood gushes forth. There's blood all over me. My hands, arms, legs, feet are trembling. Something terrible is happening to me. I can almost hear my heart sink. But I can't hear my voice. There is a cut on my wrist. Flatnose is next to me, moaning and laughing at the same time. 'Goodbye,' she says. She rises and then starts laughing and dancing again. I now realize what has happened. She hasn't slashed her wrist. She has slashed mine. There are cuts all over my body. I am bleeding to death.

You mad girl, look at what you have done. You were supposed to slash your wrist, not mine. You should have cut yourself up. Not me. You are a monster. I need a doctor. Get me to a hospital or I will die…

She goes on dancing. She can't hear me. *Look at me, you mad girl…* She continues to ignore me. It's the greatest misunderstanding of her life. She feigns ignorance of what she's done. Her terrible act will cost me my life. My life will be over and hers will… She will think she took her life and she will be redeemed forever. She will never know what a coward she is. She will revel in the despicable act. She should know she's committed a big blunder. I begin to lose the strength to even stand up and face her and show her my bloodied wrist.

Look at what you have done, Flatnose. You have mistaken me for yourself.

'Stop screaming! You aren't dying.'

She's right. Why am I not dying? I should be dead by now.

Without stopping her gory dance, she turns her mesmeric gaze towards me as if nothing has happened. She doesn't have a clue to her wrongdoing. The wicked smile on her face disgusts me and fills me with hate. I can't even complain. I can't even express my hate or my anger. I can't even take revenge. The blood doesn't stop flowing out of my veins. I look for a piece of cloth. I can't locate a thing. Silken drapes are dangling from the windows. Music starts playing. Flatnose goes on whirling like a mad person in a trance. I am dying and she's not even bothered. She has even stopped looking at me. She is lost in her own sick act. I'm just entertainment to her. Blood fills up my mouth. I am unable to scream or talk anymore.

I grab hold of her leg to stop her from dancing. She goes on and on like a maniac. I dig my nails into her skin. I bleed. I cry. She laughs.

Casting a pitiful look at me, she says, 'You have become me. Haven't you?'

There's nothing I can do to make her help me. My legs and hands have no life. Soon everything will be over.

I read her lips: 'Want me to help you?' She waits for a response.

I blink.

'Now you can't speak? You've tasted blood. Spit it out and speak. It's not difficult at all.'

I do as she says. I spit out all the blood in my mouth. And then, I regain my voice. *Go away... Leave me alone...*

I manage to stand on my legs, and throwing a punch her way, I push her away and search for a place to hide. Her gaze falls on Zubair who's been sitting motionless all the while. She grabs hold of his hand, drags him inside a glass-enclosed room, and slams the door shut. Ignoring my own plight, I make a dash for the door. I beg her to open the door. Zubair's behaviour shocks me. Not a whimper of protest. He doesn't even look at me. The way he let her take him away is scary.

Give him back to me. Open the door. Let me in. Though screaming doesn't help, I keep banging on the door to get her to open it and hand Zubair back to me.

Let him go. What do you want? I will do whatever to get him back.

My words fall flat. They don't reach her. The damned enclosure is sealed and soundproof. To my utter shock and disbelief, Flatnose fishes a pair of scissors out of nowhere and starts chopping Zubair's hair. The hair falls on the floor. Flatnose quickly lights a match and burns the hair. Small insects crawl out of the burning hair and die. Flatnose then inserts the sharp-edged tips of the scissors into Zubair's right ear.

Stop, stop, what are you doing? You are hurting him.

'Look,' her voice blares through a speaker on the door of the room, 'there's a centipede lodged inside his ear canal. It's headed straight inside towards his eardrum. It is going to lay an egg there. If the egg hatches, another centipede will be born inside his ear. It won't come out then. Your brother will die of pain. You still want me to stop? I can rid him of the centipede. Or do you want to do it yourself?'

I'm afraid of centipedes. They are vengeful insects. They take revenge by crawling into your ears and laying eggs in them.

Just as Flatnose is trying to get the centipede out of Zubair's ear canal, something gory happens. The centipede opens its dreadful mouth. The scissors slip out of Flatnose's hand and the sharp edges puncture Zubair's skin. But to my utter shock, he doesn't bleed. Flatnose makes another cut. There's no blood even now. Zubair is expressionless. Why isn't he screaming? Doesn't he feel any pain? Another cut, a deeper one this time. Nothing, even now! Not even a drop. How is this possible? One more cut. The skin is leathery, bloodless. Flatnose isn't shocked, almost as if this was what she was expecting. She's just having fun at my expense. Zubair is just an experiment. She's just amusing herself. She's insensitive to the kid's plight. She goes on inflicting cuts. Cut after cut, and Zubair neither reacts nor protests. At last, the centipede falls out of his ear, and Flatnose squishes it with the scissors. A look of relief spreads across her face.

Alright, let him go now.

'You're so heartless.'

I'm sorry. You saved him. I'm eternally indebted. Are you happy now?

'One good turn deserves another.'

Can I have him back?

'You can, on one condition.'

What condition?

'You know what my condition is.'

I will do anything to have my brother back. Hand him back to me now.

The door opens. 'I'm happy you agreed,' she says without a hint of remorse on her face. 'I will hold you to your word. But if you ditch me again, then you're accountable for whatever happens...' She's sitting next to Zubair and patting him. I rush to inspect him and his ear. He seems to have fallen asleep as though he has been drugged. 'Don't worry, he's okay now, fully rid of the deadly insect, the worst is over for the poor boy,' she says in a doctor's tone.

In Zubair's clenched fist are colourful glass beads. 'They are his,' Flatnose says. 'Let him have them. I have no use of them.'

A look of contentment flashes across Zubair's face. Maybe when he wakes up, he will spill everything out.

Don't you dare touch him now? And don't test my patience. I thought we had a pact?

'You are talking of pacts? How kind of you!'

Go away. You're not human.

'Not human? Look at me. Look at these hands and feet. Look at my mouth, my lips. You touched me. Didn't you? How dare you deny my existence? Will you deny your own existence?'

Shut up, you...

'Go ahead and curse me. No amount of cursing will change anything. You know it,' she says, walking towards a cupboard and taking out a bottle of whiskey. 'Have some of this and you will begin to see things clearly,' she adds, handing me a glass. Without thinking, I gulp it down.

Give me another.

She pours another drink. I gulp it down too. Then another and another...

'Stop, stop,' she says. 'You will kill yourself. This is not how you drink. We're supposed to celebrate and rejoice. This is our last night together. Tomorrow I won't be around. Tomorrow does not exist for me. Slow down. There's no rush. The night is going nowhere...'

Why should you be the one to give orders? Why should everything happen according to you? You're not the only one here. It's my turn now. I will decide what is good for me. I will decide what I should or should not do.

'That's the spirit,' she says, condescendingly. Clearly, she's an ace at it. But I will not let her ruin anything. I must take the control back into my hands. But something terrible is happening. The walls are spinning. This place is doing bizarre things to me. Why am I not able to close my eyes like Zubair? He's sleeping so soundly, as if he hasn't slept in ages. When will he wake up and make sense of everything that's happening here?

I rush to the window with a nasty sensation. It's horrible. I feel like throwing up but nothing is coming out of me. At that moment, I see a terrible sight. A shadowy figure—like the one in the window—has tied up the legs of the calf, and the helpless calf isn't even putting up a fight. She doesn't know her fate has been sealed. She doesn't know her end is near, that her throat will be slashed and she will be cut into pieces.

Hey you! Stop! What are you doing?

The cow is looking at her newborn with tragic eyes. It's a look of utter helplessness and dejection. She has resigned herself to it. She can't do a thing. She shouldn't have given birth to her. Another shadowy figure shows up with a knife in his hand. He pins the calf down by putting his foot on her head, and readies to slash her throat. The look in the eyes of the calf is dreadful. She doesn't even know she's looking at the world and her mother for the last time because she hasn't even really seen the world and her mother yet. She knows nothing of the world and of life. She hasn't seen anything yet. What it is to live and what it is to grow. She doesn't know what is to come. She knows nothing except the scent of her mother. She doesn't know life or death. She mistakes the two butchers for her own breed. The cow moos loudly. The calf raises her eyes towards the helpless mother for the last time, not knowing that she is fated to never see her again. It is fate against hope now. What will the cow do? Will she put up a fight to protect her calf? Or will she resign to her fate? She shouldn't give up. And then, all of a sudden, the look in her eyes changes. It's the deadliest look evoking both pity and fear. But it's just a look; the hapless look of a hapless cow. Her fate is sealed too. She's a thing to be discarded. Her survival is absolutely uncertain if nobody does anything and if Flatnose doesn't intervene. She will give up her life willingly if she's given a choice. But she won't. The imminent slaughter of her calf is a sign and a warning that it will be her turn next. And then the knife's edge moves forward and backward slowly on the calf's soft throat.

I shut the window and go back inside. I gulp down one more drink even as Flatnose is examining me and my doings as though I were a convict and she the judge. A frothy liquid comes out of my mouth. This place is accursed. Bloody humans. They know neither pity nor kindness. They have become beasts. I must save this place with or without Flatnose's help. Else I must burn it.

No end is in sight for this lingering night.

Flatnose gulps one drink after another. Soon she will get drunk and lose consciousness. Then I will get a chance to escape. A golden chance, and I must take it! If I don't make a move now, I will never get out of here.

A familiar smell comes wafting around. Whitey barges in through a window. What a relief it is to see her. She's a godsend. She seems to have come for Zubair and me. She gives me her usual affectionate and reassuring look. 'Everything is okay and we will be fine' is what the look conveys. She will help me find a way out of here, and then I can take Zubair with me.

Whitey looks hungry. Maybe we will find a bone outside. Maybe there will be a dead bird on the road and Whitey can satiate her hunger. She will know the way out of here. She will help Zubair and me get out of here.

Quietly, we step out of the house through the backdoor. Whitey leads the way. We go down a narrow path. There's an open ground nearby. Whitey doesn't make a sound but her smell gives her away. Suddenly, we hear growls. We move forward and encounter a horrific sight. Dogs from out of nowhere spring into sight. They begin to step out of their hidden dens one after another. They gather and form a circle around us. I realize my mistake. Unknowingly, we have sauntered into enemy territory. Whitey is brave and doesn't retreat. She walks by my side. One after another, the dogs come out of their dens and start growling ferociously at Whitey. We are now unevenly teamed up against each other. Whitey lowers her tail but doesn't leave my side. She doesn't retreat and we continue walking steadily. She pretends to be brave, but she knows she has been cornered and there's no escape if we keep going ahead. She circles me and as we near a dead end, some more dogs surround her. They are ferocious. They growl menacingly but don't have the courage to attack yet. We are in their territory. Then, in a trice, the unexpected happens. An alpha male with matted hair and an enormous jaw trots out of nowhere. Salivating profusely, he bares his teeth and displays his long, sharp canines. All that frothy and foul smelling saliva coming out of his mouth and nostrils drips on to the ground. His territory stands demarcated. At first, he prances slowly, digging his paws violently into the ground, raking up a cloud of dust, and then he growls menacingly giving out an unmistakable warning to Whitey and me: 'retreat immediately or face dire consequences.' This is the moment to make a call—to back out and stand down or to persist. We must act fast or else... The alpha male indicates we aren't to go any further and if we do, it will be the end of us. But we stand our ground. Whitey is fearful now. She keeps looking at me and I at her. But I don't reveal my fear to her. She believes I am fearless and will do anything to protect her from the monstrous alpha male. I look back at her to convey that we're a team and that I won't leave her side. This is the time when she needs me the most and I need her the most. Fear becomes courage; courage turns into revenge, and revenge into hate. Whitey looks at me and she sees something in my eyes that gives her the courage to confront the pack. She returns the alpha male's stare with an even more menacing stare. She reveals her pointed canines indicating battle-readiness and vengeance. It's either the alpha male and his pack or us. We are not going to budge or retreat. We are going to make the entire pack retreat back into their dens or wherever they came from.

When we start walking further towards the forbidden territory, the alpha male lunges at Whitey. Whitey doesn't give up her guard. She knows she's at her weakest right now but she has to put up a fight. She needs me now. She waits for me. She waits for a signal. I go near her and we stand together. The dogs are wary of me. They know Whitey and I are a team now. I can't leave Whitey alone amongst these salivating brutes dying to kill her. I can't let anything happen to her. She's given me the right to protect her. She has placed her trust in me. Her loyalty should not go in vain. She's not alone in this fight. This is our fight now. We against them! They want to inflict fear in our hearts so that we will never dare enter their territory. This is the point of no return.

The dogs make a formation with the alpha male leading the pack at the centre. They create a perimeter from which escape is impossible. But they don't know what courage Whitey is capable of. She knows I won't leave her now or ever and that makes her the most fearless of all dogs. Seeing the same fearlessness and loyalty in my eyes, she runs towards the pack to break the cordon. She leaps at them and inflicts a deadly bite on the second-in-command. It's the thought of revenge that has kept her going so far. This is her moment.

Whitey arches her body, and with her jaw wide open, she makes her intent clear: 'Come on, you rogues, I am ready to take you on.' She pounces at the alpha male and inflicts a deadly bite. Blood gushes out of its flesh. The alpha male concedes defeat and starts retreating. The other dogs follow suit. This is it. We win. I pose for victory.

The look Whitey throws me conveys her disapproval of my conduct. 'This is no time for jubilation' is what her look seems to say. Even in victory, her gait is dignified. She retraces as though nothing has happened. There's not a single wound on her body, not a single blemish, despite having been bitten by the ferocious alpha male.

When I reprimand her for putting herself at risk by following me, she makes a face, 'I didn't do anything and it is not my fault.'

She leads the way back to the house. I understand everything now. I am not her protector. It's the other way round. She is protecting me. She's the one who protected me from the pack of mad dogs. It is me they were after, not her. Whitey is not scared for her life. She's scared for me. She doesn't want me to be harmed. Her weakness has become her greatest strength. She will give up everything to defend me.

When we get back to the courtyard of the house, Whitey's scars reappear. She marks the gate with her scent to ensure that the strays don't follow us here and that they keep out.

We are back to square one. But at least, we are not dead.

One for Sorrow, Three for Joy

1

'A day will come when no one will believe you,' blares Flatnose. She's absent but her voice isn't. 'It is the greatest misfortune to not have anyone hear your confession. To not have anyone hear your compulsions and the reasons behind your deeds. You will beg people to hear you. But no one will pay attention. You can't even tell it to yourself. It will drive you mad. When you have no people to listen to you, you will go and beg animals and birds and trees to listen to your woes. You will confide to dogs and crows and trees and stones. Even they won't listen. But you will have me. Remember I'm your only confidante. You have already accepted my condition. Do not forget that or else you will be no different than those ill-fated souls who don't even wish to know what blunders they have committed in their lives.'

I have become an object of her desire and obsession. She has kept me under her watchful eye throughout. Maybe she's just an apparition. But what if she comes to feast upon my bones? I have nothing to offer. Maybe I'm hallucinating. But the marks on my body are real. How do I make the marks vanish? I can't speak about what I see and hear. It's a curse.

What the day gives, the night takes away. The night is a grindstone. It grinds everything that passes through it. Even dreams. I long for the night to bring me the light of a star. But this particular dreadful night is Flatnose's own creation. Only she can bring it to an end.

I didn't come here for this. I didn't come here to get robbed of reason and logic. I came here with a purpose and I have failed myself. My worries don't seem to matter anymore. I am being driven to madness. I might do something senseless. That is what she wants. She is waiting for my spirit to break. She wants to see me collapse.

I hear my name being called out.

Is that you, mom, dad? Are you calling me?

Twilight bathes the house. Zubair is a grown up lad. He's sitting on a chair with his head resting on his shoulder. He doesn't move his head. I wait for him to straighten it.

You will sprain your neck, Zubair.

'This is how I have always been. I can't always do what you ask me to do.' The tone of his voice betrays envy.

He gets up, curls up his body like a wheel and then rolls down the hall. 'Shall I drive you home,' he says. 'You can sit behind. There is room for two.' He makes sounds like that of a car engine and in the curled position he waits in front of me, indicating that I must hop on. 'Don't blame me if you fall off. Hold tight...'

Where are you taking me?

'Home! Where else?'

But we are home.

Whitey is gnawing at a bone. Zubair is happy that he's about to give me a ride.

'Hurry up,' he says, 'or else you will be stranded here forever.'

I will go and pack then.

I sneak into his room while he waits for me in the hall. I witness a horrifying sight. My worst fears have come true.

Zubair has been up to his old tricks again. He has been trapping sparrows. We haven't left the house. We have been in the same wretched house for god knows how long. Zubair's affliction is back. Maybe it never left him in the first place. Maybe the cures didn't work. The sparrows are trembling on a mat. They are stuck to a nasty glue-like substance. They can't even open their tiny beaks. Their claws are stuck. The struggle has resulted in the dismemberment of their claws and beaks. Life is oozing out of them. They have given up. They want their pain to end. But some are still struggling to escape.

Back to his original state, Zubair barges in. I want to grab hold of him and thrash him. He's fuming because his nasty little secret has been discovered again. He looks at me as if he's about to strangle me. When I scold him, he curses loudly and shouts at me. He calls me names. 'Get lost,' he screams. He pushes me away as if I am his enemy. I have never encountered such behaviour.

What right do you have to do this to me, Zubair?

He screams back at me, 'Go, run to dad. Complain to him. What else are you capable of doing?'

He looks at the sparrows with a strange, uncaring look in his eyes. He behaves as if he is their savior; as if he is easing their suffering. Something is terribly wrong. What must I do to free the sparrows? The stench of death lurks around. The entire room is a torture chamber. Zubair has no clue about his wrongdoings. Maybe the worst is yet to come. Maybe this is just the beginning. I will not let him sink deeper and deeper into an abyss from which there is no escape. He is deranged and dangerous. He should be stopped. I will do everything to stop him even if it calls for his confinement. This madness must not be allowed to go on.

Zubair looks horrible. There's hair all over his face and chest.

Moments ago, he was a little boy. He's now transformed into an adult who thinks he knows what's right and what's wrong. As I begin to free the sparrows, Whitey leaps at me to stop me from meddling into the affairs of her master. Our eyes meet and she recognizes me. She's unsure about what to do. I stroke her ears. The ominous look in her eyes starts to fade. Will she protect her master or allow me to do what I am about to do? She hasn't forgotten all that I have done for her. She sits next to me. Zubair throws a fit. He's in rage. He picks up a whip and starts flogging Whitey mercilessly. Only a beast can do such a thing. He's beyond recognition. Whitey throws her legs around me. She takes the blows and lashes on her back. She's willing to take more beating. It doesn't matter to her. Once again, she protects me. At last, Zubair gives up. He's tired. He falls to his knees and bursts into sobs. He throws himself into my lap and says the most painful words. 'I'm sorry, I don't know why I like doing such things, but I don't want you to push me into the lake and get rid of me,' he pleads, burying his head in my lap.

2

Time plays truant. It changes hands. Right now, it's on her side. It has turned partial. Twenty-four hours ago, without informing anyone, I ran away from my university, leaving everything behind to look for my father. It seems as though years have gone by already. Now I am not so sure if I will ever get to go back.

'Days have come and gone,' says Flatnose. She appears in front of me just when I need her the most. 'You haven't been paying attention. I know you don't trust me. You don't even think I am real. I have no proof but this. Look at me,' she says, lifting the scarf off her neck and revealing her mole. 'This is my birthmark. No one can erase it. How come you allowed yourself to be tricked? Look at it and touch it. It's the mole that your mother gave you. It is the same mole that the eclipse caused. Do you know what it can lead to? Do you even know what it is? I shall prove everything to you. Come with me...'

Why have you brought me here?

'Because you don't believe a word of what I say.'

Her voice turns compassionate but the dread in her eyes is still real. She isn't able to fake it.

She puts down one more condition—to live-stream her final act, 'It's going to be a worthy watch, I guarantee.'

What's she going to do? Jump off the roof of the house and fall on a thick sheet of ice without even breaking a bone? Is she going to suffocate herself until her heart stops beating? Or will she set herself ablaze? Does she intend to consume poison and die? One of her raw apples will do the job. That's why she has kept them in the bowl. She might even smash her head against the wall. But who would want to watch her die of a convulsion? Who's interested in an act that reeks of defiance? Not me, at least. Maybe she has a final speech to give in her mind. Is she going to slash her wrists and bleed to death? She has already tried and failed. Will she disembowel herself? She's too fickle to do that. But who knows what might happen to her when the time comes or when she thinks it is time? She might, at the time, even lose the last dregs of sanity and blow her brains out. But who on earth is interested in that stuff?

She thinks her final act will spell her rebellion. Her first attempt in my presence was a disaster. Maybe she has attempted earlier too when no one was watching.

She inserts her head into a transparent plastic bag and ties a knot around her neck. As she tightens the knot, her fingernails protrude and retract like those of a cat. Her eyeballs pop out of her sockets. With only a tiny hole to breathe through, she will soon start gasping for breath and then choke to death. But she doesn't. She starts humming a song and rolling her devilish eyes. I give her an angry look: *Stop this pretense.*

She doesn't stop singing. The song goes: 'Look at me… Look at my beauty… It is matchless…' She's mocking me and dragging me into her ludicrous act. I am revulsed at the very thought of being her sidekick. She's sick and she's beyond help. I have my own worries. I don't want to deal with her and her madness. She is either a girl without a cause or a drama queen or both. She is trying to lure me with her cunningness. Glorifying madness is the worst form of madness. There are no takers for her act here. There never will be. I am better off without her. I have been so wrong about myself.

Once again, she brandishes a knife and enacts a scene as if she's going to do it. But she won't. It's time to call her bluff.

What are you waiting for? Are you going to conduct a poll asking people if you should do it or not? Don't you already know that everyone will vote yes?

'Will you vote yes, too? Even after having seen everything with your own eyes?'

I won't stop you. Go ahead and do it.

'What makes you think I won't?'

You're wasting your time and mine. You're a procrastinator and a quitter.

'We will see who's a quitter and who's not. You don't even know how to save yourself and your little brother. You give up too soon. You are indecisive. What are you going to do now? I know you won't do a thing. You will just wait and wait until things happen on their own. Do you think this night will ever end? Have you thought of that? You aren't the girl I had thought you would be.'

But you said the opposite earlier.

'You still don't get it. I am on your side. Look at me. Who am I? Don't you recognize me?'

No, I don't.

'Then you will never leave.'

I will prove you wrong. Now watch me get out of here.

It doesn't take even a fraction of a second for everything to change and to become the opposite of what it is. Flatnose thinks I cannot tell dream from reality, truth from falsehood, and clarity from chaos. She thinks I am submissive. Her behaviour towards me is characterized by domination and power. She's doing her best to show me things that don't exist and never will. She believes I will begin to like it here and that I will never want to leave. But I am going to prove her wrong, now, once and for all.

If Zubair doesn't wake up, I will drag him along. I call his name a number of times. I shake him. I try to lift him. He's too big for me. At last, he stands up but doesn't open his eyes. At least, he's obedient and not defiant. I grab hold of his hand and lead him towards the gate of the house. Zubair knows the way out as much as I do. He's in a state of wakeful stupor. We walk and walk. The gate recedes further and further into a hazy distance. Something doesn't allow us to go where we want to go. Maybe it is Time that is preventing our exit. It is doing the very opposite. It shrinks its pace. Minutes seem hours. The gate is in sight but any movement seems impossible. The nearer we think we are, the farther the gate appears. But we mustn't give up. We trudge on. Zubair is motionless even though I am dragging him towards the exit. How long as it been? Hours or days or months or years? Time forbids me from measuring it. It has turned against me as if I am its sworn enemy. There is more distance to cover. We will make it happen no matter what. We are not going to give up. If I give up now, I will never make it out of here. The gate is in front of me. It isn't far. If I give up now, I will stand defeated, but if I persist I will defeat the trickery of Time. We gather pace. But the distance doesn't shorten.

I look back towards the window. Sitting by the doorstep, Flatnose is sneering at me as though she already knows the outcome of my struggle. She waves at me and blows me a kiss. Is this her goodbye or an invitation to return? Never before have I found myself caught between the devil and the deep sea.

The cow is at the very place where she gave birth to the calf. She too is motionless. She's trying to keep her newborn calf alive by not leaving its side even when it's not really there.

Time is a hydra-headed monster. You cut one head off, another one sprouts.

I find myself back in the house. Zubair is already there, at the same place he was before we tried to escape.

'Look at you,' Flatnose whispers in my ear. 'You keep doing these silly things. How many times do I have to stop you from putting yourself at risk? Leaving this place is fraught with perils, and you have seen enough evidence of that. Look at the bite marks, the bloodstains, the vomit and the grime all over you. Let me clean you up. Come with me.'

She drags me to the bath. There's steam all over the wooden walls and mirrors. She takes her clothes off and stands naked before me. She's silk. Her hands are clay. Her flesh is marble. There's not a single blemish on her face.

She bathes me as though she were my mother. She caresses me gently and wipes me dry with a soft towel. After she's done, she sprays some perfume behind my ears and applies a scented lotion on the cuts, bite marks and bruises on my skin. I start trembling. She gives me a set of clothes to wear. They look good as new, and I feel their silky softness. 'You're right... haven't worn them ever... didn't get a chance... now it's too late to wear them and go around enthralling people,' she says while dressing up herself. 'They will fit you perfectly. You will look dazzling in them.'

She makes me put on her clothes. I feel they are mine already. Not an inch loose, not an inch tight. Made to fit. Tailored for a solemn occasion like a wedding or a funeral.

As I look at my reflection in the mirror in front of me, she grabs hold of my neck and begins to massage it softly. Time slows down for the first time. Then she runs her fingers through my hair. Time slows down even more. Slowly, her hands slide down from my head and make their way back on to my neck, back and shoulders. A gentle circular motion of soft fingertips indicating expertise and precision! The touch of intense warmth! Time stops, finally. For the first time I experience genuine relaxation and pleasure. Like a masseuse trained to induce hypnosis, she works her way through the unexplored contours of my body. Our eyes meet though we aren't facing each other. We are both facing the mirror and our reflections are staring back at us. She squints at me and then gives me an envious look as though, for the first time, she is conscious of her physical limitations and fading beauty. A gentle warning is whispered seductively into my ear: 'How dare you try to become me? Take them off, hand them back to me.' She demands her clothes back. She tries to undress me yet again by tugging on the dress. I'm unable to face her. She's standing behind me. She doesn't allow me to turn. I'm facing the mirror. I look at her reflection. Her mouth distorts. Her lips curl. A hideous face is now staring back at me. Her grip around my neck tightens. It's a deadly stranglehold from which I can't escape even if I want to. I don't even try to escape. But I won't let her do this to me. Not when dawn is around the corner. I must turn the tables against her. Enough is enough. I feel like throwing her clothes back at her.

'Not just the clothes,' she says, without taking her hands off my neck.

Get off me.

I free myself and punch her on her face. I give out a piercing scream, more of a war cry, and grab her by the neck. *You're going to have no more fun now. It's my turn. I will call the shots. Your time is up. You will regret being born. I will burn you with my own hands. You have no idea what I am capable of. You have mistaken me for a passive and submissive girl. I am not.*

I land punch after punch on her stomach. She laughs at every blow. I know why she's enjoying this act. She wants me to do this to her. She's testing me. But she will regret testing me. This is it.

'Go on! Show me what you're capable of,' she screams. 'C'mon, do it. Let's see what you have got. Is that all?' She takes punch after punch. She tries to tire me out. She's bleeding through her nose.

I can't go on anymore. I'm tired. I have no strength left to punch anymore. To hide my shame and embarrassment, I persist and scream loudly. I go on screaming hysterically hoping that screaming will relieve my anxiety. It works. Flatnose lifts me up and throws her arms around me and sobs. I don't even know if her tears are genuine or not. Is this too an act of deception? Watching me throw a fit, she tries to calm me. If I don't stop myself from breaking down, her madness will intensify. She wants me to be somewhat less than her equal. This is the time I decide to take revenge. I fish out the pistol and point it at her. Her forehead is inches away from the pistol's muzzle. My forefinger is curled around the trigger. I hold it tight and steady. She squints at me, giving me a penetrating look. She wants to determine my intention first, and then wants to scare me and call my bluff. But she senses my determination. She still thinks I am kidding.

Hey you, this is neither a joke nor a dare.

She doesn't know if I am bluffing or not. At this moment, she shivers. I won't let her speak. *Now we shall see who's a coward and who's not. I won't count to three or ten. I won't do such a silly thing. I won't hesitate to blow your brains out.*

'Stop,' she says fearfully. 'Put it down. After all, we are...'

We are what? Sisters?

'Yes, how did you guess?'

I move the pistol back an inch and I know the next thing to happen will be the bullet puncturing her skull. All her false bravado will end. She will die a horrible death. She grabs hold of my hand and snatches at the pistol. Her hands tremble. The pistol is too heavy for her. She's never held a pistol in her hands. Then she shows me her hands.

'Look,' she says, showing me her empty hands. 'Listen, this whole thing is a setup. Don't do this to yourself. This is just a show. The boy you tried to drag out isn't Zubair. Zubair is sleeping peacefully. I have fed him well. I took care of him. I saved him, don't you remember? Look outside. Look at the cashier doling out tickets to the cinemagoers? He's been up the whole night. People have queued up since last night. We're going to make their wait worthwhile. They have come to watch us. We must give them a grand show.'

She looks serious, as though she has no other choice but to reveal the truth for the first time.

Before she plots her next move, I must get my act together. Whitey will be my final throw of the dice! If something happens to me, she should take Zubair out of here. She will. That's why she's here. If it comes to a choice between Zubair and me, I know whom she will prefer. I must feed her first. She hasn't even complained. She doesn't know where her pups are. She doesn't have them with her. I should be worried for her. She's the only one who cares for me. She has kept me in her sight so that no harm comes to me. She doesn't like Flatnose. She has sensed that Flatnose is a threat to me, yet she keeps waiting for a sign from me so that she will know when to come to my rescue. Flatnose is clever. She hasn't allowed Whitey to enter the house. Whitey is still waiting on the steps outside in the cold.

3

Flatnose has been lying about herself, but she knows that already and doesn't really care. She wants me to beg and plead again and again. She has been spying on me like she has spied on Whitey who, she thinks, knows everything that's happening and that's going to happen. She's right. Whitey indeed knows and has knowledge of things that are about to unfold. I would not have survived had it not been for her. No one gives a damn. Whitey does. Flatnose knows I owe my survival to Whitey and no one else. She also knows that Whitey is the only one who can get me out of this place in one piece. She doesn't know that I have kept a close watch on her secret moves. And that I have followed every move of hers through this wretched night! I have seen her go into hiding. I have watched her hide behind the trunk of a tree in the courtyard. I know why she does so. In the dead of the night, I followed her when she quietly tiptoed out of the house to feed Whitey. Her hands smelled of rice and meat. I wanted to taste the food just to check if it was safe for Whitey's consumption. At first, I thought Flatnose had poisoned the food to kill Whitey to get rid of her so that she could have me all to herself. Without Whitey I would be defenseless. Little does she know that Whitey can't be fooled into eating the food she brings to her. And that Whitey eats only when I feed her.

I hid behind another tree right next to the ditch where she fed Whitey. I know she spotted me. But she pretended otherwise. I should have been more careful. But then something unexpected happened and I saw Flatnose open the door to let Whitey in. Whitey smelled the food and ate it. And then Flatnose tried to eat the leftovers. But she couldn't even reach the morsel to her mouth. She didn't eat at all. She felt no hunger for herself. She was incapable of eating. Her only aim—to satiate Whitey's hunger and thirst. That is when I realized what a fool I had been. Flatnose wasn't to be trusted. She was trying to steal Whitey from me. And she almost succeeded in winning Whitey's heart.

I cursed her in my thoughts: Flatnose, Flatnose, may you burn in hell. I know you know everything about me and that you detest me. I'm not like the others whom you can dominate and who will be swayed by your tricks. I have neither sympathy nor pity. You know that already. You tasted my indifference. I am to blame because I gave it away. I have made it amply clear on numerous occasions. The very first time when I looked at you and allowed you to… Let's not go there. Let's not talk about it either. You know everything. But you ought to know something else. I know it has been bothering you. So I wish to tell you. I saw how weak you were the moment you went out to feed Whitey. You feel the pain when she shivers in the cold.

Whitey is not afraid of anyone. She has no milk to feed her newborns. She goes back into the ditch after you leave. She smears mud all over her body and hides so that no one can tell her from the night. Maybe she will be happier when spring arrives. She was happiest last spring. Ever since she gave birth, she's become fearful. She is fearful because she isn't sure if you will keep feeding her so that she has all the strength to nurse her pups. She has come to know fear and weakness. She has tasted love and that's making her weak. What if you don't turn up on time? What if you forget her name? What if you go someplace else? What if you…? None of these what ifs existed until now. Now, she's dangling between extremes.

But despite all your faults and frailties, you do a noble thing. Who would do what you're doing?

Whitey brought me back here, safe. Out there when I was ambushed, she didn't leave me alone, even for a second. She has not even done anything against my wishes. Even when you were insistent on hurting me! Such is Whitey's love, loyalty and obedience.

I am telling you the truth. I would never have imagined telling you anything earlier. Whitey needs you the most now. She needs you more than she needs me. Her pups will need you when they come out of the ditch and when they are hungry. You should look for them if they aren't in the ditch. They will start exploring the neighbourhood. Fox Lady has laid her eyes on Whitey and her pups. Whitey won't let her come near her pups. You know the fearsome look in her eyes. The pups whine and fight. They create a ruckus. But they go back into the ditch to hide when Fox Lady is nearby. They aren't brave like their mother. The only time they come out in the open is when they think no one is watching. But you can see them. No one else can.

Whitey is the smartest of the pack. She comes out of the ditch to meet her pups before the moonlight shines because that's the time when no one is around. Then Whitey meets her pups and they cuddle as if they are getting united for the first and the last time. They are learning how not to be afraid. They know you will show up and call their names. They know you are always watching and you won't let them out of your sight. It is you that's keeping Fox Lady at bay for she knows you will come to protect Whitey and her pups from her. Whitey does everything to please you. She still has you. She's sticking her guts out only for you. She has no one to hang out with but you.

I'm relieved you aren't crying anymore, Flatnose. I had to eavesdrop. When I go from here, I shall miss the sound of your sobbing. I will have nothing else to rely on except the feeble sound of your pain. It has made me believe in my own existence. That I am incapable of pain doesn't matter to me. I know you must think I am loony. But don't worry. I won't believe anyone. People have been filthy liars. Morons. They are scared to acknowledge your presence. I know everything that they have done and said to you. They are shameless as are their children who peep through pigeonholes just to ogle at you. Brats. When they see me, they feign innocence and ignorance. They pretend to go about their lives as if they are saints without any vices. I know very well why they give the impression that you don't exist. Would you believe it? Who are they kidding? They think I'm a fool. They don't know me. They don't know what I am capable of. They know nothing of my powers. Their days are numbered. They will rot for their lies and deception. They don't deserve mercy. I know you are forgiving, but I am not. I shall not forget what they do and say. I will prove them wrong. I will make them repent. A day will come when they will realize their mistakes. That day they will seek my forgiveness. If they don't, I will kill them one by one. Trust me. I will put an end to their misery.

Whitey and her pups still wait for you every night. Do you have any idea why they cuddle up to you? It is because they can't bear your sadness. They can't bear your absence. Nothing makes me more jealous than seeing them lick your hands. You will hate me even more now.

You must know that I am the one who took away the weakest pup. She would have died had I not taken her when you weren't watching. I nursed her. She stopped limping. She's happy at last. She's still yours. I did it for both of you.

The path leading to the ditch will soon be strewn with petals. The pups will grow and disperse. Whitey will disappear, too. So will Fox Lady who isn't as bad as she appears. What is going to happen to you when the ditch is empty once again?

4

Flatnose has read my mind. She knows I am not going to linger in her house for long now, that I am done here, and that I am now going to grab hold of Zubair and get out of this wretched place.

Even if it costs me my life! I am going to do whatever it takes to leave. She trusts Whitey to stay with her and witness her final act. She will do anything to delay my exit. She can go to any lengths to make it impossible for me to leave. Maybe she will let Zubair go. I see it coming.

Giving me a condescending hug, she whispers into my ear, 'Let me grant you your wish and relieve your torment. You can leave, but Zubair will stay here with me. You are aware by now that he likes me more than you know who.'

What nonsense! You're hallucinating.

'You want proof? Look at him carefully. Look how hard he's trying to cling to this moment of contentment. But he's not sure if it's real and if it will stay. He isn't used to it. He fears it will reject him or abandon him. He wants to express how happy he is here but he can't. He wants to express his appreciation and gratitude to me but he can't. He wants to say he's experiencing joy for the first time or maybe after a long time but he doesn't even know how to do that. He fears you, don't you know?'

I love him to death. And so does he. I will never leave him alone. Even for a moment. Not here, not with you, not with anyone else. No one can love him as much as I do.

'Well, haven't we both seen your unconditional love for him…'

What do you mean? He is sick and I have to care for him.

'It isn't Zubair who's sick. You are the one who needs help. You are making it impossible for me to keep the truth from you. You should not do what you're going to do. Let the boy be with me.'

Don't drag my brother into this...

'I'm not dragging him. It was always you.'

Me? Meaning what?

'It wasn't Zubair who built the menagerie. It was you who built it and lured him into it. The insects you tortured and killed were your trophies, not his. He simply played along because the poor boy had no choice. He loved you then. He still loves you. He loves no one else. Not even his father. And look at what you did to him. Must you make me say it?'

If you say one more word about my brother...

'I am trying to make it easy for you. If you wish you can shut your ears. But you won't.'

Here, look, I am shutting my ears. You can babble as much as you can...

'It was you who made your little brother do terrible things that almost took his life. It was you who started the fire. It wasn't him who saw things differently. It was you who mistook ducks for fish, fish for birds, night for day, day for night, water for land, and land for water.'

Oh, now it's about me? Don't bother about me.

'I thought you weren't listening...'

I am not, but you can go on with your fantasies.

'Your dad worried about you more than he worried about Zubair, for he knew that you were the one who posed a danger to Zubair and to him. It is your incurable sickness that is... Let me ease your agony. You can get rid of the poor boy by letting him be here. This is the safest place for him. You can go back to wherever you want. Very far from here! That's why your dad sent you away in the first place.'

You seem to know everything about him.

'You know very well that I do. You want me to tell you, don't you?'

Go on with your delusions.

'Before your dad went to fight his last battle, he wanted Zubair to be brought here. He even had him kept in captivity to protect him. You know everything, don't you? But you're afraid to admit it. Zubair didn't even protest or complain about his confinement. But now he's turned silent.'

You know nothing about Zubair and…

'You knew your dad's enemies might trick Zubair into committing the gravest sin. One has got to be more wary of friends. To keep winning, it is important to lose at least once. The people who went after your dad are the same who pretended to protect him. Your dad was one of them, but they didn't spare him. They must have seen something. Maybe they are wrong and know they are wrong but they wanted to take revenge by doing a silly thing. Your dad had to pay the price for being an insider. And the price for such things is no less than one's own life…'

Flatnose seems to be reading a script.

You are confusing my dad with someone else… He is not where you think he is…

'He should have quit and left this place. He should have gone to London with you. You should not have left him alone. You should have taken him along. But you didn't. This is what he wanted. Everything has happened according to his plan.'

My dad would never give up on his principles…

'Of course, he didn't give up on his principles. He knew survival was almost next to impossible. The very people he fought were his own people but he still fought them because he knew they were wrong. It was a battle unto death. Every one of his men deserted him. They took sides—some wrong, some right. Even when he was alone, he stood by his people. When he killed them, he cried. He hugged them and sought their forgiveness when they lay dying. He begged the forgiveness of the fathers and mothers whose sons lay lifeless before him. After all, these people knew that their survival would come at a price. They also knew the price they would have to pay for the terrible and unforgivable mistakes of their rebellious and wayward sons. And that price was nothing but a life of endless misery and pain. But, by that time, they had lost the ability to differentiate between happiness and sadness. Some clung to illusions and pretended to be brave. They expressed their happiness at terrible things and grieved when good things took place. They felt pleased with other people's misfortunes. But your dad mourned and cried for his people because nobody felt their pain as much as he did. He fell and then rose again like a warrior and allowed the unthinkable to happen.'

Wrong... Wrong...

'Don't jump to conclusions.'

You said he...

'No, he didn't take his life. He didn't surrender at the face of danger. He stood undefeated. He went into the bloody pit of darkness and, with bare hands, did what no human, no matter how powerful, could ever do. He protected the very people who wished him death...'

What makes you think so?

'You should know. You made him do the unthinkable. You are to blame. You brought out the worst in him.'

You're full of venom.

'Your father made the decision and stuck to it. You can't bring him back. No one can. He was on the wrong side of the battle. And now you are going after Zubair. You want to get rid of him. I won't let you do that...'

Shut up! I don't want to know. You are a liar. You want me to suffer like you. But I won't let you succeed. I won't let you get away...

'Don't say anything if you don't know what to say. Don't even mourn. It is okay if you don't know how to mourn. You don't need to say anything. You will still exist. No harm will come to you. But one day you will know what it is to mourn. That day you will mourn for those who have died for you.'

Why are you doing this to me?

'You should know by now. I'm offering you a trade-off. Want to switch sides and swap your life with mine?'

No, no, leave me alone... I will find out everything myself...

'I will find out everything myself... I want to know this... I want to know that... I want to know everything... What are you? A crybaby? Grow up... Nobody is going to pamper you here...'

If you claim to know so much about my dad then tell me if you have seen him with your own eyes and I will do whatever you say.

'You saw him, too. Shortly after you came here. Didn't you? He was wearing the coat you gave him?'

I don't believe you...

'Who do you think made it happen?'

Oh come on! Stop joking now...

'Ask your brother if I'm joking,' she says, turning her gaze to Zubair. Zubair nods in agreement just like he often does when he is dreaming. A wicked smile plays on his face.

'You trust me now?' says Flatnose with a sneer on her face. 'You see I never lie. I would never lie to you despite all your provocations. You think I am your enemy? I am not. I need you more than you need me. Don't you understand? What will it take to make you understand?'

5

Flatnose stops rambling. She begins polishing her boots as if she's about to step out. After she's done polishing the boots, she puts them on and starts walking in a strange manner. She rubs her palms and a flower appears in her hand. She runs her left hand through her hair and another flower emerges. A woody scent fills the room. The repulsive stench that permeated the room is gone. Everything turns fragrant in an instant. Flatnose places the flowers in her hair and ties a knot using a string. She is now a danseuse about to step on to the stage for the performance of a lifetime. But there's no audience except Zubair and I. She mistakes us for the invisibles that she thinks have come just to laud her. If she thinks this whole act is going to be streamed live to the outside world, she's wrong. She will be disappointed with the reality. She can do whatever she likes. I am not going to stop her now. She adjusts her scarf and hums a song. A mysterious smile is etched on her lips. She poses in front of me and waits as though I am still at her beck and call. She wants me to please her and cheer her so that she can take the next step. The look in her eyes indicates disappointment at my unwillingness to reciprocate her advances or applaud her bravado. She waits and waits. If she's still hopeful that I will dance to her tunes, then she will soon realize her folly and stop this theatrical act. She's mistaken. She can't test my patience any longer and I am not going to test hers anymore. She can do whatever she wishes and I am not going to give a damn. We close in on each other. Our eyes meet and everything becomes clear to both of us. She gives me *that* look: 'I have been in your place before and I know what will happen to you.'

And then, without waiting any further, she looks away making it clear that she's not going to look at me ever again. The urge to end everything is the strongest now. There will be no turning back. This is it.

I give up, Flatnose. I lose. You win.

She looks most gorgeous and most radiant like a firefly about to perform her last dance and vanish into her own glow. She has now tamed her only fear. She's going to attain the unattainable. She shows me something that I am not supposed to see. What no human is supposed to see because to see it is to reject oneself and do the unimaginable. I can't even tell you what I see. You won't be able to bear the sight of it. You should be spared the horror. This is going to be her chrysalis. I could be engulfed in whatever is left behind. It could consume me. But I am not going to let that happen. Wild laughter erupts.

She starts singing:

> Yesterday they loved you for you sang their songs;
> today they hate you for you're singing someone else's songs;
> tomorrow they will come after you for you shall know how
> to sing your own song...

In an instant, and as if by some unseen force, a flame appears on her fingertip. She moves it gracefully up and down, right and left three times, and then bringing it closer, she holds it underneath the scarf she's wearing around her neck. And then begins the ritual she's been waiting to conduct for the whole night. Her tango with flames! A circle of fire forms around her. Guarding her from any external intervention, it doesn't allow me to go close to her. Nothing can extinguish the fire now. Nothing can douse the flames. I can't even touch her in this final moment when life isn't life and death isn't death. I see her fading, dissolving slowly. The blaze is brightest at the moment. At this point, I give up. I want her to go on until the very end because I want to watch her go. She moves in circles with her arms around the flames until she's one with them. She keeps her promise. I will now have to keep mine.

But before the flames swallow her completely, she does the unthinkable by making one last attempt to drag me into the flaming sphere of dissolution. Wrapped in flames, she leaps at me like a lioness leaps at an unsuspecting prey. This has been her plan all along—to not go alone, to take me along with her, and for the fire to consume me as well. But she doesn't know me. She has no idea of my ability to thwart such devious stratagems. I've kept my defenses ready. I push her back into the flames—her own creation. Her time is up. The next moment, she's gone completely as if she never existed. Nothing of her remains!

You got what you wanted, Flatnose! You had your moment of glory and I gave you that moment. But tell me. Are you happy now?

6

I am not worried or sad because dad lied to me. He had even sworn upon my life that he's not a coward. I am distraught that he pretended to treat me as an equal. What do I do now? How am I to make sense of his sayings? 'Don't let history stop you from doing what you have got to do. If history comes in the way, you must get rid of it too. You must go on…'

It is time to make a move now that night has passed.

It doesn't irk me that Flatnose didn't make such a big deal of her generosity. It's a pity that she didn't know her flaws. This is what she wanted. This is how she scripted her end. She believed, mistakenly, that I owed my life to her and that I would give up my freedom to free her. She believed I would remember her and her act for the rest of my life.

When I think of Flatnose, I think of a life gone to waste. She could have come out of her delusions and made a difference to the lives of so many others who have nowhere to go and nobody to turn to. She could have won hearts. Despite her constant bickering, her charm was beguiling, her looks tantalizing, her intuition precise, and her beauty matchless. Her tenacious intimacy towards me nearly drove me mad and nearly made me do what she wanted me to do.

She could have come with me. I had thought of asking her, but I knew what she would have said. She would have laughed at me. Her fits of laughter were maddening. She was hysterical all the time. Her jibes were aimed at me. She had no one but me to ridicule. Who else did she have but me? Yet, she couldn't tell the difference between living and not living.

Whitey, who's been so brave until now, is very afraid. She's kept guard so that everything goes uninterrupted and unseen. Her eyes are watery as she stares at the trail of ash left behind by Flatnose. She clings to me. She doesn't want to let go of me. She knows the time of parting has come. She looks me in the eye. I can't make out what she is trying to communicate to me. But it doesn't matter. She makes me see herself in me and myself in her. Our joys and sorrows are one.

At last, the smell of dawn! The chirping of birds and the rustle of trees! Obscured by the twilight, the moon is gone, finally. The calf has fallen asleep next to her mother in the shed. The cow hasn't let her calf out of her sight. Zubair takes hold of my hand and prods me to get out of the house.

As we prepare to leave the house, Flatnose's voice rises out of the lump of ash: 'Where are you going? You can't go anywhere now. You belong here. Outside the gates of this house you will perish. You will end your life just like I ended mine.' She's still around because her voice is not gone. She's still calling to me. She keeps her word.

'No one who comes to this house can leave without my permission,' she had said. 'But you have my permission to do anything. I have nothing to call mine. I have nowhere to go and no one to call my own. I am free. I see only freedom and that's beautiful...'

Will you believe me if I tell you what I think of her? I won't lie to you. I still know nothing of her—who she was, where she had come from, why she did to herself what I would never be able to do. She was gifted but she had lost interest in her talents. She had no use of them. She wouldn't know how to put them to use. I know you will not believe me. You will never see and experience what I saw and experienced. No one will believe me. But it's okay. A time will come when you will know and believe everything. Because this will be the only thing worth believing when everything else will seem like a dream. A girl with unfulfilled desires and burning ambition is dangerous to herself.

'Do you not see what your presence has done to me?' she had said. 'I was about to let go of the strings but then... You gave me reason to put off my departure. You took my courage away and left me with fear. I will never forgive you for causing that. But I am to blame. Pretence, you see, isn't my thing. I am grateful to you. Don't ask me why. Who would have thought I would say this to anyone ever? Every day I used to wonder what tomorrow would bring. People wait for many things imagining that these things will come to them. I haven't told you about myself but that isn't important. Your guesses haven't been as good as mine, although you think you're good at guessing. You will not fail if you keep guessing. I know what you think. You must be wondering why I did this to myself. Everything must seem inconceivable to you. I am decidedly much better at deception than you are. I am not a lost cause. I don't cause trouble by inciting people and luring them into hell. I am not against myself. But don't let my pretty face and beauty beguile you or mislead you. I am not any of these girls...'

Now that she's gone I'm beginning to doubt if she was the one who said all these things. Maybe she didn't say these things after all. Maybe she made me imagine that I was hearing an inexistent voice of an inexistent person trapped in the mirrors or lurking in the dark.

I call her name one last time. Maybe the prankster will come out of hiding. *Flatnose, Flatnose...*

She had said she would respond if I called her name. But she is gone for sure. Even in her dying moments, she remained an exhibitionist. Let her be. She's at peace at last. She's silent, once and for all.

Goodbye, Flatnose!

She shows up one more time, possibly her last appearance. It looks like she still has some unfinished business to carry out. Shadowing her, the damn night is back as well. It too is yet to empty its coffers. In her curtain call moment, Flatnose is black as the night. The next moment, she is a flaming ember. It's blinding to even look at her.

Beauty, unfortunately, isn't a fortress. Sometimes, it is the victim.

A flower lands in front of me and transfers its scent to me. I place it on the lump of ash and shut the door behind me. Zubair refuses to let go of the glass beads he's clutching in his hands.

As we step out of the house and start walking through the avenue towards the main gates, the unexpected happens. The whole house goes up in flames. There's no point in looking back at the burning house and waiting to see what will happen to it. There's no point in waiting to see what will remain of it when the flames have nothing left to feed on.

The sky lights up. I have left night behind me and everything that happened through it.

7

Will dad or Uncle Dar show up now that the night is over and time has resumed its stride?

I should have placed a bet that night would end and dawn would return. I must follow the light now.

At the far end of the avenue leading to the road, the two saluting guards are still standing at attention in the same place they were when we came here. Even now, they don't turn their heads when they see us walk towards them. As we close the distance between them and us, truth comes to light. I look at them closely. They are frozen and expressionless like mannequins in a shop. A tiny bulbul is perched atop one of the guard's peaked cap. The guard's left arm is broken from the elbow down. The forearm is lying in bits and pieces on the ground. The other guard is intact. I should have known. They aren't human guards. They are statues.

When we reach the city, we find ourselves next to the hospital where Zubair was born and where, upon his birth, he was placed into his mother's lap and she didn't know what to do. He had slipped off her unsteady hands and fallen on the floor. It was the scariest moment. The sight of his tender head smashing against the tiles on the floor had caused my heart to stop. Mom had blamed herself. It was the beginning of her madness. But Zubair's miraculous survival was ordained.

The birds are leaving their nests. They are chirping about the dreams they dreamt in the dark night. One day, these birds will fly North and everyone will think that the North is where they must go.

A girl with golden hair is holding the hand of a boy who's crying inconsolably by the roadside. The boy is holding a dog in his lap.

'Don't you see he's dead?' whispers the girl into the boy's ear repeatedly. She's trying her best to console him. 'We have got to bury him unless you want to die of disease.' The stench is unbearable and the carcass is stiff. The girl doesn't give up. She tries to free the carcass from the boy's firm grip. But he refuses to part with it. His grip on the carcass is steely. Running out of patience, the girl slaps the little boy. The boy's eyes are blank. He is indifferent to the girl's admonitions. The girl doesn't know what to do. She tries to make the boy laugh but he starts crying. Then she starts calling him names and swearing at him and the boy stops crying and starts giggling. It's a strange condition that seems to have stemmed from the union of fear and loss. It can do terrible things to children.

The boy turns his gaze towards me. His eyes are misty and grey. I peer into them. The girl indicates that the boy can't see.

'What are you doing to yourself?' whispers Zubair to me. 'Why are you doing this?' He wraps his right arm around my waist. I feel the warmth of his dependence on me for the first time. 'I won't let you down, Zooni,' he says.

After yet another failed attempt at letting him go, I throw my arms around him.

'Are we going to meet Papa?' Zubair asks. I nod because he will listen and forget instantly. 'Look Zooni, flowers,' he says, turning his gaze to a row of flowers.

Those are winter tulips. They defy everything to bloom even when not a blade of grass can survive. Even nature can't stop them from blooming in winter.

'Look Zooni, snow,' says Zubair. 'Shall we go to our secret place?'

Zubair's offer is tempting. It's been a long time since we went there. I nod at him and pretend to marvel at the snow he is seeing.

Yes, it's snowing, I say to him looking at the inexistent snow on his face. He shows me the most gorgeous caterpillars I have never seen.

The lake is in front of us. The same lake by which we had once stopped, hoping to swim over to the other side. Zubair stops. He hasn't forgotten my promise: *Do you want to give it another try now? It will be fun and you won't feel a thing.*

A boatwoman is singing about her exploits: 'Do not tell anyone. No one should know. Someday, my silence will force you to return…'

It is evening, and dew's trail is splattered all over the boulevard.

We go to see Rani one last time at the house. She's sitting next to her unfinished nest with a twig in her beak. She's building the nest at the wrong place. She knows this isn't the right place to build her nest, yet she persists. She knows the nest is inside a cage and that her chicks won't be able to fly out of it. She won't be able to teach them how to fly. But she doesn't give up. She continues building the nest hoping that someone will dismantle the cage someday and her nest will be free. The place is cramped. And her chicks are already creating a din. Rani's piercing and ever-watchful gaze is fearful as if she has a foreboding of what is to come. She's eyeing me as though it's my turn next.

Zubair points his finger at a ferocious-looking bird sitting atop a tree. It is the same bird whose life I had spared during a hunting trip with dad. Dad's prediction—she will let you in on a secret—is about to come true. The bird is watching Rani's nest with her black eyes and keeping a close guard. Every now and then she sharpens her menacing beak against the frosted bark of the tree. Not only has she decided to spare her prey but she is also keeping vigil over Rani's nest. That's what is so strange. The bird is going against her nature.

Rani flutters her wings, takes flight, circles the house, returns quickly, bringing along two mynahs, and then settles back into her unfinished nest. The two mynahs start whistling. Zubair's eyes light up at the sight of the mynahs. He reciprocates by blowing them kisses: 'One for sorrow, three for joy, one for sorrow, three for joy, one for sorrow, three for joy…' He doesn't stop. I don't correct him. In my heart, I repeat after him: *One for sorrow, two for joy, three for a girl, four for a boy.*

Rani takes off again. She soars higher this time and flies higher and higher until she is out of sight. Just a faint trace of her flight remains. Ismail's prediction—a day will come when Rani will surprise us all—has come true.

8

A newspaper lands in the courtyard. The headlines read:

Commandant Salim Dar of J&K Special Forces
killed by militants

> Within hours, his teenage daughter walks to her death by entering her burning house. Government announces an ex-gratia relief of 50,000 rupees to Commandant Dar's next of kin.

A photograph of Uncle Dar and a beautiful girl accompanies the report. I take a closer look at the girl's face. Is she who I think she is?

The rest of the news report reads:

> Dar was kidnapped from his house on Friday night. Hours later, his disfigured body along with the killers' note was found in an orchard nearby. Claiming responsibility for the kidnapping and killing of Dar, an unnamed militant outfit said that enough time had been given to Dar to comply with the 'final warning'—to resign from the Police Service by December 19. Dar had reportedly rejected the militants' warnings and had issued a counter warning to them to surrender or else face his wrath. A day earlier, Dar had successfully eliminated eight militants in an operation in a village in North Kashmir. This is the 127th incident involving the kidnapping and killing of a Special Forces Police Officer in Kashmir this year. Police and other investigating agencies have launched a cordon-and-search operation all across the valley to hunt down Dar's killers…

I can't take my eyes off the photograph. In the photograph, Uncle Dar's daughter, whom I'd spent the night with and whom I called Flatnose, is smiling and happy. I never got to know her real name.

A message from Sridhar flashes on the phone, 'It is the winter equinox. I am going to the lake with you by my side. The day is not going to end. Time will rest at last.'

No message from Sara.

Dad's diary that I have retrieved from the house is in my hand. My bags are packed. Tomorrow begins the search for the man who has vowed to sacrifice everything for the well-being of his people and for his beloved land.

Book III

The Journal of Abdul Aziz

Faceless, he could represent only two alternatives: that he was either a conscious agent of harm, or that he would unknowingly harm me anyway.

—Agha Shahid Ali,
The Veiled Suite

Dear Zooni,

Remember that pale autumn night when it was our turn for the power cut. The wind slept mute on the naked boughs of the poplars in our garden. The Great Bear stood framed in the windowpane. And then just as a bright star made an appearance, you prepared to go to bed. The neighbours' children were already in bed because they couldn't watch television. Your grandpa had listened to the news at seven-thirty and then gone to bed early. The newsreader had babbled the usual stuff:

> The Chief Minister went to Lal Chowk and made a speech condemning the massacre at Kavdor. He said, 'Such incidents should not incite us.' Earlier that morning the Chief Minister attended the funeral and announced a cash relief to the next of kin of those massacred. 'I am going to recommend to the Centre to disband the Special Forces,' said the Chief Minister, 'because they have lost the sense of right and wrong.' People are storing firewood for the impending winter, burning dry leaves and twigs to produce charcoal. Leaves of the chinars are auburn. Snow is expected early this year.

The bored newsreader had yawned as if the occurrence of such things was of no interest to anyone anymore. Nothing important had happened that day except the usual bloodbath at a bridge. Everything appeared fine when you gazed out of a window and looked at the houses and the moonless sky. Silence prevailed! Everyone stayed indoors. Crows sat on electric wires and sharpened their beaks against the surface of the wires. The power cut would last the entire night.

At ten-thirty, footsteps intruded upon the silence. I heard whispers. We were in the living room on the first floor. I peeped through a chink in the curtains as though I were a thief in my own house. Two young men paced the narrow lane outside. One of them was holding a pistol in his hand. I squinted at it. It fit perfectly in the youth's firm clasp. The two kept whispering into each other's ears. Your mother swallowed her fright when she peeped at the two men brandishing a pistol. Your grandpa was sleeping his old snoring sleep in his room. One man lit a cigarette.

'What does he want?' your mother asked.

'Nothing,' I said to her. 'They must be mistaken. This is the wrong house. They must have come for those there.' She believed me.

'But what have they done?' she asked.

'Nothing! But they are the ones to be…'

'Shall we scream?

'No, no! Be quiet! Not a word. They will leave soon.'

'What if they don't? What if they have come for you?'

For the first time, I had no answer. My gaze didn't lose the intruders. Fear lost me. I pretended to be brave. A knock at the gate! Then, a pause! Another knock! A third one! The other man whispered into the ear of the young man with the pistol.

The knocking persisted. Never had the knocking been more spiteful. 'What shall we do now?' your mother asked.

'Nothing, be still, quiet.'

Till twelve-thirty, we sat still and continued to hear whispers. The moon came out lighting up the lane. Your mom's breathing was slow. You looked at me and saw anguish on my face. I can never forget that look in your eyes. You thought you would never see me again.

Then I heard another whisper at the gate: 'Are you sure this is the house?'

'Yes, this is the Commandant's house.'

The Legend of Salim Dar

I started writing out of compulsion. I had no choice. There were days when I couldn't write because I had seen things that can't be written about. Those things should never have happened to me. Such things should never happen to anyone anywhere in the world. But they did happen and I blame myself for their occurrence.

I will now start from the beginning when I had thought everything would be over in a matter of minutes and I would never get to hold you in my arms again.

It all started on a winter day, a little more than two decades ago. My men and I were at a hideout and were about to blow up a building. We had laid the wires and everything. We were just waiting for the right moment. Salim Dar had been tasked with the job. He pressed the button and the entire building went up in one giant ball of flames. We were to flee the place immediately and go underground. But we couldn't. The entire thing was an ambush, a trap, not for me but for Salim Dar on whose head was a bounty of a hundred thousand rupees—a fortune those days. Shortly after, men in camouflage uniforms barged in and shot down everyone except the two of us. They held Salim and me at gunpoint. By then it was too late to do anything. Salim became suspicious the moment he was captured alive and whisked off to an unknown location.

Sparing lives of the likes of us was unheard of in those days.

After all, we had blown up a building, and Dar's name was on top of the hit list of Special Forces. The forces could simply have pumped two bullets into our heads. That's what they did in such cases. That's what is still done. It is simple. Shoot to kill. But killing Salim Dar, the legendary commander, wasn't a good idea.

What happened that day was no unusual exception. We were granted a reprieve that day. Our lives were spared for a reason. And we owed our lives to the men who didn't pull the trigger. We weren't supposed to come out of it alive. We were supposed to die that day.

But there is another truth. I knew something that Salim didn't.

The truth is that Salim saved me that day and on several occasions, he put his own life in danger to protect me. Even today, he will give up his life for me because he mistakenly believes that I saved his life once.

'We must save ourselves because no one will save us' was his call, not mine.

A Dream of Freedom

I first met Salim Dar in the summer of 1990. He would come home for tuitions. His father owned a hardware store near our house. 'If you ever find yourself in trouble, just take my name,' Dar said to me one day. Besides being a storekeeper, he was also your grandpa's student. He was grateful to him for the tuitions. But studies held no interest for Dar. 'Studying is useless,' he would joke. 'Real education lies in taking up the cause for our people. And dying for the cause.'

Dar claimed to have been appointed the Area Commander of the Kashmir Liberation Front (KLF). 'This part of Kashmir,' he said, 'is under my command.'

Those days, Hizbul Mujahideen (HM) lured the youth more than KLF—it had risen to be the most feared of the insurgent outfits, given its links with the Jamaat-e-Islami that professed Kashmir's merger with Pakistan. Dar, however, dreamt of azadi. 'My heart bleeds for Pakistan, but I shall live and die in azad Kashmir,' he would say.

One afternoon when I stopped by at his shop, he spoke of his ambition, 'I am going to be made the Regional Commander of KLF soon,' he said, elatedly. 'And, god willing, if I do well and succeed in all the missions assigned to me, I will become the Divisional Commander someday.' Heroism, idealism, utter contempt for school and college education, loyalty for his teacher and fondness for his teacher's son characterized Dar.

He laid out an ambitious vision for Kashmir, 'It is going to be a long struggle for the liberation of our beloved land. It could take years or decades, maybe...'

'What if it doesn't happen?' I had asked, knowing very well that most people were made to believe freedom was around the corner. Belief gave people hope. The broadcasts from Pakistan were encouraging. 'We will sip *kahva* in Shalimar Gardens in azad Kashmir next spring,' blared the voices on radio and TV. Euphoria prevailed in households.

'Azadi is a matter of days, you will see,' some people said. But Dar suspected otherwise. 'We have a long way to go,' he kept saying. 'We have taken up arms but we aren't afraid to die...'

That day when I asked him what if azadi didn't happen in our lifetimes, he spoke of a second wave. 'The great AM Khan has spelled it out in his vision,' said Dar, emphatically. AM Khan was the Founder and Commander-in-Chief of KLF. 'The second wave, which will succeed us in the years to come, will be more determined and primed for action than us because it will fight a battle on the soil smeared with the blood of their elders. But there won't be any second wave if we don't lead from the front... and if we don't go down fighting... we have to sacrifice ourselves for the second wave to take birth...'

Dar was very mercurial and the way he operated was unusual. He had scant regard for his own life. He would do things no other commander would do. But he wasn't irrational and impressionable like most youngsters I knew; he was very methodical in his approach. His belief in the cause and his determination towards the armed struggle inspired a generation. People swore by his name. He was a legend for everyone—those who hadn't met him and those who had.

I didn't see him for the next few years. He simply vanished and I thought I would never see him again. I was almost certain that he had been captured and killed either by a rival group or by security forces. In the days to come, I forgot about him as if he never existed. But whenever I walked past his shop, which had remained shut ever since his disappearance, I thought of him for a moment and remembered his face.

Three and a half years later, in spring, I heard his name again. At first, I thought it was someone else. There were several Salim Dars who were notorious and famous for acts of bravery and valour. I didn't expect the Salim Dar I knew to come out of his grave. I didn't imagine he had gone into some sort of hiding only to emerge years later. The news about him came to me through Special Forces' agents on the ground. Salim Dar has been given the command of Gurez valley, I was told.

Dar's mission was to set up a base for KLF in Gurez, and then to establish a zone somewhere there that would act as a launch pad to carry out KLF's activities all over North Kashmir. But to be able to do that Dar had to recruit people. That was when the Special Forces were set up and I was the Commandant incharge of North Kashmir. My job was to establish surveillance, gather intelligence across all districts in the region and to monitor infiltration from across the border. Dar was the Regional Commander of KLF. He had achieved his goal, though his ultimate dream—to become the Divisional Commander and to witness the liberation of Kashmir under his command—was yet to come true.

I wanted to know if the Salim Dar about whom I was informed was the same Salim Dar I knew. Nobody had a clue to my induction into the Special Forces though I knew about Dar's secret ambition of launching his own liberation outfit in case it came to that. I went undercover to Gurez to keep a tab on the goings on there and to find out more about Dar and his plans.

After his arrival in the Gurez valley, Dar went from house to house to understand the issues of the people who lived there. He tried to find out about the kind of lives people led, what kind of concerns they had, what they thought of India and Pakistan, what they thought of the border security posts fortifying the villages, and if they would be willing to allow him to address their concerns.

But soon after Dar started his work there, people mistook him for a government official. They thought Dar had been sent by the government to help them. The village headman treated Dar as though he was the most important person of the government machinery in the whole of Kashmir. He gave him his own outhouse to stay in. The house was next to a beautiful stream that descended from a mountain and merged into the river at the foothills of a meadow. The headman's son was a cricket fanatic. His wanted to organize a cricket tournament in the village. When he told Dar about it, Dar offered his services instantly. In exchange for the favour, he would help Dar in all matters pertaining to his *mission* in the meadow.

One evening, when I showed up at the house where Dar was staying, he was surprised to see me. He asked me if I still owed my allegiance to the resistance and liberation movement. I said I did believe in it still but wasn't really doing anything of importance on the ground. As expected, he wished to know everything about me. He wanted to know how my father was doing, what I had been up to in the years gone by, and what had made me come to Gurez.

I have come here to evade capture is what I said.

In the city, everyone our age was under watch by some agency or the other. Even a word uttered in private could land you in trouble. Disillusioned youngsters were manipulated into joining secret groups and offered bogus jobs in bogus agencies. People like me were constantly rounded up and made to vanish.

'You know how it is in the city,' I said to Dar, preempting further questioning on the matter of my sudden appearance in Gurez. 'Nobody trusts anybody. Friends have become foes and foes have become friends.' He nodded.

'But weren't you planning to go to London to study, and from there keep our struggle and resistance alive through activism?' Dar asked, displaying his infallible memory. I was expecting this question because we had spoken about it in the past. I had no answer. I remained quiet although I figured he had guessed the real reason. Dar's initial impression about me, right from the early days of our association, had been somewhat misplaced. To him, I had always been a boy without a cause. Someone who vacillated between extremes—emotion and reason, for instance, always unsure of himself and everything else, and looking for easy routes! But Dar wasn't to be blamed. The impression he had of me wasn't completely untrue. It was my doing. I wanted to give him that impression. Everything was for a reason.

'I know how difficult it is to get out of here,' he said in a sympathetic tone, sensing my hesitation to admit my own failures. 'And going to London is no mean feat. After all, you had a dream too... and the dream must be kept alive through other means... it mustn't be made to die... maybe we can realize it together... let's see if we can make it happen for you...'

He said he remembered his teacher fondly and missed him.

I got the impression that Dar was happy to be reunited with

his long-lost friend-without-a-direction. 'Together we will do wonders,' he said, excitedly. 'We can bank on each other.'

Dar made the decision without even consulting me. Such was his blind faith in me. The fact that even after so many years he was still my well-wisher was both reassuring and problematic. Those were times when to trust one's own family members was fraught with peril, and ours was a case of two estranged friends meeting after years without the faintest idea of each other's last whereabouts, affiliations and actions.

Dar even said that going to London should not be impossible if I made the right moves. 'I stand for arms and you stand for ideas,' he said, demolishing the distinction between the two types of struggle—'armed' and 'ideological'. 'Both are inseparable and they lead to the same destiny. Our cause is one.'

Clearly, he had gotten his causes mixed up.

A Life for a Life

Dar returns at dawn. He can't conceal his impatience and exhilaration. I ask him what the matter is. At first, he refuses to speak. Later in the evening, we go out into the meadow and he reveals the details of a mission assigned to him.

'The order has come,' he says, with a sense of anticipation as if he has been waiting for it his entire life.

I wait for him to fill me in. 'In a few days' time, I am to help some mujahids sneak into the valley. But the Border Security Force is going to intercept us. There will be a tradeoff. Some mujahids will be let through along with arms and ammunition. Money will change hands. Big money! In exchange for the mujahids, I am to hand over at least twenty boys from the village to the Border Security Force. I am to testify that these boys are the infiltrators. Photos of the boys with an arms haul in front of them will be taken. And then you know what is going to happen. Some of them will be captured and some will be...'

It's as expected. Such tradeoffs aren't unusual. These are win-win tradeoffs.

I ask Dar if he is going to take this deal forward. He says he is committed and that he has no choice but to make it happen. 'It must be done. It will be done. I will see to it that the mission is accomplished no matter what. Sacrifices have to be made if we are to succeed.'

'But twenty boys? We may not even have twenty boys in the

village. Are you suggesting that we get hold of minors?'

'It doesn't matter. Age is immaterial. As long as the boys look old enough to carry rucksacks and traverse a mountain, we should be fine. The aim is to select the boys and take them across the mountain to the designated spot where the swap will take place. They mustn't get to know of anything or suspect our intentions.'

'But what if people get to know? After all, twenty is a big number. We aren't talking about five or six boys here. Twenty boys mean twenty families.'

'What are twenty boys for a worthy cause?' says Dar, emphatically. 'Nothing. Not even loose change. Let's go ahead and select the boys. We will handle any exigencies. That's what we are trained to do.'

Dar says he can't make it happen on his own and that he needs my help. 'I'm counting on you,' he whispers into my ear as we walk back to the house. 'The village headman's son, Aijaz, is already on-board. He's waiting for us in the house. He has already identified the boys and chalked out a plan. We must tie up any unforeseen loose ends now...'

'What about their parents? What are we going to tell them?'

'It's the easiest thing to do. I have an argument ready. The boys will disappear one night and not return. The blame will be put on someone else. This will serve our purpose. We will then work on the next steps. Everything will happen as per the plan.'

Each of us—Aijaz, Dar and I—is in sync. In a few days, we are to leave with twenty boys on the pretext that they will be given employment in the government. The headman has been briefed. My job is to assist Dar. But Dar mustn't know of the counter-plan I am hatching to thwart his mission. He mustn't get to know who I am and what my real purpose is. He mustn't get a whiff of anything I am about to do.

The night of departure arrives. At midnight we are to leave for the designated place. It's going to be a long trek. If we leave at midnight, we will be at the designated spot by dawn, provided we don't stop at all. Dar will lead us. The boys assemble in the courtyard of the headman's house. Some of them are wearing new clothes. Some of them are barely in their teens. Their parents have packed food and clothes for them.

'Don't worry,' assures Aijaz, 'they will send us off with hugs and kisses.' There are no tears or goodbyes, only parental blessings for success, good luck and see-you-soon parting messages. Barring a few minors who're sleepy and disinterested despite our reassurances and the rosy pictures we have painted, all others are excited at the prospect of being selected and landing jobs that will earn them money. It has taken some amount of crafty persuasion to explain the value and benefits of money to these boys. We will be back by tomorrow, we say to the parents and then, we set off on the journey.

The script is ready. Shortly before dawn we are to reach the designated spot. The Commandant of the security post is to intercept us. He will make it seem like a routine check. Dar is to instruct the boys to take rest in an empty tent. The two of us will go into the Commandant's tent where he will explain the execution of the deal. They will have made all the arrangements. Two of the Commandant's men will be ready to carry out the orders. Money will already have changed hands. Some newly trained muhajids will be waiting in an adjacent tent to cross over to Kashmir via the meadow. No one is to know who will die and who will escape and survive. Not even the Commandant or Dar. Luck will play a major role in life and death. Randomness will prevail. In such a situation what matters is numbers. The lives of ten of our boys will be spared in exchange for some 30 or 40 militants who will be allowed to sneak into the valley while others will be detained. Some of our boys will have to be disposed of. That's the arrangement. It's simple. Some mujahids will be let off; some detained to be paraded later as the captured ones; and the bodies of the rest will be used by the Border Security Forces as proof of success. By dawn everything will be over. Dar will be asked to leave with the fortunate ones. And we will head back to the village. The entire thing will be stage-managed to look like an encounter in which militants crossing over into the valley opened fire on the border security personnel and the BSF fired back in retaliation, resulting in the death of some of our boys. When we get back to the village, we will have accomplished the mission. It will then be a piece of cake to get the rest of the boys to join KLF. Having witnessed everything firsthand, especially the role played by the BSF, they would already be motivated enough to take up arms and avenge the deaths of their friends, siblings and neighbours. A perfect win-win for Dar and for the BSF. For Dar, it will be like killing not just two but three birds with one stone. But if you take into account Dar's own aspirations and ambition—to make it to the upper echelons of power in KLF—it is killing four birds with one stone.

The same day, after the operation, BSF will announce that it stopped a major infiltration bid into Kashmir by eliminating many militants and seizing their arms and ammunition. They will be rewarded handsomely in cash and kind by both parties—the government as well as the mujahideen groups.

But none of this happens. Shortly before we take the turn at Chicken's Neck, we hear gunshots. Dar is alerted. 'Something is wrong,' I say to him. 'We must turn back or else all of us will be killed and everything will go in vain.' I feign absolute shock at the happening.

Dar turns to me to gauge my reaction. He's already trying his best to cook up an alternative to go ahead. He's an ace at circumventing unforeseen problems and obstacles. Taking split-second decisions in life-and-death situations is his forte. 'Abandonment should neither be the first nor the last option,' he always says. 'We go or we die.'

'I can't abandon the mission, you know me very well,' he says to me.

'But the boys are scared. They don't know what to do. Look at them. They are all ducked down with their heads inside their laps. They are trembling. If they suspect our intentions, then we are finished. We must retreat now. We're running out of time. Any more delay and we will be in trouble. We can't let our efforts go to waste. I have a plan. Trust me. We will turn the situation around to our advantage...'

He relents: 'All right, we will go back, but this mission is far from over...'

He instructs the boys to descend. At dawn we are back in the village. No one has slept. Everyone is still assembled in the courtyard of the headman's house. When we enter the courtyard, we see horror on people's faces.

Before they open their mouths, I explain everything to them. The boys corroborate my account. When I finish speaking, the people are jubilant. They get up and surround Dar. Women hug him and plant kisses on his forehead. Men lift him in their arms and carry him on their shoulders. They shower their blessings on him. Kids salute him. Everyone is in tears. Chanting erupts,

'You're our saviour, our hero. You saved each one of our boys. Long live Salim Dar…'

Dar falls silent and gives me an intimidating look.

'What have you done?' he whispers into my ear.

'Look, they are celebrating your homecoming.'

I reassure Dar that this is not the end of his mission and that I will help him again the next time, 'We are going to give it another try. I won't let you down…'

'I must not disappoint them otherwise they will spit at me,' says Dar, looking at the adulation and the welcome he has been given. 'I must give them a reason to believe in me. I won't be given another chance…'

'Of course, you will not disappoint them.' The trick works. Dar believes I am talking about his commanders.

At daybreak, people start making preparations for a feast as if it's a big festival. Twenty sheep are slaughtered.

Dar is now the de facto leader of the people of Gurez. He is a hero to the kids. He's the greatest government official Gurez valley has ever seen. 'May he become a minister,' people say, triumphantly. 'Why just a minister? He deserves to be the Chief Minister or the Prime Minister…' They give him their blessings and shower him with gifts. He's the talk of the town. On everyone's lips is only one name, and that is Salim Dar. Little do they know that there's no Salim Dar—the government official.

The next day, the unforeseen happens. The villagers come to Dar's hut and offer him their children. 'Make them do whatever you wish,' they say with gratitude gleaming on their faces. 'At least, they will be of use to you and we will get to repay the debt we owe you for saving their lives. They will have a good life under you. Make them your servants. We will be happy with the thought that our children work for the government. They are yours now. We give them to you. Do whatever you wish to do with them…'

Dar is stunned that his wish has come true in a matter of a few hours and without even batting an eyelid. Things fall into place finally.

I look him in the eye: 'You got what you wanted.'

He is lucky. The parents' offer is a boon. Dar knows he has hit a jackpot. A failed mission spells doom for any Hizbul commander. Without delivering on the mission, he could face dire consequences. His future could be at stake. He might be passed over by others. There are others who are willing to do anything to see a mission through even at the cost of their lives and the lives of their families. And with this offer now, Dar has a chance to redeem himself and prove his worth in the outfit. He knows the rewards for success and the penalty for punishment. Without giving it even a second thought, he seizes the opportunity and takes a chance.

The headman tells Dar the same thing his commanders keep telling him, 'The entire village is under your command and control now. You know what to do. Not even a fly should enter here. We have to keep the infidels and enemy out. You know what it means to be a leader. You control everything. You take the lead, we will follow you…'

Dar agrees to take two boys immediately and promises to take the rest of the boys in the days to come. His selection of the boys is random. The two boys he picks belong to two different families. A small boy insists on tagging along with his elder brother, Arif. He begins to cry when he's told he is not going.

'It is not god's wish that you leave us yet,' says the boy's mother to him. 'You're too small.'

'When will god wish?' he asks his mother.

'You have to listen to me. Do as I say. Then god will wish and you will get to join your brother in the big city.'

'I won't be a pest. Please let me go with him,' says the boy.

'Wait for some time! Grow up a little and we will send you too.'

'No, no, I want to go now.' The boy is beyond convincing.

'He's just like his brother,' others say, stunned at the closeness between the two brothers. 'Very caring and diligent! He never leaves his elder brother alone. They have always been a team. And both of them are always together and look after each other.'

'Uncle will take you soon, my child. He's promised us.'

'No, no, I won't stay here without Arif. I want to go with him...'

'You are a good boy. Don't be so adamant. Who will look after us? You will. Won't you? Who will help us chop wood and float logs in the river?'

'But I want to go,' says the boy repeatedly.

'You are too young for a government job.'

'I want to go with Arif. I want to go,' he insists, throwing a tantrum. His mom hugs him as his brother prepares to leave with Dar.

'Your passion is commendable,' says Dar to the boy, patting him. 'I will take you very soon.'

'Arif,' the boy cries. His brother gives him a comforting hug and then walks away with Dar.

The next morning, Dar sends the two teenagers off to a training camp for induction into his outfit. 'They will now work for the government,' he says to their parents.

'We won't ask you about them from now on,' they say, reassuring him and insisting that they have forgotten about them already. 'You are everything and everybody to them now.'

Of the two boys, only one is to survive. The other will never return.

A Dangerous Idea

Dar and I are to go to Srinagar for an important meeting, but incessant rain and consequent landslides have cut off Gurez from the main valley. The only road out of here is submerged and the only way out is to either wait for the road to clear or else undertake a treacherous trek through the mountain passes. It will take us three days to get out of here if we do undertake the trek. We evaluate our options. We decide not to trek because it is too dangerous. The border posts are nearby and you never know what might happen if you are spotted by a sniper. One mistake and it's all over. In our line of work, there's no room for even a single error.

Every morning, we go out into the meadow to inspect the condition of the roads. We now know what it means to be posted in a remote meadow where no people come and go. Days are like picnics. Nights are for dreams. We don't feel the absence of people. We eat and talk and smoke and sleep. We wait and wait…

The baker opens his shop before sunrise. We go to him as soon as he opens his shop and sit there until dawn watching him light up his oven and knead the dough with the care and affection of a man who has no worries in life. He is the most contented person we have ever come across. When he kneads the dough, time slows down. A cat slinks in out of nowhere and lies down next to us. The baker's skillful hands can revive a dying man. Such is the mystic power in his hands. When the bread comes out of the oven, he gives us two pieces to eat. The bread is so sweet that it makes us abandon our day's work. It makes us fall asleep and dream of ethereal things. The baker speaks of things that are unheard of. He speaks of love and nature and contentment.

At dawn, we see nomads roaming the hills. They are carefree. They have no place to call their own so they claim the whole world. The mountains are their home. The meadow is their courtyard. The sky is their roof. At noon, we sit by the Kishanganga and marvel at people making a living out of timber. The river goes into Pakistan. Nearby a carpenter is at work, making boats. He requests Dar to help him obtain some modern tools that he has heard have arrived in the city. 'I want to build a big boat,' he says, 'so that should the need arise, we can all board it and take it down the river.' We help people collect logs of wood and float them in the river. We hop on to two large solitary logs floating in the river and take a ride right up to the last bridge where India ends and Pakistan begins. We do this over and over again just for the heck of it. We leave in the mornings and come back in the evenings. We spend evenings at the shrine of Peer Baba of Multan and observe men and women offering prayers silently. They have no big demands, only a desire for two simple meals a day and boundless contentment.

When we get bored, we climb a mountain in front of us but dare not go to the summit. The mountain won't allow us a safe passage. We spend a night in an abandoned nomad shanty. We see visions. We dream of falling in love with beautiful women and marrying them. We dream of settling in the meadow. We dream of a life we have never imagined.

A month passes. Two months. We are happy. We want nothing. We desire nothing. We possess nothing. We are free.

Spring gives way to summer. The road opens and we spot a chance to leave the meadow and go to Srinagar. But we don't. It is too late.

Dar wants people to come to him with concerns about their lives. He thinks people will come to him with wish lists. He wants to hear their unspoken demands and pleas: 'We have no hospitals here… Can you establish a school here? Look at our children… They have become lazy and wayward… They will turn into vagrants if left idle… You promised them jobs… When will you make it happen?'

But nothing of that sort happens. Dar expects men to come to him with all sorts of problems. He thinks that they will confide in him about their women and that the women will come to him with their share of worries about their husbands. But people are happy about their lives. They have no desires, no wish lists, and no grievances. There are no squabbles. How is this possible? What makes people happy here? What gives them the strength to be content all the time? They are very happy to have Dar living amongst them. Should anything bad happen, Dar is there to help. But there are no problems to solve.

'Praise be the rulers for having sent Dar to this place,' people say. 'Long live Salim Dar.'

A Hero's Welcome

Dar is back in Srinagar. He is to set fire to a shrine on the outskirts of the city. But he has to do it on his own. The town wears a look of desolation. Shop hoardings have fallen. Houses wear a sombre look. The clock tower has collapsed.

Dar is ambushed. He's alone and there's little chance of his escape this time. But he escapes miraculously and takes shelter in the very shrine he's supposed to torch. The townspeople come to know that Dar is inside. They will do anything to protect him. They will even take a bullet for him. Dar is their liberator. His life is more precious than the lives of all others. People realize they must do what Dar cannot. They have to repay him for all the favours he has done them. The only way out is to set the shrine on fire so that Dar gets to escape uncaptured and unhurt. And people do what they would never do in any circumstances. They burn the shrine. They complete Dar's mission for him. The forces storm the shrine but Dar is nowhere to be seen. A rumour is started that Dar has perished in the fire. But Dar is inside where the flames can't reach him. The forces surround the shrine from all sides. Dar comes out wrapped in flames. He comes out of the blazing fire wearing protective armour. The forces start firing at him. Hundreds of people form a human chain. The forces stop firing. There is nothing they can do. Dar pulls off a daring escape. In a trice, he is gone.

The next day, Dar makes an appearance in Gurez. He receives

a hero's welcome. When the people see him burnt and bruised, they pray for his recovery. They stop eating until he starts showing signs of recovery. Each family makes an offering for his recuperation. People send packets of food floating in the river hoping that it will end up in the hands of some hungry souls.

'We won't let him go now,' they say. 'No harm should come to him. His life is precious. He's the saviour of our children. He's our only hope. He will stay with us forever. We will let him guide us. He's our leader. Long live Salim Dar! Long live his tribe!'

As days go by, Dar recovers steadily. One morning, the village headman brings him a marriage proposal. 'You should see her for yourself and decide,' he says. The meeting between Dar and the girl is arranged. Dar takes me along to the headman's house. She's the most beautiful girl I have ever seen. Dar says yes instantly.

'Are you sure?' I ask him. He looks me in the eye and I get my answer. The next day, Dar marries Rubaiya, the village headman's daughter. 'I have already thought of a name for my daughter,' he says. 'Her name will be Rabia.'

Dar changes in an instant. He's a different man now. I see desire and longing in his eyes. He asks me a question: 'What will you name your daughter?'

'What if I don't get married?' I say to him.

'You should and you will. And you must name your daughter Zoon. She will be like Habba and sing the most beautiful songs. Rabia and Zoon will become friends like us. They will rewrite our history someday. They will live in beauty and in freedom…'

Honest Betrayal

Two years have gone by. Rubaiya still does not know the truth about Dar. Dar loves her desperately. Rabia is yet to be born.

The day of reckoning has arrived. I decide to do the unthinkable because he's about to undertake a suicide mission. This is the third time. This time he's been entrusted with an operation to kill a top-ranking army officer who's going to visit Gurez for the first time. Dar can't blow his cover at this stage. He knows what's at stake. So far I have done nothing but played along. But I can't let Dar go on any further with his plans. He will die if he attempts to kill the army officer. Everything will have been in vain if he dies at the hands of the security forces.

Dar has his orders and I have mine. But I won't carry it out myself. I decide to have someone else do it. It's easier that way. I won't be around when it happens. Dar's killing will be a severe blow to KLF. But it won't take long for the news to reach Gurez. What will the people of Gurez make of it? What will Rubaiya think? That Dar was a traitor?

This is the moment I have been waiting for. It's now or never. Such instances won't come again. Dar must remain alive. He is useful. But for that to happen, I have to stage-manage the situation in such a way that he's left with no choice but to surrender.

Dar's commanders are told that Dar is planning to go rogue and is not to be trusted. An example must be set. And the example will be Dar's killing. The news of Dar's imminent killing must reach him. The explanation: 'You will be killed so that no other men from KLF will commit the same mistake.'

An order is issued and in two days, Dar will be killed.

When the time comes, two men will shoot at Dar. He won't know who they are. No one will know if they are HM or KLF or the police. That's when I come in and play the most important part. But before that happens, I reveal the plan to Dar and explain the pros and cons in such a way that he will do exactly as I say: 'You will die for sure. But if you wish, I can save you. Rubaiya should not lose you. Think of Rabia. She's yet to come into your life. You can't be reckless and put your life in danger. You have to live for Rubaiya and Rabia. You will have to surrender and then you will be taken into custody. After some days, you will join the Special Forces. It's a government job. You won't have to live with the burden of not being able to reveal the truth to Rubaiya any longer. The truth will continue to shield you. It will save you from ruin. You and Rubaiya will shift base to Srinagar. You will be under my command. But there's a condition. No questions asked. You will do exactly as you are ordered.'

He disregards my condition: 'What exactly do I have to do? Kill my own people?'

'If you don't kill them they will kill you or we will. You know very well how many KLF men have been hunted down by HM. And KLF hasn't been able to do a thing about it. In this game, death is certain, but I give you my word that I won't let anything happen to you. We have the power to do anything. It is up to you now. You have no options left. This is your only chance and you have no choice but to accept it. Think of Rubaiya. Think of Rabia.'

Dar doesn't believe me. He thinks I am joking. But he weighs his options. The scales are tipped against him.

We spend the night together. In the adjacent building is Dar's target. He is under the protection of his men and my men. Dar will never learn the entire truth. At midnight, the building housing the officer and his men is to be blown up. On my orders, Special Forces will barge into the house and capture Dar alive. From that moment onwards, Dar will do as I say.

Rubaiya's love will render him weak. But henceforth, it will also give him the strength to undertake the most daring missions for Special Forces. It will give him the power and courage to go after the very people he once idolized! But his pictures will be taken off the walls of people's houses. He will be declared an outcast. He will be branded a renegade. Those who glorified him will bay for his blood. And if he dies, he won't be given a hero's or a martyr's send-off. No one will cry for him. Even his own people will disown him. Simply put, he will not be remembered. He will neither be theirs, nor ours.

Moon Rises from the North

When you were born, I named you Zoon. You now know why. Dar was very happy that day. 'Someday she will save us,' he said, marveling at the glow in your tiny eyes. 'When she grows up, you should send her to London. What you couldn't do, she will. She will give wings to your dreams. And a day will come, she will return to Kashmir and bring peace to this place...'

That day Dar vowed to take the responsibility of looking after you and protecting you in my absence. He showered you with gifts of all kinds. Once again, he showed me what he could do. He showed me what I must do.

I didn't want Dar's wish to come true. He had wished for you to follow in my footsteps. He had pinned his hopes on you. Who else could he pin his hopes on? 'Someday, Zoon will rise like the moon, not from the south or the east or west, but from the north, and people will look at her and forget their grief,' he said.

When Rabia was born, Dar didn't tell anyone. It was too risky to let the word out. After all, he was on the hit list of every militant organization.

On the orders of their handlers and commanders across the border, HM boys were on a catch-and-kill spree. All former KLF cadres and men who had joined the Special Forces were on HM's hit list. More and more people died on the streets. Bloodshed became so common that people didn't even know how to grieve for the dead. Everyone stood divided on religious, sectarian, ideological and political lines. Suspicion, mistrust and betrayals created partitions within the society and human relationships lost their meaning. No one knew who worked for or against whom. No one knew what to believe and what not to believe. Daily life became more and more paradoxical and full of absurdities and contradictions. Even today, to live in Kashmir is to have your freedom snatched away from you and you remain trapped in an intricate web of insurgency, counter-insurgency, espionage and counter-espionage.

Rubaiya took Rabia with her to Gurez. She couldn't live in fear. She had never known fear in all her life. But, with Rabia's birth, she experienced fear for the first time. It was unnatural. Both Dar and I agreed that Rabia should grow up in Gurez and that she shouldn't know about her father. To stay away from his own daughter was the most difficult decision of his life. In his eyes, I saw sorrow and helplessness for the first time. He didn't want to reveal it to me. I heard his unspoken plea: 'If something happens to me, will you protect Rabia? She shouldn't be made to pay for my decisions and deeds. My doings are mine alone. If something has to happen, it should happen to me. Rabia deserves a beautiful life…'

Dar wasn't in any need of assurances. Giving up the cause and abandoning his duty weren't even the remotest options. The thought would never occur to him. It didn't bother him that people called him a deserter. 'They are insane,' he said. 'They have lost their senses. They are fools. They are suffering from the worst delusions. They don't know what fate awaits them. They will die for no reason, before everyone else and much before they are supposed to die and thus an entire generation will die for a lost cause. We will do what's best for Kashmir…'

Lion's Den

When I was pursuing Salim Dar, first to kill him, then to make him surrender, and then to recruit him, I had a sense of what would happen. But I had never imagined that he would ask me to kill him should the need arise.

'If at all I am to be killed, you should be the one to do the job,' he said to me. It was his only condition. 'We will not talk about it again until the very end. I will not remind you ever again. You will just have to keep your word. I have complete faith in you. I know you will never betray me.'

It wasn't for the sake of redemption or to salvage honour and regain the adulation of people. It was just between us. His desertion of militancy and induction into the Special Forces had come with this condition. It wasn't an impossible condition to fulfil.

The first attempt on his life took place when he was on his way to inaugurate a cricket tournament in Gurez. After years, the village headman's son's dream was going to come true and he owed it to no one but Salim Dar. Dar had given Aijaz his word that he would come for the tournament. Though the tournament had been Aijaz's idea, without Dar's help it wouldn't have ever happened. The real reason behind Dar's intention to go to Gurez wasn't the cricket tournament. The real reason was Rubaiya and Rabia. Dar wanted to see them from a distance. That day when he was on his way to Gurez, an unidentified man shot at him. But he survived because of the timely intervention of Special Forces. He felt invincible. He returned to base without seeing his wife and daughter.

The next day, Dar received his first warning letter: 'We didn't want to kill you without a warning. After all, you have been one of us. But you have betrayed your own brothers. You are a disgrace. Do you think we will ever forgive you for what you have done? The bullet was your first warning. We are giving you another chance. You know what you have to do. There won't be another warning. Don't make us do what we don't wish to do. Quit before it is too late. If you do as we say, no harm will come to you and your family.'

The letter was signed: A well-wisher.

Someone had snitched on him. They had gotten to know about his family. The next day, two of Dar's recruits—people whom he had inducted into our Force—declared insanity and resigned from the Special Forces. They had received warning letters, too. They asked him to follow suit. 'We are lucky,' they said to him, 'to have been warned and let off without an attempt on our lives. There might not be a next time. Think of your wife and daughter. No cause is worth it. No cause is greater than family and life.'

The two militants-turned-cops showed him their letters in which they confessed to having lost their minds. The letters were published in all the newspapers.

To Whom It May Concern

I, Rouf Jan, resign from the Special Forces of Jammu and Kashmir Police with immediate effect. I had lost my senses and was tricked into joining the Special Forces. People from Special Forces had threatened me and I was left with no choice. But now that I have regained my senses, I will not commit the same mistake again. I apologize for all my mistakes and sins. I beg the forgiveness and mercy of the freedom fighters. I appeal to them to pardon my family so that we can live the rest of our lives in shame and repentance. We stand with the freedom fighters. We stand for the liberation of Kashmir.

Signed: Rouf Jan

The second letter that bore the exact wording as the previous one was signed Farooq Ahmad.

'Cowards,' Dar fumed at the two men. 'You think you have secured your safety and security by publishing such letters? You think you are now free to live and do whatever you can? You think you can now go wherever you wish? You think your *tanzeem* will take you back? You think these muhajids are fools? Don't you know how it works? We have seen it all, haven't we? You will still be killed. Your death will be made an example. By quitting, you have denied yourself the only chance at living honourably and with dignity. Your days are numbered. Who will protect you now?'

'Won't you?' they said. Dar laughed at the suggestion. He knew they weren't wrong. But both men knew that by declaring madness and quitting the Force which was considered an ignominious entity, they had not averted death. They had merely bought some more time. A day, a week, a month or maybe a year! Postponement of death was life. But the trickiest part was their unwavering belief in something far more dangerous and deceptive. That was hope. Hope had no meaning in Kashmir. It still has no place in our lives, and those of us who fall for it and nurture it are headed towards imminent disaster.

The same deal had been offered to Dar and he had made his decision. He wouldn't be a deserter again. He pledged to go after those who threatened him and his family. He banked on the protection of the Force. The very Force that continued to desert its own men in times of need! It had done so in the past and it would do so in future.

Dar pinned his hopes on only one person. And that was me—his commanding officer. I gave him the freedom I never had. No, I shouldn't lie. I didn't give him the freedom. He seized it and made it his armour. It scared me watching him walk fearlessly on the roads, going into people's homes, sniffing them out at will and thrashing them until they confessed to their guilt and wrongdoings. He dragged boys through the streets as though they were animals to be slaughtered. He beat them until they couldn't drag themselves away from him, until they couldn't show their fear any longer, until they couldn't even cry and plead for mercy, until they couldn't raise their hands for help, until they couldn't open their mouths and until they lost consciousness. People watched in dread, unwilling and unable to intervene. They feared for their lives and the lives of their kids. Dar's monstrosity made their blood boil. They wanted to avenge the merciless beatings and tortures Dar inflicted on them on a daily basis.

Dar went about his duty in the most unusual of ways. The separation from his wife and daughter had turned him into someone I wouldn't want to deal with. I had no choice but to stick with him.

A day came when people took a chance. Dar was returning to the place where he lived. He got off his vehicle and started walking towards his quarters. Out of nowhere came a bunch of masked youngsters with sticks and rods in their hands. Dar found himself ambushed. Without losing time and without giving Dar a chance to resist or to escape, the boys threw themselves on him and started throwing punches at him. A deadly fistfight ensued. Dar stood outnumbered. One against a dozen! In a matter of minutes, Dar started bleeding from his nose. Blows were exchanged without any words.

A woman came out of her house and saw what was happening in the street. She saw Dar, her neighbour, being beaten mercilessly by the youths. She saw how he wasn't even able to defend himself. She rushed towards the beaters and started hurling abuses at them for not showing mercy. She threw her arms around Dar and took the blows on herself. The beaters stopped.

'Mother, why are you intervening?' they said, shocked at the woman's behaviour. 'Don't you know who he is? He is the one who took our lad—your son. Instead of siding with us, you are protecting him…'

The woman looked at the beaters with pity in her eyes. 'You won't understand,' she said. 'My son was wayward. He went against us. This man must have kept him in a safe place. You think he will do something bad to him? This man saved him and us from doom. I don't want the same to be done to him…'

People who had gathered witnessed the scene with disbelief. 'Look what she's doing,' they said. 'She's protecting the very man who's hell-bent on siding with the enemy and making his own people's lives miserable. He's not even bothered by our suffering. This is what happens when people are pitted against each other. We have been driven to become our own enemy. We have become numb to pain. How are we to reconcile? How are we to understand each other? How are we to save ourselves?'

The woman asked for water and a bystander rushed to get some. She poured water into Dar's bloodstained mouth. It was at that moment Dar realized he had been saved from certain death. And that the next time he might not be spared by the furious mob. But as long as the woman was near him, no one would dare touch him.

The woman picked up Dar's assault rifle from the pavement near a drain where it had fallen, ran her ageing fingers over it as if it were a thing not to be stained, wiped clean the dirt off its metal, and then handed it back to him. 'Go now and do what you have to do,' she whispered into his ear. 'Do your job. Save us from damnation.'

Dar tried to stand on his legs but collapsed soon after he rose. The woman helped him put his shoes back on and then buttoned up his shirt for him. She offered him her arms and Dar stood up on his battered and bruised legs and started limping his way back towards his vehicle. He was trembling.

The woman rushed to him with a last request. 'Will you find my son?' she begged. 'I have waited enough. Now please bring him back to me. I will beat him with my own hands and send him away from here. He has no idea what he's done. He's been fooled. He thinks he's a rebel like Salim Dar. He thinks someday he will become a hero like him. But he doesn't know that there can be only one hero in this place. That hero is you. May god bless you and your children! You too are my son,' she said, placing her hand on Dar's head. She wiped her tears with her scarf and walked back towards her house. Her husband stood mute at the door. He put his arm around her and led her inside.

Some people thought that the woman defended Dar because

she feared for her son's life and because she was fearful herself. But like most others who turn a blind eye to the truth, they were wrong.

Such people believe in lies. They don't want to accept the truth because it is against the very cause they believe in. And the realization of truth will make them fall to pieces. They don't even want to look at the truth, for if they do, they will have to live in abject shame and regret for the rest of their lives. Years wasted believing in a grand lie.

There was neither fear nor revenge and contempt in Dar's eyes. Only the desire to see Rabia one more time!

Kill Us Before We Kill You

The clamour for the disbandment of Special Forces is growing among politicians and people. These politicians are not to be trusted. They change colours faster than chameleons. My men want me to tell them what is going to happen to them in case they are ordered to stand down. They come over to my house in the dead of night like thieves. They ask questions they aren't supposed to ask, 'What will happen to us if we are dissolved? We will be hunted down one by one. What are we to do? You're the one who recruited us. What lies ahead for us? Should we also bring out apology letters and step down? Maybe we will be forgiven for our mistakes… Maybe our lives will be spared…'

I can bear anything except fear and cowardice. Except for Dar, all the others demand answers to their stupid questions. Dar is furious. He screams at them, 'We are the best of the lot. And you talk of stepping down and hiding in holes? Who will do the job then? As long as people like us are out there in streets, there is sanity. Once we are gone, you will see what will happen here…'

Nissar Wani, a young recruit, sides with Dar, his superior. He's steadfast in his resolve to honour the oath he's taken. He is ex-Hizbul Mujahideen. He and his elder brother were trained by Hizbul to be Fidayeen bombers. Their mission: to blow up a government and a military establishment. Wani still carries a photograph of his brother. Strapped to his brother's waist is a belt full of grenades. With a gentle push of a button, he blows himself up. Nothing of him remains. Wani, his backup and second-in-command, is then promoted and given charge of a solo operation. He enjoys the solidarity of the masses, and that solidarity is evident in the graffiti on the streets. His name, along with his brother's, is still painted all over the town walls. Next to the names are the words: 'Freedom. Liberation. Nationhood.'

But when Wani's commander, the elusive daredevil, go-getter, and another hero of the people, is shot dead by Salim Dar, he is on his own without the protection of his outfit. His partners order him to go back to the battlezone but don't stand by him when he needs them the most. People chant slogans in his name to rouse him to avenge the killing of his commander. They shelter him and give him food and clothes and money. But he is on his own.

Wani still sports the look of an idealist. He claims that he and his brother were not lured or tricked into joining Hizbul. 'We didn't want to be left out,' he asserts. 'What if the dream of freedom was about to come true? I saw it coming true. It seemed possible. My parents wanted me to become a doctor. It was their only wish. But it wasn't meant to be...'

People still don't know that Wani is Special Forces now. They believe he will never change sides.

Had he not surrendered he would have ended up dead like his commander. He's a quiet yet daring officer. Once he dreamt of leading a rebellion, a revolution. He dreamt of making speeches. He had been made to believe that the world was in his hands. That he could do anything. Even the impossible! That he was next to the Supreme Commander. He had thought he would be given the reins to an entire district or maybe the whole of the valley. He isn't the only one with such beliefs. There are hundreds who still fall for such illusions. Dar has gone through all this himself.

Wani is our best catch so far. The most promising recruit! Nothing is impossible for such recruits. They can get anything they desire. Power, wealth and whatnot... Nothing is beyond their means. Crushed dreams, betrayals and disillusionment bring out the best in them. Wani gets us valuable details about Hizbul's activities in some villages. He's trying to persuade others in Hizbul to surrender. He's still at it. He says he will succeed. He's playing a double game and he knows the risks. But he's unafraid. He has made his peace with his new job. He's been an insider and Dar is mentoring him. But the anger in his heart is palpable; anger towards both Hizbul and the state. He thinks we are monsters and that he has no choice but to be a monster himself.

Dar tells him things that are scandalous and horrible. Just to incite him and fuel his passion for revenge. But Dar doesn't lie to him. He speaks the truth and he speaks it for himself and for the rest of us too, 'Don't you remember the times when in the coldest of nights, we boys were made to stand naked outside our own homes, that too in front of our mothers and fathers; we were forced to lash ourselves with rusted chains and knives and then made to revel in our own punishment and suffering? Don't you remember the days when we were tied to the bonnets of army jeeps to be used as human shields and paraded naked through raging mobs of stone throwers? Don't you remember the times when we were shoved into dingy boxing rings and made to fight each other and then bets were placed upon us until one of us killed the other? Don't you remember the times when we were made to chop each other's fingers off one after another and then force them into each other's mouths? Don't you remember the times we were forced to beg for our existence? When we were asked to do so day after day, week after week, month after month, year after year until we ran out of years, months, weeks, days, hours, minutes, and seconds. And until there was no time left in the whole world! Time was taken out of our lives as if we didn't deserve it. It is the remembrance of that vanishing time which should make us do things no human must do...'

Wani listens stoically as if whatever Dar is saying is inconsequential. The look on his face indicates he doesn't give a damn. He nods derisively and then retorts, 'First they got my brother killed. Then they came to offer condolences. They said I should celebrate the martyrdom of my only brother. They even gave me money. A lot of money! They said it was good money. They said the days of our sorrow and suffering and oppression and subjugation are numbered and good times are going to return. They said freedom is only an arm's length away. Look at me now. Here I am, born again, ready to die one more time...'

Dar's tactic works. He throws in another provocation, 'And then along come those two-faced leaders whose only job is to mourn and celebrate at the same time. They come and tell you to prepare for battle when their own children are flourishing elsewhere. They don't allow their own children to utter a word. To them they say one thing; to our children and us they say something else. They come and sell you your own martyrdom. And they sell it cheap. They have neither shame nor morality. Their only aim is to make us weak and render our lives hollow. To suit their duplicitous agendas, they don't even hesitate to betray their friends and befriend their enemies. They are the opposite of themselves. These are the people who don't want a solution to the Kashmir problem because keeping the problem alive has, over the years, been incredibly profitable. A simmering Kashmir keeps their coffers full. Falsehood and greed is what unites them and not love for Kashmir. Now they can't even set themselves right. They are forced to stay together to peddle each other's lies. Now that they know we are watching them, they are doling out certificates of greatness to each other. You must know that they will continue ganging up against us for the fear of being exposed even among the commoners. What will these let-Kashmir-burn people do when the fire is doused and when all of us die? How will they derive sustenance? What will they do then? And now after all the sacrifices we have made, we are made to question our own past and justify our existence by denying the past? Why this, why not that? When, where, how…these questions do not matter any longer… What good will come out of it all? Only one thing matters now, and that is what we must do and what we are capable of doing. We are people who know how to exercise our power over others to decide their fate, not just to decide how they will live and die, but also how to curtail their desire to live so that they beg for death. Our power is such that the oppressed become happy in oppression. They begin to get used to it and like it…'

Another officer looks at Dar with disbelief, 'But what about their mistakes?'

'They needn't commit a mistake for us to punish them. They are used to being punished regardless of their actions…'

'But the political parties have promised the people that Special Forces will be disbanded. They are begging for votes on this promise. They are pledging to set up inquiry commissions to investigate each one of us. They are accusing us of custodial killings and making people's lives hell. They blame us for everyone's miseries as if we are criminals. Not a word about the militants and their cohorts. What have we done to deserve such apathetic treatment? After all, we carry out orders of the very people who now seek to oust us. We would take a bullet for them. We made a mistake by covering their asses so far because now if someone has to be punished, it will be us. They think we are the monsters.'

'You are right,' nods another officer. 'First they create us. Then we are made to go after our own. Then we are called harbingers of evil. Then others are made to go after us. The bottomline is that a time will come when none of us will exist. Neither they nor us! Our homes will be empty. Only ghosts will live there. Maybe even they won't stay when they come to know what we did to each other...'

There are arguments and counter arguments. I listen to everyone. What good will come out of talking? All we have done year after year is talk and talk. Nothing has come of it. No solution is in sight. The truth is we have become killers of our own people. We kill people who don't even exist and should not exist. If we kill people who are adamant on killing us, what wrong are we committing? There are no rules to this game. We are saving others. We are saving the young from dying young. This is why we were created in the first place. This is why we exist. People believe what they want to believe. We should not let their tears bother us or deter us from our duty. People cry a lot and shed crocodile tears. Are we to allow ourselves to be swayed by them?

You know why our own people are hounding us? Because they think we are theirs. It's their job to instill fear in others to keep them from siding with us. So that they do exactly what's required of them. It is simple. You kill your own to keep the flock together. That's not betrayal. That's loyalty.

'We are going after the wrong people,' says another recruit, indignantly. 'We are saving the wrong people. Everyone out there is fixated on saving the perpetrators and punishing the harmless.'

Dar corrects him, 'We can't expose our weaknesses to anyone. We may not be as strong as our enemies put together but we are no weaklings either. You know that. We don't want anyone to know that. Better be a monster here than a weakling ready to be slaughtered.'

'You know what people are saying about us... They wish us death...'

'You're wrong. They don't want us to die...'

'But they don't want us to live either...'

'People don't know what they really want.'

The meeting starts taking a dangerous turn. If I order everyone to shut up, they will think I am not with them. I have to keep the flock together. What do I say to them? You know what makes people dangerous? When they don't know what they really want. Such people in large numbers spell doom for a society. How can we be considered good? We are running after something that's unattainable. Kashmir, for the present-day militants, is an unfinished business worth fighting and dying for. For us, Kashmir is just a posting to guard the crown. For the ordinary folk who wake up in the morning and leave their homes to earn a living, not even bothering if it's safe to go out or not, Kashmir is just another hopeless day.

Listen up everybody, I want all the bloody mess to end. But you will have to help me.

'With due respect, Sir, our children are asking us why we are doing this,' says another senior officer. 'Ours is a wretched existence. A sorry state of affairs! What kind of a force have they brought into existence? We are pitted against each other. And we revel in the extermination of our own…'

'At least we don't make people suffer every day,' says Dar.

'Yeah, we just silence them with a bullet,' quips the officer. 'The day of judgement will soon be upon us. We shall have to face ourselves and there won't be a place to hide…'

Things You Mustn't Know

Dear Zooni,

You keep coming in my dreams; sometimes against my wishes. I don't want to dream anymore. You are far away from me and you ask me the same question over and over again, 'Have you ever felt the loss of something precious? What if you wake up one morning and realize you have lost the ability to do the things that define you? What will you do that day? How will you live?'

Not a day goes by when I don't think of you. How I wish I didn't have to return from work and think about the rights and wrongs. You don't even look at me. You don't even question my doings. You still have faith in me even though I tell you things you mustn't know. How long will I blame myself for others' wrongdoings?

In my dream, you are here in Kashmir. You are searching for me among hordes of people whose only aim is to keep us apart. In the dream I say to myself, 'They are going to make us kill each other.'

You keep me alive day after day. I reveal my flaws to you because you rid me of them.

For years you kept asking me a question, 'Dad, why do you have to be the one to pull the trigger?' I brushed it aside and told you anecdotes that no one knew. Truth—plain and simple! Like cold water from a spring. I can hold it no longer. If not me, then who? Don't you wish to know why I haven't returned yet? I don't want my reappearance to destroy your longing.

I see people I haven't seen before. Their gazes are fixed on me. They aren't afraid anymore. They follow me like my own shadow. They speak to me without uttering a word. Their looks do the talking. Their eyes fix the blame. 'Look at us,' they say. 'Look here, you thief. Face us. Don't you see what you have done? You have taken our life and called it your own.'

'Won't you ask me why?' I plead.

'No,' they scream. 'You must go through this pain.'

They don't even ask me for explanations. They are real. Not like the sketches you make. I never thought they would come back to haunt me. But now they have. I can't escape. They follow me like a shadow. They are in front of me all the time. When I wake up and when I go to sleep. Even when I am asleep they surround me. They come to me in my dreams to persecute me. I want them to go away. I want this to end. I want to kill them again. But can you kill anyone twice?

Someday, we will go back to the place that doesn't exist. Someday, you will find what most of us think doesn't exist.

You have your eyes set upon the world, Zooni. But always remember who you are and where you have come from.

All my love,

Dad

Surprise Inspection

'Have you ever wondered about the *isness* of Time and of things we think are ours?' the Head of Psychiatry at the mental hospital asks while showing me around. 'There was a time when this hospital was empty. But now all you see are remnants of Time splashed all over here.'

My purpose of going to the mental hospital is to ascertain the facts of a strange case pertaining to some unknown people who, I am told, go in disguise to hide there. Dar suspects that the unknown people are mujahids on the run. At first, I debunk the inference. It seems ridiculous that militants, for any reason, would take shelter in a mental asylum. Why would they or anyone else for that matter hide in a mental hospital? Because nobody would suspect that they are here? There's no dearth of hideouts here. But when Dar comes up with some credible evidence, it becomes necessary to pay a visit and find out the truth. He vehemently refutes my dismissal of his suspicion.

'Using a mental asylum as a hideout is an ingenious idea,' Dar says. 'You can do almost anything there without fear and without attracting attention.' Dar implies we storm the asylum and smoke out the militants. But it isn't so easy to storm a hospital, so we decide to go undercover and pose as officers of the health department, which even today is in shambles. We decide to make our visit look like a surprise inspection. Nobody there will be alerted, and nobody will even think of cross-checking our credentials with the health department. After all, who gives a damn about mental hospitals?

When we reach the hospital, a doctor introduces himself as the Head of Psychiatry and Mental Disorders and greets us in a manner that suggests his foreknowledge of our arrival. We present ourselves as officials of the Health Department. 'Yes, yes, I know,' the doctor says, gleefully. 'I was told you would come. I've been expecting you for months. Thank god, you showed up at last.'

We explain the purpose of our visit and set out our expectations, 'A quick tour will do. We would also like to go through the roster and meet a few patients.'

'You won't be disappointed. We maintain our records immaculately. And the patients are extremely well-behaved. Some are even in the process of being discharged...'

'We're in a hurry. You see we have to inspect more hospitals in just a day. So let's get started.'

Walking in a funny manner, the doctor guides us through a long corridor. We realize he has a limp. Maybe it's a faulty bone, we think. Dar points to labels pasted on the doors of the wards. He winks at me to convey his suspicion and doubt, 'What do you make of them?'

The label on the door of the first ward towards the right reads: 'ALMOST FIT AND FINE'. The label on the door towards the left reads: 'READY TO BE DISCHARGED.' Reading the labels and trying to make sense of them, we walk past the rest of the wards to the left and the right of the hallway.

Label on the door of the third ward: CHILDREN BELOW 15

Label on the door of the fourth ward: NO HOPE

Label on the door of the sixth ward: PERMANENT INMATES

Label on the door of the eighth ward: STAY AWAY

Label on the door of the ninth ward: YET TO BE DIAGNOSED

Label on the door of the tenth ward: VERY IMPORTANT INMATES

We notice something peculiar. Going by the sequence of the wards lined up on the two sides of the corridor, the labels for wards 5 and 7 are missing.

We arrive at a room and the nameplate on the door reads:

Dr M RIYAZ, MBBS, MD (NEUROPSYCHIATRY)
Head of the Department

The door is half-open. A man is seated on a chair. We figure that the man in front of us is the head of the department. He appears familiar. We exchange looks and it becomes clear to me who he is. We know each other from before. There's an awkward silence between us, but he gets the drift. We shake hands and he apologizes for not greeting us at the gate.

'If only I had known about your arrival earlier, I would have made proper arrangements,' he says, ruefully. Very gently, he ushers the doctor who greeted us at the gate to a separate room next to his.

'Pardon me, he has a habit of impersonating me,' Dr Riyaz says, referring to the other doctor. 'He's doing okay. Not a serious case anymore... What can I do for you?'

We aren't undercover anymore. I decide to take Dr Riyaz into confidence and explain the real purpose of our surprise visit. But the situation is tricky. If Dr Riyaz is indeed shielding militants in the hospital on the pretext that they are mental cases, then he's complicit, unless he's blissfully unaware of their real background—which doesn't seem unlikely. After all, what does it take to feign madness these days? It's the easiest thing to do here in Kashmir. Half the people have been made to go mad anyway. The other half is almost there.

I signal to Dar whether we should call off the mission. He thinks otherwise. We decide to proceed as planned. Dr Riyaz agrees to show us around.

'What's with these labels?' Dar asks him.

'It is Professor Hamid's doing,' he says, pointing to a photograph on the wall. 'The impersonator, I mean. He was a history professor at a college. The principal of his college referred him here. He's been here for a year now. In the beginning, he was quite unwell. But the treatment seems to be working and he's calm now. He's not a threat anymore. He's free here. He derives solace out of impersonating me and others. It keeps him busy.'

'Who else does he impersonate?'

'Lots of people. You wouldn't believe. He becomes them.

'Name a few.'

Dr Riyaz gives us a few names. Among them are former rulers and others we haven't heard of.

'Are these real people?'

'For him they are.'

'Are there any inmates in the wards? Why is it so quiet in here?'

'The wards are empty at the moment. The inmates are in the polo ground. Let me take you there.'

He calls Professor Hamid and asks him to join us. Upon

seeing us, the professor starts flipping through an imaginary newspaper and makes a face. He walks towards us holding the inexistent spread-out newspaper firmly in his hands. His limp is gone. His gait is different now. He looks somewhat authoritative. He pretends to be in charge of things.

'Why aren't there any labels on the doors of the other two wards?' Dar asks. Dr Riyaz brushes the question aside. Dar is insistent. He walks up to the door of the unlabelled ward and peeks inside. I follow him. He signals me to take a look. It's a small, dark and dingy room with a bed and some electrical equipment. 'Shock therapy...' Dr Riyaz butts in, 'for the worst cases...'

We arrive at the lobby in the second floor from where an open ground is visible. 'That is the polo ground,' Dr Riyaz says, pointing at a large ground almost the size of a football field. 'Look over there...'

Men and women are sauntering in the ground. By the look of it, everybody appears normal. Nobody is behaving abnormally. There's no screaming and running around and frolicking like mad people. There are no fights and arguments. There is no incessant laughter and crying at the same time. There are no ludicrous gesticulations. The inmates are just idling.

Dr Riyaz seems like an honourable and honest doctor. I remember hearing about him several years ago when he was in the news for having won a prestigious award for his research work on mental illnesses. He's now the state's foremost authority on mental disorders. Although he has a degree from a top-notch medical college in the United States, he didn't choose to settle there. He chose to return to Kashmir and serve the people here. I take him aside and tell him the real reason behind our visit to the hospital. We take our chance, 'We had intelligence that some people come to hide here. We thought of dropping by to rule out any foul play and to… But everything appears to be normal here…' Dr Riyaz listens quietly and then suggests we go back to his room.

'You're late by a year,' he whispers, struggling to keep a straight face. 'Some health department officials did come here a few times to conduct inspections. At first, I thought they were very influential people and indeed from the health department. I had no choice but to let them stay and do whatever. You know how these bureaucrats are. They seemed no-nonsense people. There was no way to authenticate their real identity. Who knows what's real and what's unreal here in the city. The times are bad, as you know. But when the officials brought along new faces during subsequent inspections, I figured out the real purpose of their visits. What they can't get outside, they are able to get here…'

Dar interrupts: 'What do you mean? What are the visits about?'

'At night, when the children are singing to one another in their dreams, the visitors enter the children's ward like ghosts and do whatever pleases them. They have a free hand. No one comes to know. There is not even a whimper. No ruckus is created. The chosen boys and girls don't even realize what's being done to them because they are not conscious. They believe this too is part of their treatment. Those who are spared think their turn will come the next time. Who knows what they think and feel? It doesn't matter anyway. The inspectors leave behind nothing except stains. We haven't had the visitors in some time now, but I suspect they won't come back now that you have gotten to know.

It's good you are here on a surprise inspection. I wish I had the guts to confront the visitors despite knowing they were imposters of the worst kind. I would never have the guts to leak the matter to anyone, let alone you in the police or the health department. I have to keep my job. No one will ever come to know who the visitors really were. If you still insist, I will show you around. You can get to meet some of the children.'

Dr Riyaz takes us to a ward at the far end of the corridor. 'It's the children's ward,' he says. 'Take a look around and decide for yourself.'

In the ward are children from ages five to fifteen. 'Let me show you something,' Dr Riyaz says, taking us towards a ten-year-old wearing a loose fitting Che Guevara t-shirt. On the front of his T-shirt, below Che Guevara's face, are the words: 'I know you are here to kill me. Shoot, coward, you are only going to kill a man.'

Politely, Dr Riyaz asks the boy to show us his treasure. The child is shy and hides behind the doctor. He doesn't even look at us. He has an inscrutable look in his eyes. The same look Zubair has in his eyes when my fellow officers come home.

Dr Riyaz opens a rickety cupboard and takes out a bunch of paper airplanes. He hands one over to me. 'There's more,' he says, showing us creations we have never seen in our lives.

'This boy has done all this? What are these things?

'No one knows. He's suffering from PTSD. His mother left him here a year ago. She visits him sometimes.'

Dr Riyaz shows us a certificate. On it is written a name in bold letters: MASTER SUFI MIR. The citation reads: 'For standing first in the inter-school art competition.'

Dr Riyaz says the boy's mother holds it in her hands and kisses it whenever she drops by. 'This is his home now,' he adds. 'But I hope I can send him away from here soon. He will bring us glory someday. He will make us proud. He's not the only one. There are others. Each one of them possesses a gift. If only I had the capability to discover their potential…'

I inspect the faces of the children in the ward. They aren't even aware of the presence of strangers. Who knows what we are to them. Their gazes are elsewhere.

This is the strangest place I have ever visited. And you can imagine the kind of places I have been to and set foot on. Dar is trying hard to swallow his rage by holding his breath and clenching his fist. Before he does something unwarranted, I decide to take him away from here.

When we are about to leave the ward, Dr Riyaz takes me aside and whispers into my ear, 'I gave up my practice in USA and returned to Kashmir, hoping to do wonders. But now I am struggling to come to terms with my own inadequacies. What do I do? How do I treat these children? There's only one cure which will rid them of their ailments, and it looks like I can't even bring that cure to them… In my entire career, I have never come across a child like Sufi. You know he can see things that none of us can. Things that don't exist… It takes a certain amount of faith to believe in the inexistence of god. The only thing that brings these children happiness is the sound of Sufi's paper airplanes. Their faces light up when Sufi flies them through the windows. They are all smiles as if someday they will get to fly too…' He pauses for a fraction and then begins again. 'People fail to recognize the illnesses within themselves. And they think these kids are ill. Normal is the new abnormal here and abnormal the new normal.'

Dr Riyaz stops. He is struggling to tell me everything. For the first time, I see fear in his eyes. In school, he was the brightest of us all. His dream—to go abroad and become a doctor—has now come true. I still remember the sermon he gave me on the day he left school, 'You will not live for more than a year if you too join the resistance movement. Don't be a fool like the others. Leave this place and make a life elsewhere. This place is headed for disaster. You don't want to waste your life and be killed for nothing…' He had meant every word. I had envied him that day. He wasn't alone in his assessment of me and the others who stood together for a common cause. There were others like him who dismissed us as fools for choosing Kashmir over greener pastures. After leaving school, he thought he would never see me again. I had never thought our paths would ever cross again but I was sure of living to see his name plastered all over the best of magazines in the world. That his name and fame would take him places had been on everybody's mind those days.

He's gotten used to the state of affairs now. He's become an inmate too. He doesn't even realize what a blunder he has committed by allowing terrible things to happen in the hospital. He doesn't know what his weakness has done to him and to the children. He doesn't even want to know what his silence has caused. He is happy to look the other way like everyone else. His willful blindness might have bought him some more time at the hospital but someday he will have to pay for his silence and inaction.

He points to the clock on the wall and signals it is time to gather the children to offer prayers. Professor Hamid makes another appearance and, this time, he's dressed like a cook. He brings food on a trolley and calls out to the kids. The children assemble around the trolley and start examining the food. Professor Hamid lifts a plate full of rice and cooked vegetables, makes a small morsel using his right hand, and then starts feeding a child who's sitting quietly in a corner and looking at the world outside through a window that doesn't exist. The look on that child's face is inscrutable. He opens his mouth obediently and accepts the morsel of food. But the defiance in his eyes is frightening.

'He is the only one who refuses to offer prayers seriously before breaking his fast,' says Dr Riyaz about the boy. 'That's why he's the first one to eat.'

Dar is furious. His contempt for Dr Riyaz is swelling every moment. He's the real culprit and we must get rid of him is Dar's verdict. 'We must finish him off. We won't get another chance,' he thinks. As always, Dar is proven right. But we are late by a year. I must get him out of here or else he will take matters into his hands and land us in trouble.

I thank Dr Riyaz for his support and cooperation in showing us around the hospital. 'Aziz...' he sighs, 'I am sorry... I thought all you would do in your life is distribute pamphlets, but I was wrong...'

I will come again, I say to him out of courtesy. To see Sufi.

'If you do, will you be able to recognize him?' he says with a hint of sarcasm on his face.

Before I leave, I want to shake Sufi's hand but I can't get myself to look him in the eye. I can't take my eyes off the t-shirt he's wearing. I want to offer him a new t-shirt in exchange for his, but I know he wouldn't trade it for all the t-shirts in the world.

Sufi reminds me of Zubair. But I cannot go back to Zubair now because he too is in a place that no longer exists.

Truth of Life

Arif, the boy from Gurez, has resurfaced after many years. He wasn't supposed to have survived.

He brings information that Dar is not going to be spared and that the date and time of his killing have been decided. 'I have come to repay the debt,' he says tearfully. 'How do I meet him? I just want to see him and tell him everything in person.'

Arif is caught between two hells. He's become a double agent, meaning he's neither here nor there. Showing me his mobile phone, he brandishes chat transcripts with the who's who of the security apparatus and the militant groups. He shows me his conversations with militant commanders, intelligence and counter-intelligence agents, army and police officers, other informants and dubious people with code names who claim to know everyone and everything.

Going by his attitude, he thinks he can decide people's destinies. He has the appearance of a person who thinks he can prevent or trigger an event or change the course of someone's life or make people disappear. Such is his delusion. He's working for everyone and no one. He's come to ask a favour in exchange for a favour done to him by Dar years ago when he was just a teenager and when Dar had taken him away from Gurez and brought him to the city to get him a job.

At first, he takes off his shirt and reveals his scars. 'Look,' he says, pointing his finger at the marks. 'This happened in the first year, this in the second year, and this in the third. I have stopped counting now...'

He's not blaming anyone. He thinks he's invincible. He doesn't know what mistakes he has committed and what blunders he will be made to commit. I decide to send him away with a warning, 'Do not be misled by these people who you think are your benefactors. A day will come when they will have no use for you and that will be the end of it. And that day isn't far. It will be upon you sooner than you think. You won't even be given a chance to repent or make amends. These people, whose patronage and protection you are enjoying right now and who have made you believe in lies and fabrications, have already figured out what to do with you when the time comes and when they are done with you. You and thousands like you mean nothing to them. Do not be seen here. Go away right now. Leave everything. Destroy whatever you have got. Take nothing with you. Leave no trace. Do not return.'

He returns shortly and asks me if I would be willing to help him. 'My wife is in trouble,' he says. 'She's in pain and I have left her alone. I couldn't even take her to a hospital. But now I know what to do.'

Taking pity on him and for Dar's sake, I accompany him to his quarters. A young woman is lying on the floor and she's unable to move. Her condition is indescribable. There's no point in describing how she looks. I can't do that. You shouldn't even try to imagine. If you do, you will fail. I used to think I have seen the worst and there's nothing left to see. I was wrong. Sometimes you look into a person's eyes and you shudder. You choke. You don't know what to do. All you want to do is look away. You try to imagine all the things that the person has been made to endure. But you fail. You can't even imagine those things. You think they don't exist in the world. You can't even imagine people are capable of doing such things. You think this is not who we are. Humans are incapable of such things. There's nothing that can allow them to do such things. Things that shouldn't be spoken about and can't be spoken about! And then you want to turn your back on the person. You want to leave immediately, and you pray you never get to see the person ever again in your life.

It's a miracle the young woman is even alive. Well, this is the land of miracles. Some people don't die even after there's no life left in them. At least she's alive. Arif must thank his stars.

'She's been like this for days now,' he says. 'She refuses to go to the hospital. She has a death wish, I know for sure. She thinks she will be cut to pieces if she's taken to the hospital.'

The woman looks at Arif and me and screams. 'Don't come near me,' she yells, taking out a knife from under the mattress and brandishing it at us as though she will have no hesitation to stab us. 'I will kill myself if you try to...'

Arif goes near her and tries to snatch the knife out of her hand. The woman's grip on the knife is firm and Arif is unsuccessful in getting rid of it. What more can a one-armed man do? He looks reluctant to force himself on her.

I advance toward the woman to free the knife, and she starts trembling violently like someone who's having a seizure. Her mouth is frothy and there's blood all over her abdomen.

'Who did this to her?'

'She blames me,' Arif whispers to me. 'I'm not responsible for her plight. I told her whom to blame but she's not even willing to listen to me or talk to me. I am doing what I have been advised to do. But now I need your help.'

'What do you want me to do? We can take her to a private clinic right away. Nobody will get to know.'

'No, that's not the help I want.'

'Then what?'

'I was going to take her home to Gurez but...'

Arif takes me aside and tells me what he has in mind. At first I think he's joking but he's not.

'Do you know who you are talking to?' I yell at him. I hold myself back. I feel like grabbing hold of him and strangling him to death. He senses my outrage and anger. 'Don't misunderstand me,' he says, rushing to defend himself and clarify his position. 'Do you think I want to do this? I'm Commander Dar's protégé. Under no circumstances will I ever think of doing such a profane thing. But you must place yourself in my shoes. What would you do if you were in my place? I have thought things through. There is no other way out...'

'And what will you do afterwards?'

'I will do whatever you say.'

'Okay, I will help you. But from tomorrow onwards you shouldn't be seen here or else you know what is going to happen. I have warned you. There won't be any more warnings. Nobody will give a damn. Not even I.'

'Sir, what makes you think I'm afraid of dying or any other eventuality? I'm not here to defend myself. I'm here to protect Commander Dar. Had it not been for him, I would have died years ago. You know what he means to me. You were there when he took me under his wing. His life is more precious than mine for he will guide us and show us the way. He won't let the sacrifices of the children of this land go in vain. He will bring us closer to our cherished dream...and we shall see the truth of life...'

I correct him: 'Dar is not a Commander. He's the Commandant of an elite force, you fool.'

He lowers his head, and says, 'If you ever happen to go to Gurez and meet my parents, tell them I have just lost an arm. I am fine otherwise.'

The Keeper of the Gates of Paradise

Hundreds of thousands of people have come out of their houses. More and more are coming out into the streets. There's no more room for people to assemble. Not an inch is vacant now. Some have parked themselves on rooftops and on trees. Some are peeping through the chinks in the windows of their houses. Everyone is marching towards the place where the bodies of those killed in the encounter are lying. Preparations for the funeral are under way. People are chanting slogans in the names of those martyred. The news has reached the world. News channels are broadcasting the event live. Journalists and reporters are commenting.

One television anchor sums up everything in a few sentences: 'The dreaded Jaish-e-Mohammed and Lashkar-e-Taiba that have successfully altered the meaning of Jihad form the core of the second wave in Kashmir. If at all the second wave is contained, or even eliminated in the years to come, what assurance do we have that a third wave, which perhaps will inflict damage at a catastrophic level, won't rise? Indoctrinated by ISIS ideology, the present-day Jaish or Lashkar militants operating in Kashmir are willing to tackle the forces, spread havoc, put people's lives at grave risk, take a bullet and die for the sake of a lost cause—Pakistan or Islamic State or jihad...'

Dar is peering out, his gaze fixed at the movements of people. The scene is much more horrendous than what is playing on the television screen. A sea of people is marching from the east to west where the funeral procession is to take place.

Lighting up a cigarette, Dar says, 'How are we going to be remembered? Years from now, people will know the opposite of what actually happened. Because there are people out there right now who are scripting history. We are going to be remembered as villains. It will be the worst thing to happen to us. It is better not to be remembered at all. To be forgotten and erased from people's memories as if we never existed...'

He stubs out the cigarette. 'With your permission, Sir, I must leave. There's one last thing I must do before everything ends.'

'You have never asked my permission before. So why now?'

'You know why.'

'On one condition!'

'You have never believed in conditions.'

'I'm making an exception.'

'You leave me no choice.'

'We go together.'

'You don't trust me?'

Dar's intentions are suspect. He might blow his own cover. We go out. He leads the way. He retraces his steps to the place where once he was thrashed for having dragged a young boy out of his house. He knocks on the door of the house. A woman opens the door. She's the same woman who had saved him from a lynch mob. She doesn't take a second to recognize him.

'What's the matter?' she asks. 'Have you got him back?' The woman surveys the street for any traces of her son. She calls her other son—a boy aged no more than ten. He rushes down the stairs and stands in front of us. He gives us an unforgiving look. The woman breaks down. 'What's the matter?' she goes on asking. 'Where is he?'

Dar looks at me, and then turns his gaze back at the woman.

'I am the one who did it,' he says. 'With these hands... I had my face covered so that he doesn't... I didn't want him to look at me...'

'No, no, don't say that. You're lying,' the woman sobs. 'I know you're hiding the truth. You're incapable of such an act. You won't do it. You will never do it. I have seen it in your eyes. You are supposed to be the protector and not the destroyer. You promised to bring him back. Now go and get him back and I will not say a word...'

'I am not here to apologize to you. I am here to tell you the truth and offer myself up to you. If you let me go, I will do it again and again and again until not even a single one survives. You must accept the truth and face the reality.'

Upon hearing Dar's admission, the woman grabs hold of his arm and collapses. Her son rushes towards her and throws his arms around her. Dar takes the woman's hands in his hands, rubs them and then sits next to her until she regains consciousness. 'Won't you ask me why I did it and why I am here?' he whispers into her ear. The woman shakes her head, unable to recover from the shock.

What Dar is doing is insane. It will destroy him forever. It will turn him into a beast. This is the point of no return. This is the moment when you are hurled down an abyss without even the remotest possibility of coming out unscathed.

'Go away,' the woman says, regaining her consciousness. 'Do not return until you find my son and hand him over to me. When he returns, I shall feed him with my hands one last time and then send him back to you if you wish.'

The woman's husband comes close to Dar and without

uttering a word begs him to step aside so that he can explain. He has the look of dejection on his face.

'She has lost her senses,' the man whispers, remorsefully. 'She wakes up in the night and screams her son's name over and over again. Rizwan… Rizwan… Rizwan… She goes on and on without stopping. She feels his presence. She feels guilty. Rizwan had asked her what he should do. If he should surrender or not! She said no to him. She said it's better to die with dignity than to surrender out of cowardice. Rizwan was alone in his fight. Had everyone been together, he would have seen his dream come true. To see Rizwan happy was her dream. It is because of the love she has for our son that she is behaving abnormally. She doesn't know she's not alone in this loss and there are thousands of others who have reconciled to their fates without uttering a word. There are mothers who have lost not one son but two. Unlike thousands of such women she hasn't learnt how to handle loss and death. Day after day, I remind her of the meaning of martyrdom, but she's stubborn as a child. She should know that dying for one's motherland is to live forever. It is life. But she throws tantrums. She's blinded by her love for her firstborn. Her problem is that she is full of hope. She believes in it. She thinks it is real and it exists. I keep on telling her that hope isn't hope. Yesterday it was hope. Today it is despair. Tomorrow it will be betrayal. She thinks her son will return. How does one return from Paradise? Why should our son even come back? He's free at last.'

Dar isn't even listening as he's used to listening to such sob stories all the time. In Kashmir, even the pebbles on the streets will tell you sob stories and fairy tales.

The man pauses. He walks up to a shelf and brings a photograph to show Dar. The photograph is of a boy who's barely in his teens. There's a sparkle in his eyes. The man runs his fingers on the photo. Caressing the boy's face, he says: 'We will always have him.'

A cat comes out of a room and rubs herself against Dar.

'Rizwan loved her,' the man continues. 'He rescued her from certain death. He used to say cats have nine lives. By that logic, she has eight more to go. She's soon going to have kittens. Now we have her and our younger son. He's too small to understand what's going on here. But he misses his brother. He says he will get him back if we allow him to go out. But he shouldn't stay here. When he grows up, he should leave this place and get a job somewhere else. I have only one appeal now. We have been demeaned enough. We don't care about anything. Not even our life. We are facing hell. Say this and say that is what people tell us. Blame them and blame those, they say. Don't give up; we are with you, they say. And then they abandon us only to resurface when another misfortune strikes. They think we are fools. They want to claim us. They think they own us. They mistake our silence for blind acceptance and servitude. We are not yours. Don't impose your voice on us. We want nothing. We don't even want your help. Let us be. We want nothing else now but to be left alone with our grief. We will grieve and handle whatever happens to us. All our lives, we have been forced to utter lies. We are forced to say what people want us to say. Now we don't even know what the truth is...'

Dar is silent. If he's thinking his job is done, then he's mistaken. If he's thinking the confession is over and now he is free from all burdens and guilt, he has no idea of what is to come. This is just the beginning. Everything looks deceptive. There are no conclusions. He can't run away now. What does he think is going to happen? He will have to pick up the thread and carry on doing what he's supposed to do. That's who we are. That's what we have become. The process is irreversible. We don't have the luxury of facing ourselves and searching for answers. We don't have the compulsion of being answerable to anyone, not even to ourselves. There are no questions to face and no answers to seek. That's the whole bloody point of our existence. Our existence is built around the premise that we will finish the job and then cease to exist for anyone. No one will give a damn. No one should give a damn. Playtime is over. It's time for action. But Dar is unfazed.

Turning his gaze towards his wife, and then facing Dar once again, the man says: 'She was so happy when she realized that the body of a teenager in the morgue wasn't her son's. Her faith in you should not die. It should remain alive. If only our son came home for one last meal… But you don't worry… You have suffered enough… You deserve forgiveness…'

The man stops but doesn't seem to be finished yet. He grabs hold of his wife's hand and takes her inside. She obeys helplessly. 'Tell them to give me a few minutes with him. Even a minute will do,' she begs, mournfully. He whispers into her ear, 'they have promised me, they will send him to us, your prayers have been answered.' He makes sure his whisper doesn't remain unheard.

Before leaving, I offer the man a final word. Truth must be upheld: 'There is something you should know. Your son came under the wheels of a truck. It was this Salim Dar who tried to save him. But it was too late. The boy shouldn't have been out there, fighting those who were trying to save him. It was not his fight. You shouldn't have let him go out of the house. People die because they make mistakes in places they aren't supposed to be.'

The man isn't even listening. He is lost in his own thoughts.

Or maybe he is used to such excuses and justifications. Nothing matters to him.

'You must be getting late...you have far more important things to do...thank you for coming...you should leave now,' he says and then shuts the door behind us.

A neighbour who's been waiting at the door all this time musters up his courage and whispers terrifyingly into my ear: 'The boy had arranged to send them for Hajj next year, but...'

I was wrong. Something has stirred in Dar. He is walking in a manner as if he has nowhere to go now. I haven't ever seen him in such a pitiable state. That he would fumble and break is unimaginable. He has the heart of a lion. He's supposed to roar and frighten everyone. But right now he's disintegrating. He's being consumed by his own demons lurking within him.

The streets are teeming with mourners. Firepots are hanging off the branches of trees and off rooftops. The first coffin is seen. And then the second! The thirds follows. And then out come the fourth and the fifth to loud chants: 'Paradise for the martyred and freedom for the land'. It's an endless trail of coffins surrounded by hundreds of mourners ready to meet the same fate as the slain. Countless torches light up the place. Mothers cling to the mounds of moist earth—final resting places for their sons. One woman is holding the lifeless body of her son in her lap. The boy is dead but his fingers are still quivering. There's some life left in him and it's refusing to end.

Standing behind a tree are three men, talking in hushed tones.

Man 1: Look at me. I am still alive. Nothing has happened to me.

Man 2: I survived too. Nothing has happened to me as well.

Man 3: Ali's son hasn't come home for two days now. But

my son has. I have locked him up now. You must also lock your sons up.

As more and more people come out from all directions, the slogans start growing louder and louder until no other voice is heard: 'Freedom… Freedom… Freedom…'

Is this the march of death or of freedom?

'Look, freedom and death are walking hand in hand,' Dar screams into my ear.

He stands all by himself, unarmed and unnoticed, ready to plunge into the lava flowing in front of us. A mother of a slain boy is going around in circles like a woman possessed. She's singing and crying at the same time. Her gaze falls on Dar and she starts laughing hysterically. She seems to be laughing as though her grief has been taken away and as though her hope has been restored. She goes on laughing without stopping. She doesn't know she is in the throes of a wicked dream. I don't want her to wake up from the dream. She continues laughing until she can laugh no more.

She stumbles against Dar, grabs hold of the collar of his shirt, and says, 'Do not grieve for them; do not cry; they will come back; it's been foretold; they will return to their mothers and fathers; do not grieve for anyone; do not shed tears, my son…'

Dar's lips tremble as more and more slogans rend the air: F…R…E…E…D…O…M.

Lion's Roar

The final battle is about to begin. Dar and I will go into the bloody pit of horror from where there's no coming back. But as long as I am alive and in command I won't let anything happen to him. I won't fail him. I will stand by him. There's one last thing to be done. I'll send him home to be with Rabia before he returns to finish the unfinished business.

When Dar arrives in Gurez, I expect the people there to swear and hurl abuses at him. But the opposite happens. People welcome him with open arms. 'Our lion has returned,' they chant. They bring forth their newborns. Sons are named after him. There are countless Salim Dars all around. The ground where once he taught cricket has been named SALIM DAR CRICKET GROUND. The baker has named his shop, SALIM DAR AND SONS. The signboard over the door of the village dispensary reads: SALIM CARES. Next to a lumber mill in the timber market are truckloads of logs ready to be dispatched to various places. On each of the logs is an engraving: FROM SALIM DAR—THE STAR OF KASHMIR—WITH LOVE. For the first time, people have installed nameplates on the wooden doors of their shanties. The nameplates bear only one name: DAR MANZIL. The message on the Welcome-to-Gurez signboard reads: SALIM DAR—LION OF KASHMIR.

When Dar leaves, people send him off with hugs and kisses and with hope in their hearts. But they know that he might never come back again. He doesn't say a word to them. His silence is his tribute and gratitude to the people who still believe in him and who accepted him as their only leader from the very first day of his arrival there.

The night is going to be short. No one will sleep for it is the month of Ramazan. The dawn whisperer starts making his rounds. He is beating a drum and singing a ballad. His job is to awaken the people before dawn.

'Wake up,' his drum beats, 'it is time to break the fast.'

He sings: 'Wake up, O people of faith, I offer you my body, I offer you my soul, don't keep me waiting, for I won't sing for long. Wake up, O people of this great land, it's time to break your fasts, it's time to stay awake…'

Dar and I are going to break the fast together. It's going to be our first time. But one of us will go back on his word. The ceasefire will end when we go into the hideout and make sure that no one escapes. Dar has cooked a meal. We're to break our fasts before twilight and then set off for the hideout. The drumbeater beats his drum again: 'Remain alert…remain cautious…the enemy is within…stay awake, O innocent sons and daughters of the beautiful soil…don't fall prey to foolish dreams…'

It is the final hour before the drumbeater stops beating the drum and retreats. Salim Dar rises, gets dressed, and, facing me, stands at attention as if he's about to be administered an oath: 'I, Salim Dar, do hereby declare that I am neither mad nor rational, that I am neither loyal nor deceitful, that I am neither a coward nor brave, that I am neither a hero nor a villain, that I am not here to obey you or to betray you, that I shall neither destroy you nor protect you, that henceforth I shall do as I please, and my actions will be beyond reproach.

'I, Salim Dar, do hereby declare that from now on I shall not run away, that I shall be free from everything—money, ambition, fear, favour, greed, hope, dreams and love. That I shall reject even freedom, for freedom is a curse.

'I, Salim Dar, son of Fayyaz and Rahat Dar, husband of Rubaiya Dar, father of Rabia Dar, do hereby swear in the name of Fayyaz, Rahat, Rubaiya and Rabia Dar and by the power vested in me by myself, that I shall neither quit nor belong... that I shall neither discharge my duties nor renege on them... that from now on I will never go wrong or right... for Salim Dar, there are no wrongs or rights... there are only rights... that I shall bear allegiance to only one thing, and that thing is yet to come into being... it never will... until then I shall go on and on and you can't do a thing about me... you will have no choice but to follow me, but you won't be able to reach me...'

'Sit down, Commandant Dar, I order you. Do not take this madness any further or else you know what's going to happen.'

Dar disobeys for the first time. He goes on and on: 'I, Salim Dar, the Dar of Dars, Salim of Salims, do hereby announce that nobody can save you from ruin... that your fate is sealed... that it is pointless to do anything... you may do whatever but nothing can help you escape...'

'Stop it, Commandant. I order you. Stop this madness and take control of your senses. We have but one hour to go. Remember your mission. Do not falter. This will be your moment of glory. From tomorrow, you shall be hailed as the Lion of Kash...'

'No, Sir, you're wrong,' he raves. 'Everything that we've earned will be snatched from us. We will be reduced to nothing. People will spit at us. I don't care about myself but I care about those who don't know what is being done to them and what they are being made to do. They don't know what they are turning into. It's their ignorance that is driving me mad. Not that they deserve to know the cold truth but that they don't deserve to die for nothing. They shouldn't die as deserters and villains. After all, they have given their blood too. They have traded their dreams and lives for the comfort and welfare of those who don't deserve to live… Go to people. They will listen to you. Talk to them. Explain everything to them. You must plead our case. Not just for us but for our land and its people. We saved many, but who will save us if not you? Who will do it for our own people if not you…?'

'You're right. We have saved many people. We will go on saving people. People will remember that. They will…'

'Yes, yes, we saved many people. We will keep saving them. We only save. We do nothing else… For how long will we keep turning our backs on the truth? Our real job, Sir, is to sniff out our own people and just make the numbers. We are still doing the same things we did when we were mujahids. For how long will we live in denial? The tactics are the same. Nothing has changed.'

'Salim Dar, don't cross the line. I shall repeat for the last time. I order you to grab your weapon and finish your job. Do not forget who you are. You know the consequences of not following an order…'

'I will not do it. And I will not allow you to do it. It is over.'

'Is it because you have once again come to realize that they are your people and not mine?'

'I haven't forgotten anything. I never will. Remember the day when you ordered me to go full throttle and I did exactly that.

Slow down, slow down, that's enough, you had said. I spared no one that day. You didn't want to leave any traces. And I did exactly what you wanted me to do…'

'I need you one last time, Salim. I need you now. Much more than ever…'

'No, wait, I haven't finished yet,' Dar interjects. 'You must know why I kept following your orders blindly. You must know why I killed people at the slightest suspicion. It is because they like to suffer. That's all they know. Only suffering. Nothing else. It gives them hope and I like to see them die with hope alive in their hearts…'

'And the same people believed in you and looked up to you…'

'Yes, they thought I would perform miracles for them and make their dreams come true. They thought I would fulfill each one of their wishes. But I was wrong about them. We haven't even seen the threshold of their endurance yet. They can suffer more than you and I can ever imagine. Their suffering will outlive mine. I will die only once but these people… they will die again and again and we will never be able to do anything…'

I run out of patience and time. I can't risk it any longer. This is a do-or-die moment. I give it a last shot. Maybe Dar will obey this time.

'Yes or no?'

He doesn't budge. He stands his ground, 'If I don't do it, you will. This is the place where to break the law isn't illegal. You know what to do.'

He is defenseless. He stands down without any fear or obligation to obey my orders. Outside, the voices bellow: 'The forces are digging trenches to keep people out. Those who try to cross over will be buried alive.'

'You heard it, Sir. Something good is about to happen,' Dar says, resignedly, ignoring me completely. 'But what if it happens only after I am gone?' He starts walking away.

'This is subversion, officer, and you shall have to pay for it.'

'I am ready for anything, Sir.'

'Do you realize what you have done? Do you even know what you are doing?'

'Do you? Tell me... Do you? Or do you not, Sir?'

A Dream of Life

Dear Zooni,

You are in my dreams again. We are going hunting. You're an ace at hunting now. Better than me and everyone else I have trained. But unlike others you're compassionate and forgiving. You look at people shooting down birds indiscriminately and it makes you cry. You know when to stop. It's a gift you have. It can't be taught. You are my teacher. But I am not a good learner. I stand next to you and watch you take aim. And I wait for the moment when you take your finger off the trigger. A beautiful black-necked crane's flight remains uninterrupted. It will fly back to its nest and keep returning here. It will bring back a thousand cranes. It gives me happiness of a kind I have never known.

Our house is by the side of a river. It's a beautiful place and nature is bountiful and benevolent. You always wanted a house by a river. Across the river is a forest where we haven't gone yet. I am teaching you how to take aim and pull the trigger. I teach you how to be fearless. I test you. But I don't offer an explanation. I will walk away from you and cross over to the other side of the river. I must save myself from an invisible enemy that's determined to take me down. You must not allow the enemy to get to me. You must either stop the enemy or let me go. You won't say no. You will act firmly and in the best interests of both of us. You won't ask any questions. You will understand everything. Even those things, which aren't understandable! Neither you nor I can spot the enemy, but the enemy is present at a striking distance from us. It is someone who wants to take me down. Will you allow that or will you do what I am asking you to do? If at all I must be stopped and taken down, you should be the one to do it. Not some unseen force.

I want us to win. I want the enemy to be defeated forever. There's only one way out. It will spare me pain and disgrace. It will stop me from committing more blunders. For if I survive, I will still not do what I am supposed to do! The enemy will get to me and, in front of you, do terrible things to me.

I cease to be your father. You cease to be my daughter. But this won't be the last time we will see each other's faces.

I start running away from you. You take aim. You don't flinch. You don't falter. My teaching will work. Nothing can deter you. Nothing will come between you and me. Your eyes are set on the target. There are no thoughts. Nothing exists except the target. And then you do exactly what is required of you. You take the shot. It's on target. You pass the test. So do I.

The dream doesn't end because I never wake up. Even if it is made to end, you will still be by my side and we will still be hunting. Nothing will come between us. We will be happy. We will protect ourselves with dreams of each other.

With all my love,

Dad

The Night of Communion

Autumn has set in. Everything is floundering. A smell of decay permeates all around.

Dar has taken all the money out of his bank account and burned it. He wants to burn his house and possessions. He says everything he has accumulated so far must be destroyed. He spends his nights in an empty sewer pipe in Eidgah and refuses to come out of there. He doesn't sleep or eat. I remind him of Rabia and he sneers, 'You say that as if you care about her.' Giving me a suspecting look, he adds, 'When she gets to know what happened to me and what I did, will she ever forgive me? She should not have been born. I should not have…'

I stop him from uttering atrocities: 'She will never think that.'

He goes on: 'The same is true for Zooni and you know it already. Years from now, when you are gone, she will ask herself if what you did was worth it. What are you going to tell her when she gets to know what you have become? When she comes to know that you did everything for her and in her name? When she's told that each drop of blood that spilled on this soil because of her father is cursing her. It will be too late to do anything then and too late to repent and seek her forgiveness. Will she forgive you that day? She's going to return some day and demand answers. Or maybe she won't because she will know there are no answers.'

'What has happened to you?'

He strikes a match against the floor and lights up a cigarette. 'You know we can end this with this match,' he says, stroking the flame with the tip of his forefinger. 'Just this one match and everything will be over. But do you have the guts?'

'You want to burn yourself…'

'Cinders don't burn,' he retorts, putting out the flame with his finger. 'They destroy whatever comes in contact with them.'

'Why are you doing this to yourself?'

'Today it is me. Tomorrow it will be you. The day after, someone else…'

'You're wrong, Salim. It will always be you.'

'I'm asking you once again for the last time. For how long do we keep this act going? For how long do we keep looking away? Aren't you tired of all this?'

'This is what we are now, Salim…'

'Do you think we could have had a different fate had we chosen a different path?'

'We have to go right up to the end.'

'This is the end. Beyond this, there is nothing.'

'You want to die, Salim?'

'For years, I courted death because I always dreamt of dying young. Now I wish to live so that I don't die for nothing.'

'What should I do for you? I don't want you to… You know I want you to…'

'You still have a 50-50 chance. I have none,' Dar says, tossing a coin in the air.

'Are we now making decisions by the flip of a coin? Rabia and Zooni still count on you to protect them. If you leave now, a day will come when they will disown us. They will want us to die.'

'That day is already here, my friend. It is our fate to die no matter what we do.'

For the first time, Dar is speaking of things like fate and chance and life and death. He's losing grip on reality and questioning his own sanity, thereby subjecting himself to unwanted scrutiny. He's losing the will to fight. But he isn't wrong, though he knows I will never admit that he's right. He knows that his fate is tied to mine and mine to his. And that our fates are tied to the fates of others, and to the fates of even those who are yet to come into existence... And to the fates of those who have come and already gone without leaving a trace.

Dar is forgetting the only code that defines him. Fate is for cowards. People like him chart their own destinies.

You might wonder what I think of all that's happening to Salim Dar. Was he always like this? No, he wasn't. Did I see his fall coming? No, I didn't. Now that the unexpected has happened and I don't know what lies ahead for him and what he might do to himself and to others, I have only two choices—to let him go or to ease his torment. But I think of Rabia. She's still clinging to the belief that her father is a hero. What will she do when she sees him? She will go mad. She's already displaying the signs. She says she knows what's going to happen and what she's going to do. She makes predictions about herself and the days to come.

I have been thinking of taking Dar to the mystic's place. But I can't because only his chosen followers are allowed in his house. He summons them to his place at short notice and they drop everything and go. Such is their faith. Blind faith, I used to think. But not anymore! Blindness is the greatest virtue. It shows you doors that no light can illumine. For the sake of Dar, I decide to go against the norm and take my chance. There won't be any more chances hereafter.

We arrive at the mystic's place. Men are making preparations for the night of communion. We are going to stay awake for the whole night. Gulzar is going to sing. Dar is vacillating between extremes. He's dreaming of his old days. For the first time, he tells me his dream: 'Father is taking me to the dargah. He raises his hand towards the holy dome of the shrine and prays for a boon. He wants me to leave home and build my life elsewhere. Years later, his prayer is answered. I'm to leave home and join the freedom struggle. Father is heartbroken at my disobedience. I try my best not to disappoint him. But nothing is in my hands. History has already decided for me. I am to give up my father's dreams for the dreams of twelve million people who are betting on me.'

The mystic enters the room. He's in a trance. He senses our presence in the room. He's forgiving. He looks at Dar and gives him a compassionate look.

Evening falls. People start assembling at the house. Gulzar and his entourage take their seats and begin to tune their instruments. Gulzar begins to sing. The chorus follows. A young boy with a broken leg starts dancing. The voices converge and become one. Slowly, Time spreads its wings. The wings are not seen but their rhythmic motion is felt. A circle of energy forms around us and the moment doesn't seem to end. The singers' voices permeate our being. Everything ceases to exist. Everything except a sense of touching the untouchable, of attaining the unattainable! We are transported somewhere else—to a place that doesn't exist. A place beyond time and space and dream and memory! A place that's ever changing, yet still non-existent. The music reaches a crescendo. And then, as if by magic or divinity, it gives rise to a new creation—it is multi-dimensional. Notes blend with beats in perfect harmony as if the communion has been scripted by the masters themselves. As if their union has happened previously in some other realm or dimension. As if the very occurrence of this event has been rehearsed infinitely so that nothing can ever go wrong because there are no wrongs in this creation.

And then, there's no end. A strange light flickers.

I snap out of it. Dar is reclining against a wall. He doesn't know where he is and who he is. He doesn't even know if he's alive or gone. He's beyond happiness and pain, freedom and bondage, hope and despair. A smile has settled on his face. He's dreaming a happy dream.

For the first time, I feel the urge to reveal the truth to him. That I wasn't the man he thought I was. That I was always an officer, but he had mistakenly thought otherwise! That I had sent him into darkness because his rage was inexhaustible! What I made him go through is hard even on me. It is unfair that he should go on this way. But now, I won't deprive him of his last dream, no matter how false it is. I shall not stop him now. I shall not come in the way of his freedom. He shall dream again and again of a life that was not to be.

Tomorrow when I ease his pain, everything will be set right. But I won't keep my word. I won't do it myself. I don't have the guts.

Justice is not blind. Justice sometimes comes in the garb of deceit. I hope you will prove me wrong someday.

The hour before a disaster is always beautiful. Especially when you know that the end is near. By then it's too late to do anything. That's what makes everything beautiful. You embrace truth. You see beauty for the first time. You see freedom. Right now, I am seeing what I have never seen in my entire life.

The North Star is peeping from behind a cloud, and Jupiter is closing in on the Crescent. Is this a sign of change and of the good times to come? Or is this nothing but a passing tide?

Spring's Last Song

Dear Zooni,

All my life, I have let go of things that I should have embraced and embraced things that I should have discarded. I fell in love with your mother only after she died. The day she gave birth to you, I knew I had been a fool to not love her. By the time I started pining for her, it was already too late. I never spoke the words that could have saved her life. But the day she died, I wanted to die too. There never was and never will be a woman like her.

I realized my mistake only after I first held you in my arms. You had your mother's eyes. You looked at me the way she would have looked at me if I had told her that I didn't want her to go. You gave her a mole when you were in her womb, and she gave it back to you so that I would never forget her. Don't lose the mole for it will keep love throbbing in my heart forever.

I was guilty, but I pardoned myself over and over again. As we grow old, we begin to notice more and more things that we have forgotten and lost. I learnt my lessons the hard way. I kept avoiding mistakes after mistakes. But I became so obsessed with preventing small mistakes that I lost the ability to even spot the big ones. And then came a time I was beyond any mistakes.

You are now the same age I was when I gave up my passions and set off on a journey that took me far, far away from home and ended only in the permanent separation from those I love. I should have stuck to history. But now even history won't accept me.

Writing has taught me that one can never flee from the truth. And that if you ever try to hide from the truth, it will come to haunt you in different forms.

Someday I will gather courage to stand in front of you and ask you for a verdict. After all, you are a student of law, and justice is what you must pursue and deliver no matter how trying the circumstances and choices are. Someday you must tell me everything about justice. What meaning does it hold for people who are bereft of all meaning? What value does it hold in a place that has no values left? How must we keep it alive? How do we see its light?

Everything seems very far away. But to you everything is within grasp. I want you to hold my hand once again. You mustn't do to yourself what I did to myself and to you.

And when all this is over, we will sit quietly, somewhere far away from here, and count our losses and gains.

Spring has arrived and people are coming out of their homes in search of sunshine. The snow is melting and stains of desolation have started shimmering once again. The spring will now lure everyone into its trap and no one will be able to tell if the land we rest our feet on is a garden or a graveyard.

Everything that happened until yesterday will be a distant memory. Everything that's going to happen tomorrow will also be a memory. 'We have seen everything, even things that are yet to happen, for they will happen again and again in the same fashion as they have happened for years,' Salim Dar had said soon after deciding to abandon me. 'What else is there to see? What else can happen that has not already happened? That we are still alive is no longer a blessing.'

Dar's insubordination and mutinous behaviour were forgivable. On certain exceptional occasions, such an otherwise unacceptable attitude is acceptable. It gives us the strength and aggression to fight and win without going into the rights and wrongs. What was unpardonable, however, was Dar's sudden and inexplicable descent into disorder and madness. What Dar endured is what humans go through when they mistake the bad for the good and the good for the bad. He had broken down that day. It is only after the horror has ended that you cry.

Dar is now at a place where neither the good nor the bad can ever emerge victorious. Where defeat and victory are not two separate states but one and the same thing. Where everyone is the same.

Sometimes, the most important story we forget to tell is our own. Dar played his part and then crossed the Rubicon. I am now playing mine.

People aren't tired anymore. They haven't resigned. That they are coming out one after another is proof that nothing is lost yet. They are ready to face whatever is to come. All they desire is for the spring sunshine to last longer.

They have decided to be happy for the sake of their children who still don't know what happiness is. Spring is the season of hope and happiness. Spring gives birth to new people in us. Spring gives us the courage to live for one more day. It makes us pine for new life. Everybody has been saying so since the arrival of spring. Is this true? Do you also feel the same about spring? Does it do similar things to you? Does it show you things that make you long for more life?

I have come out too. Sunlight has flooded the city. The scent of flowers is all around me. I am sitting in the shade of an almond tree and looking at a family of four picnicking in the garden. Father, mother, son and daughter spread a mat and open the lids of their tiffin boxes. Food is served. A fifth plate full of aromatic dishes is placed on the mat for either a stray or a mendicant or a missing person.

We start eating like a family.

A little village girl your age is singing an old Habba Khatoon song that's sung by a hundred girls on sighting the first buds of spring. She's the soprano among them all. If you close your eyes, you will hear her song too. It will take you away to a place where you get to meet everyone you have ever loved.

But this isn't the time to close your eyes and shut your ears. Now is the time to see and hear everything.

I will stop here now. I will not find a better place and time to stop. I don't know what's going to happen after the day ends and the song stops, but the way the little girl is singing and everyone is listening, it doesn't seem that the day will ever fade or the song will end.

All my love,

Dad

Epilogue

I am, once again, at the Arrivals lounge of an airport. People landing from cities I have never been to are coming out in hordes. Momentarily, they stare at the placard in my hand and walk away, dejected. Eyes meet eyes. Hands do not greet hands. Another flight lands. No sign of him. I look for a gesture, a habit, a hesitation of the heart. The placards of those next to me are met with smiles of joy.

Welcome Joanna (University of Oslo)
European Springs welcomes Mrs and Mr Simmers
Welcome Mr Han San (General Electric, Tokyo)
Miller and Sons welcomes Peter Cooke

Welcomes are readied. Sons meet mothers. Daughters meet fathers. Wives meet husbands. Lovers meet lovers. Strangers meet strangers. Tales of adventure shine in their eyes. Even their baggage conceals secrets.

'Who are you waiting for?' a bystander asks, trying to make small talk and hoping to kill time until the person he's waiting for shows up at the meeting point. Or maybe he's not even waiting for anyone. He could be anyone—an idler or an observer.

All arrivals have their names written on placards. There are no failures. The connections work with clockwork precision.

I wait and wait. Honeymooners, business people, tourists, homecomers, tired air hostesses for whom the world is still a beautiful place, and strangers walk through the gates, and disappear.

Last come the pilots with glum faces. Carrying packaged drinking water and dragging black suitcases, they exit too, without paying attention to the solitary comings and goings of the very people they ferried from one continent to another. It must be summer somewhere.

Another flight lands. People in fur coats bring remnants of a distant winter.

The flight status monitor flashes:

Istanbul Arrived
Moscow Arrived
Tokyo Arrived
Abu Dhabi Arrived
San Francisco Arrived
New Delhi Arrived

Hours pass.

The monitor flashes one last time—ALL FLIGHTS HAVE LANDED—and then goes off.

The lounge assumes a deserted look as though the airport has been shut down. I am the only one left behind, still waiting and hoping that my wait isn't futile and endless. What am I doing here? Who am I waiting for?

A tall man wearing a rugged coat walks towards me. His stride is steady, his stare certain yet compassionate. Behind him is a small boy with blue eyes, his hands clasped together, walking with a spring in his step.

Waving happily at me, the man smiles enigmatically, 'Hello Zooni, your placard is blank. It's been a long journey, and we're tired and famished. Mind taking us home?'